A MEET WITH MURDER

This first edition published in Great Britain in 2008 by
four o' clock press - a discovered authors imprint

ISBN13 978-1-906146-28-3

Available from Discovered Authors Online -
All major online retailers and available to order through all UK bookshops

Or contact:

Books
Discovered Authors
Roslin Road, London
W3 8DH

0844 800 5214
books@discoveredauthors.co.uk
www.discoveredauthors.co.uk

Printed in the UK by BookForceUK (BFUK)
BFUK policy is to use papers that are natural, renewable and recyclable
products and made from wood grown in sustainable forests where ever
possible

BookForce UK Ltd.
Roslin Road
London W3 8DH
www.bookforce.co.uk

A MEET WITH MURDER

THOMAS JENKINS

four o'clock press

To all who love horses, hounds and hunting

PRINCIPAL CHARACTERS

George Ashley	A London detective
Edward Radford	His assistant

Soldiers of Prince Albert's Troop, Royal Horse Artillery

Captain Raynham	Adjutant to Prince Albert's Troop
Lance Bombardier Green	A junior NCO
Trooper Tom Noad ('Tom One')	Nephew to Ashley
Trooper Tom Marsh ('Tom Two')	Best friend to Tom One
Trooper Scott	
Trooper Sorrell	

Staff of the Gidleigh Hunt

Colonel Hargreaves	Master of Foxhounds
John	Senior huntsman
Robert Brookes	Kennelman and whipper-in

Other inhabitants of Chagford

Margery Noad	Sister to Ashley; Mother to Tom One
Lavinia Ashley	Aunt to Margery and Ashley
Prebendary Stephen Trevis	Rector of Chagford
Mrs Alice Trevis	His wife
Primrose Armishaw	Owner of a livery yard
Katherine Stone	A widow; great aunt to RobertBrookes
Evelyn Warren	Distantly related to Katherine and Robert
Betty Trenchard	A corpulent cleaning lady
Peter Masters	A solicitor
Norah Dyer	A garrulous shopkeeper
Farmer Crane	An ugly agriculturalist
Mrs Crane	His ugly wife
Mark Overland	A vintner

Police

Inspector Simkin	Of Exeter CID
Sergeant Craggs	His colleague
Constable Harry Sefton	Of Okehampton police station
Ernest Yeo	A special constable; also a bell ringer and odd job man

Plus other inhabitants of Chagford, police and many horses

AUTHOR'S NOTE

Chagford is a real town, isolated and magnificent, in the heart of Dartmoor National Park. I hope that many readers will recognise descriptions of the area and gain as much pleasure as I did when calling them to mind. I have not, of course, portrayed any resident of the town in these pages. Two friends, unconnected with Chagford, appear in the novel; all other characters are fictional, as is the Gidleigh Hunt.

This novel was written in the Summer of 2004 and the events described are those of Christmas 2003. At that time, hunting with hounds was still a legal activity. The Gidleigh Hunt, like all others, continues to exercise hounds, to follow trails and to hunt within the letter of the law. With more supporters than ever, its members wait patiently for the return of the great sport in all its glory.

I am grateful to Gunner Matthew Wood for showing me around the kennels of the Royal Artillery Hunt and explaining the routines and traditions of the hounds. If any mistakes appear in the book, they are all my own.

Thomas Jenkins
April 2007

CHAPTER ONE

- PROLOGUE -

A grey, mizzling, dismal mid-December morning. Heavy, lowering clouds exert an extra burden on the shoulders of working Londoners. The rain is so fine that umbrellas seem ridiculous, yet without them, and without the protection of raincoats, the unforgiving moisture steadily penetrates layers of clothing until the body is wet and the soul more miserable than it might be in harsher conditions. Instead of scurrying, the citizens plod; their collars up, their shoulders hunched, and their necks bent, they stare at the shining pavements and pick their way through sodden litter.

* * * * *

In the North London barracks of Prince Albert's Troop of the Royal Horse Artillery, a thin column of mud, called Tom, creeps wearily around the perimeter of the parade ground, his left arm swaying under the weight of a steel-framed army saddle. Days of steady rain have transformed the neighbouring park and the scrubland beyond into a shining, slithery no-man's land. Tom has been spattered with mud by cantering horses and splashed with red-brown water by the wheels of antique guns. His boots and spurs are crusted over with the solidified consequences of a dismount into six inches of faecal London clay. The brown and green swirling patterns of his combat jacket seem to have been created by an ill-advised sprawl in the quagmire, and his face, streaked and dirty, appears to have been decorated with inferior and badly-applied camouflage cream.

Unlike most of his fellow Londoners, Tom is not miserable; he is simply exhausted. The riding, indeed, had been exhilarating, but grooming his horse afterwards was a long, dirty and sweaty process; the combined effort of both activities has left every muscle in his body aching. As he creaks his way towards the harness room, he debates whether to attempt cleaning his saddle and bridle now, or to postpone the task until the free time after his evening meal.

'You're looking good, Tom One.' Lance Bombardier Green emerges, grinning and immaculate, from the harness room just as Tom reaches the steps leading up to the door. 'There are hippos in Africa achieving climax in less mud than that.'

Tom smiles wearily: 'Thanks, Lance, that makes me feel much better. Tell me how they do it, and I'll give it a try.'

Green considers. 'Well, my guess is, they start by putting the kettle on. I was just going to make a brew in my room, but I can knock one up here, if you fancy it.'

Now it is Tom's turn to ponder. The lance bombardier is famous for his appalling tea; a repellent orange fluid produced with two teabags per mug, powdered milk and enough sugar to rot through the enamel of the strongest teeth. Still, he had been Tom's first mentor in Prince Albert's Troop and, despite the difference in rank, the young trooper regards Green as one of his two best friends. Perhaps the lining of one's stomach is a reasonable price to pay for a rest and half an hour's comradeship.

'Thanks, Lance - you're a hero. That'd be just great.'

Tom staggers up the steps into the harness room and heaves his saddle up on to a bracket, where it can wait until after supper. He hangs up his bridle, leans against the nearest work surface and, for the first time since six o'clock that morning, relaxes.

* * * * *

As Tom lifts up his saddle, four undertakers raise to their shoulders a casket containing the remains of Ellen Cleghorn, late of the parish of Chagford, in Devon. The weather here has been frosty, rather than wet, so the men wear rubber-soled shoes, lest their feet should slip on cold granite. The Rector of Chagford, Prebendary Stephen Trevis, looks on dispassionately as the men adjust themselves to spread the weight of the deceased's wizened body more evenly. When this is done, a fifth black-coated professional takes a minute or so to place a few small floral arrangements on the lid.

The rector uses the time to glance around at the bystanders who have lingered to watch the cortege before continuing their shopping, their exercise, or their gossiping. Among them, Norah Dyer from the corner stores, stepping out from behind her counter to get a better view; ugly Mrs Crane, preventing even uglier Farmer Crane from entering the pub until she has seen the whole show; Robert Brookes, the young whipper-in of the Gidleigh Hunt, mounted on one horse and leading another. Robert removes his hard hat and cradles it respectfully in his right hand, controlling both horses with his left. Mrs Crane, spotting his gesture, nudges her husband vigorously until he doffs his scruffy tweed cap and holds it awkwardly in front of him, rolled up in both hands. Prebendary Trevis assumes that the huntsman has paused, not out of curiosity, but because one of the horses might take fright at Mrs Cleghorn's pine-veneered corpse. She was, after all, pretty terrifying when alive.

And now the flowers are arranged and the men have shuffled around so that Ellen Cleghorn can meet her maker feet first. Mr Mortimer, the director of the funeral parlour, leads the slow march to the church and the pallbearers follow behind. There is no family: the few mourners are already inside, so the rector completes the procession. As they move between the yews, he ponders the sudden death of this nasty old woman. Perhaps she had decided that a heart attack was a cheaper option than buying Christmas presents? He hopes that the Holy Spirit will inspire a few well-phrased platitudes for his homily.

The church clock strikes eleven as they pass underneath an ancient granite arch, through the porch and into the church itself. The rector discards his private thoughts and loses himself in the ageless prose of the funeral service:

'I am the resurrection and the life....' The barrel vaults echo to his words.

Outside, the onlookers disperse: Mrs Dyer returns to her neglected customers; the Cranes refuel with a pint of cider and a cup of coffee; Robert Brookes heads out towards the moor.

* * * * *

At about the same time as the rector climbs into his pulpit and makes reference to 'Our dearly beloved sister, Ellen Cleghorn,' wondering whether his nose will grow like Pinocchio's at this outrageous lie, Tom, dryer and refreshed, but slightly queasy from a second lurid mug of tea, climbs the staircase of his accommodation block. There is time to shower and change before the midday meal: both activities are very much to be desired. He turns along a corridor towards the room he shares with his other best friend in Prince Albert's Troop; confusingly, his fellow trooper is also called Tom, and is therefore known as Tom Two. They had joined up on the same day and Tom One is the military senior by all of fifty seconds.

Tom Two had been due to ride on the scrubland as well, but was plucked from the section at the last minute to put in a trumpet part in a fanfare. He is now sitting cross-legged on his bed, reading a letter. His riding kit is distinctly cleaner than Tom One's and he wears a green military sweater rather than a combat jacket. His discarded spurs and his valveless cavalry trumpet lie on the cupboard by his bed. He looks up as Tom One enters and gives a wry smile.

'Hi, One - it looks as though I got the better deal this morning.'

'I think, Two, that you could just about be correct there. I had a couple of hours of mud-wrestling, an hour of grooming and two whole mugs of the Lance Bomber's special brew.' Tom One peels off his combat jacket and flings himself back onto his own bed, taking care that his muddy boots remain well away from the blankets. One of his spurs clanks against the metal frame of the bed. 'How about you? Was the fanfare practice all right?'

'Fine. Apparently Trooper Grange was kicked by his horse yesterday when he tried to pick its hoofs out, and he's going to be pouting like a tart with silicon lips for the next week or so. But he's only fourth trumpet – it's an easy part. I got to ride afterwards, as well.'

'Really?' Tom One turns his head and observes that the polish on the inside of Two's boots has been scuffed and that a few short, chestnut hairs have attached themselves to the leather. 'How did you manage that?'

'Blondie Lang gave me a lesson. He had a letter yesterday telling him that he's been chosen for the Riding Instructor's course in the Spring.'

'Hey, that's really great! He'll get promotion as well, won't he?'

'Bound to. Anyway, he asked Sergeant Miller to give him a

session on basic instructing techniques, and I acted as guinea pig.'

'Was it good?'

'From my point of view, it was: it's the first time I've been in the riding school for a Miller lesson and not come in for most of the criticism. Still, I reckon he was quite pleased with Blondie; we did some simple jumps towards the end and it felt really smooth. There's a Christmas card for you, by the way: I think it's from your mother.'

Tom Two nods in the direction of the desk, which they share. Half sticking out of Tom One's inverted service cap is a large envelope, on which his mother's backward-slanting, querulous handwriting is easily recognisable, even from One's distant, horizontal position. He regards it with suspicion. It will doubtless contain a long letter with the usual account of Chagford goings-on, together with a re-iteration of his mother's latest grievances against her friends and neighbours, the army and, of course, Tom himself.

'I'll open it after lunch; mother's communications usually require more ballast in the stomach than a couple of flagons of the lance bomber's gut rot. What about your letter, by the way? Girlfriend?'

Tom Two regards with distaste the double sheets of lavender writing paper which have fallen off the edge of his bed. He leans over, scoops them up and crumples them into a ball, which he projects inaccurately towards the metal waste paper bin.

'*Ex*-girlfriend,' he replies, emphatically. 'Louise droopy-udders Trotter is a two-faced, scheming, hypocritical bitch.'

'Oh – sorry.' One feels inadequate. 'So it was a "Dear Tom" sort of letter, then?'

'That's about it. If you're going for a shower before lunch, I'll join you – I want to wash that cow out of my system.'

* * * * *

15

George Ashley, a moderately successful private detective, and uncle to Tom One, is looking forward to revitalising himself with stronger liquid than that which is splashing over his nephew and Tom Two. For the sake of their livers, which deserve a respite before the onslaught of Christmas, he and his assistant, Edward, have agreed not to drink before midday. During the last half-hour or so, they have been glancing irritably at the clock in the sitting room of Ashley's Lonsdale Square apartment, exchanging grumpy remarks and rustling unread newspapers. Edward periodically tosses his head impatiently, so that his floppy blond hair lies first one way, then another. At length, the clock gives a wheezing prelude to the Westminster chimes and they both leap in the direction of the drinks tray. As the four quarters sound, Ashley shoots generous portions of gin and ice into glasses and Edward slices a lime. Once the fruit is added, Ashley dashes in just enough tonic water to make the drinks respectable, and by the first 'bong' of the hour they are ready to glug away.

'My God, that feels better.' Ashley gives a deep sigh and returns to his armchair. Edward re-occupies the sofa, putting his feet up and allowing his body to slide down. He keeps his head just high enough to be able to drink.

'You don't think,' he muses nonchalantly, 'that we might be teetering on the edge of the ravine of alcoholism?'

'Toppled over and holding on by our fingernails, more like. Still, in these dreary winter days, we have to find consolation where we can. Shall we do the Christmas cards now?'

Ashley has strong views concerning Christmas cards, deeming it deeply sinful to open them without a drink in his hand. He also has very set ideas with regard to their position-ing around the apartment: expensive religious cards with glossy reproductions of mediaeval Sienese masters are displayed on the chimney piece; other expensive, but non-religious, cards are allowed in the sitting room and clutter up small tables and an otherwise functionless what-not. Among these are a couple of cards showing the famous portico of the Minerva, Ashley's club, and a regimental card from Tom, with the crest of Prince Albert's Troop and a silk ribbon in the green and cherry colours of the unit. By far the grandest, however, is a copy of a highland scene, supposedly by Landseer, from a painting which Ashley knows to be a forgery. Mr Joshua Robbins, a barely respectable art dealer on the Portobello Road, made a good deal of American money out of that painting and therefore selected it for his annual greeting. Mr Robbins has no belief in Christmas but he believes in keeping up good business relationships and he likes to have Ashley on his side, in case of emergencies.

Other cards, of the 'buy-fifty-for-two-pounds' variety, are relegated to the kitchen. Edward's collection, almost entirely from like-minded friends with a taste for the grotesque or obscene, remains in his room, though occasionally one is deemed sufficiently funny to be pinned to the inside of the lavatory door.

'What have we got today?' Ashley reaches out for the four cards that make up his share. On the envelope of the uppermost he recognises the same script that had peered out of his nephew's cap:

'Oh dear – my sister.' Reluctantly and distastefully he opens it, putting the kitchen card ('Peace and Joy from Chagford') to one side and unfolding the letter inside.

'And how is Margarine? Any seasonal cheer from the old bat?' Edward looks up from a card in seaside style, showing two large Christmas puddings steaming in a brassiere. There is an unrepeatable caption.

'Well, old Mrs Cleghorn has died suddenly, which is about as cheerful as it gets in Chagford. Funeral,' Ashley becomes aware of the coincidence of time and glances at the clock, 'Finishing about ten minutes ago, I should think. If it's a churchyard burial, they'll be shovelling the earth on her even as we speak.

Oh, – and my sister sends her love. The death must have put her in an unusually good mood.'

'My God – she'll be inviting me to stay next.' Edward shudders at the thought.

'Don't worry; I think Chagford would have to be wiped out by the plague before she became cheerful enough to take that step. I shall brave her all by myself, as usual.'

'When do you depart?'

Ashley weighs up the possibilities for a moment. 'When are those ghastly "Carols in the Square"?'

'On the evening of the twenty-third.'

'Then I shall travel that afternoon. Are we rich enough for me to go first class?'

'Not really, but I dare say another gin will make you reckless enough to book the ticket anyway. Shall I pour this time?'

'Thanks – and go easy on the tonic. We need to conserve it, in case there's an outbreak of malaria this summer.'

* * * * *

Tom Two sticks his head under the powerful jet of hot water and massages the soapy lather from his scalp. He and Tom One have the large, communal washroom to themselves, so they feel free to talk loudly above the noise of the water and their conversation ricochets around the steamy tiled chamber. Having rinsed his hair, he resumes his narrative.

'So, basically, when I was destined to be a boring accountant behind a boring desk in a boring office, it was, "Oh, Tom, I really love you and one day we'll get married and have two point five children," and all that sort of thing, but never, "Oh, Tom, my parents are out – let's go upstairs and have a quick shag." She was all prim and proper about that sort of thing. Now that I've joined the army – and in the ranks, not even an officer...'

'Quite right too,' Tom One interjects supportively.

'Absolutely. Well, as you can imagine, I can forget the whole matrimonial side – but she hints between the lines that she's always quite liked the idea of doing it with a soldier, so if I want her to give a two-legged salute, the offer's there.'

'That's a revolting expression, Two.' Tom One shows no signs of being shocked: 'The army's coarsening you, just like mother warned. Anyway, isn't that what you wanted?'

'I dare say it was, once, but her attitude just turns me off completely. Are you done?'

Tom One looks towards the central drain. What had at first been a muddy rivulet is now a flow of clear water.

'I'm done.' They turn off the water and rub themselves down with green army towels before returning to their room, where they lounge amidst the debris of discarded uniforms and toppled-over riding boots.

'The worst of it is,' Tom Two continues, combing the front of his short hair into a tuft, 'That we always spend Christmas with her family. We're neighbours, so it's always been Christmas Day at her place, Boxing Day at ours. It's going to be awful.'

There is silence for a few moments, then One has a bright idea.

'Come and spend it at my place – it'd be really good to have a friend to stay.'

'I'd love to, but….' Tom Two recalls the subject of numerous conversations: 'What about your mother? Won't she mind?'

'She'll be glad for me to have someone of my own age, I should think. Otherwise, it's only dotty Aunt Lavinia, who's about a trillion years old and Uncle George, who spends most of the time hitting the gin. They both drive her up the wall; Aunt Lavinia's got pots of money, so mother has to be nice to her. She buys great Christmas presents – it should be really good this year, because she's pleased I've joined the army. Shall I phone mother and ask?' Tom reaches for his mobile. Tom

Two takes a moment before making up his mind:

'Could you? Look, One – this is, well, really decent of you….'

'No problem, Two.'

By the time they descend to the cookhouse for their meal, smartly kitted out for the afternoon's duties, it has all been arranged. They tuck into pie and chips cheerfully, making plans for the Christmas leave.

In Chagford, Ernest Yeo, the gravedigger, having patted down the last clods of earth over Ellen Cleghorn and arranged her flowers on the mound, settles down to an identical meal in the Three Crowns Inn.

* * * * *

CHAPTER TWO

- AUNT LAVINIA'S CHRISTMAS PRESENT -

Over the next few days, the frost, which had already touched Chagford, moved eastwards and descended on the parklands of London. The rusty brown puddles in the scrubland, where the Toms did so much of their training, froze over and there were satisfying cracking and crunching sounds when any of the horses penetrated the ice during their early morning rides. Every so often, a particularly well-placed hoof would cause a great spurt of dirty water to shoot out, often striking the soldiers with uncanny accuracy. So far, on this score, the Toms had been luckier than most.

The riding track in the park was altogether more civilised. On an apathetic Friday afternoon, fed up of the sight of his office, the adjutant to Prince Albert's Troop telephoned George Ashley to see if he fancied a ride.

'It won't be much more than a plod and a trot, I'm afraid, but we'll probably have the park to ourselves. I don't know about you, but I could do with giving the cobwebs a blast in some civilised company. We should be able to get a decent amount of time in before it turns dark.'

It sounded a good idea to Ashley, so a little more than an hour later they were trotting along the track, exchanging news. Frank Raynham was an old friend and, since he had been posted to the 'Patties', Ashley had become accustomed to these sessions in the park. His horsemanship had improved enormously, though he was still a long way from being up to Raynham's impressive standard.

'How's my nephew coming along? You've had him back for a couple of weeks now, haven't you?'

'That's right – he came back from his basic training early this month. According to Lance Bombardier Green, he and his chum are completely bonkers, polishing every bit of kit in sight and volunteering for extra riding sessions with Lang. We even suspect them of practising sword drills in the privacy of their own room. You get the idea?'

Ashley did: it was a great contrast from the rebellious schoolboy of seven months ago. Unlike his sister, Ashley had been delighted when Tom signed up for the army; a decision for which, according to Margery, Ashley himself was entirely to blame. Raynham continued:

'Green's arranged for the pair of them to take our horses when we get back, so you'll have a chance to catch up with him. Incidentally, this stretch of the track is in quite good order – let's make the most of it.'

The horses were as keen to go as their riders. Ashley applied the slightest of leg aids and his chestnut mare sprang into a canter so enthusiastic that the ride could have turned into a race, had he and Raynham not held the pace back. As the adjutant had predicted, they had the park to themselves: only a member of the ground staff looked up from his work to view the two riding in tandem and to admire the controlled energy of the chargers beneath them. He watched them until they disappeared around a corner, then returned to his tasks. It was a sight of which he never tired.

The light was fading as they turned their horses into the barrack gates. Raynham responded to the salute from the sentry on guard duty and then to a further pair from Ashley's nephew and Tom Two, who were waiting outside the stable block. Tom One moved over towards Ashley's mare.

'Hello, Uncle George, sir – shall I take your horse?'

Ashley made a slightly less agile dismount than Raynham, took the reins over his horse's head and handed them to his nephew. He then ran up the stirrups while Tom eased off the girth. Over the back of his horse, Ashley observed Tom Two and Raynham going through the same steps. Light from an unshaded bulb within the stable gave a chiaroscuro effect to the evening scene; the brilliantly polished leather of Raynham's boots, saddle and bridle flashed as they moved, while the dull greens of the troopers' coveralls transformed into a dirty grey if they moved out of the light. Ashley enjoyed the picture, the more so because his nephew seemed to fit into it so naturally.

'Thanks, Tom – or am I supposed to call you 'Trooper Noad' now? It's a very grand title.'

'I'm not sure that it feels it when you're mucking out at six in the morning, Uncle George, but it does sound good, doesn't it? Just wait until I'm a lance bombardier – that'll be *really* grand.'

'Dream on,' Tom Two remarked from somewhere behind the other horse.

'Thanks a lot, Two.' Tom One looked as though he would have liked to keep the banter going, but the presence of the adjutant was a restraining one. 'Are you coming into the stable, Uncle George, or are you off into the mess with Captain Raynham?'

Raynham correctly assumed that uncle and nephew would like to spend some time together, so interrupted tactfully:

'Actually, George, I've a couple of letters which I ought to get off before the weekend so, if you don't mind, I should probably spend half an hour or so at my desk. After that, I'm up for a gin – if you feel like it?'

Ashley did feel like it, so Raynham departed in the direction of his office, his khaki service dress appearing progressively more drab as he moved away from them and into the darkness. The Toms, who had sprung to attention, relaxed again and led the horses into the stable block. While they went through the process of untacking and grooming, Ashley squatted on a bale of straw and took pleasure in the sight of other people working. No strenuous grooming was required, but the task came at the end of a long day, so Tom One's dark hair was soon glistening; individual strands began to stick together, and little lines of scalp could be seen through the gaps. Tom Two's large, protruding ears began to glow red; when he bent down to pick out the horse's hoofs, they formed natural gullies for the trickles of sweat from his head. Two's hoofs were finished first; when he began the easier work with body brush and curry comb, Ashley opened the conversation.

'So, Tom Two, you're joining the remnants of the Noad clan for Christmas.'

'That's right, Mr Ashley, sir – hope you don't mind.'

'On the contrary, I'm delighted: it means that my sister's conversational auto-control will be switched to 'polite' rather than to 'moan', and that can only be a good thing. Have you been briefed on Tom's other relatives?'

'Yes, sir, but don't worry – I don't believe a word of it.'

Ashley speculated briefly on the grotesque thumbnail sketches his nephew would have provided, then asked the pair if they planned to travel together. Tom One prised out a sizeable chunk of parkland from a hoof and answered for both of them:

'That's right, Uncle George – we've got travel warrants for the twenty-third and we come back a week later to relieve the chaps who've been on duty over Christmas. Then they can go off for the New Year.' He let the hoof down gently and moved round to another. 'Apparently, there's a huge party in the NAAFI on New Year's Eve and then we all go for an early morning gallop in the park on New Year's Day to blow away the hangover – it should be fun.'

'It sounds it – but don't put it quite like that when you tell your mother about it. I'm travelling on the twenty-third as well.'

'Great – we can catch the same train.'

'We can – but if you think I'm squatting on a couple of kitbags at the end of a crowded cattle-truck, just for the pleasure of your company, Tom, you can think again – I'm travelling first class. We could meet in the buffet car for a drink, if you like.'

'That'd be good, Uncle George.' Tom paused in his work to call over the stall partition to Tom Two: 'Hey, Two, Uncle George has offered to buy us drinks on the train.'

'That's very kind of you, sir – One and I had been wondering how two poor soldiers would manage to keep body and soul together during the long journey to the West Country.'

Ashley took his stitching-up with good grace.

'All right, the drinks are on me – but you're carrying my luggage. Agreed?'

'It's a deal, Uncle George.'

The telephone call came about forty minutes later. By the time the horses were blanketed up and the saddles and bridles deposited in the harness room for later cleaning, Raynham's offer of gin had seemed increasingly attractive. However, an avuncular sense of duty persuaded Ashley to postpone it when it became clear that his nephew was anxious to show off his accommodation.

'It'll only take a few minutes, Uncle George – and we can knock up some tea, if you like.'

Ashley had felt that this invitation needed clarification before acceptance.

'When you say 'tea', do you refer to the soothing beverage of the civilised world, or the evil witches' brew that your lance bombardier ferments in a nosebag hanging from the harness room ceiling?'

'Don't worry, Uncle George, this is the real thing – we've got a pint of milk on the window ledge and Two's mother sent a hamper with all sorts of groceries in it.'

Tom Two confirmed this. 'The lance bomber won't touch it, Mr Ashley – he says it's only fit for officers and Nancy boys.'

'It sounds perfect: lead the way, and we'll all pretend we're, er, officers for a few minutes.'

Ashley had seen army accommodation before, and the troopers' room was exactly as he had imagined it: utilitarian furniture, a portable television (permanently switched on, it appeared, with the sound down) and heaps of kit everywhere. Green clothes and khaki clothes, disruptive pattern combat jackets, boots and head dresses, were variously arranged, waiting to be ironed, bulled to a brilliant shine, or otherwise tended to. Christmas cards, including his own, were displayed wherever there was space, and a mixture of boot polish and male hormones provided a characteristic fragrance. This, Ashley noted with relief, was understated. He smiled and made appreciative grunting sounds, which were sufficient to please the Toms. Having thrown his forage cap accurately onto a hook and stepped out of his coveralls, his nephew cleared some chair space for him, while Two began preparing tea.

'I'm sorry, Mr Ashley – we've only got horrible enamel mugs from our basic training course,' he apologised, throwing a bag in each. 'We're going to get a set of regimental ones from the Troop shop, but it'll have to wait until after pay day.'

'That's all right – I'll survive.' Ashley made a mental note of a possible Christmas present. Then he nodded towards the desk where the Toms, in service dress, smiled from separate frames. 'The photographs are good – were they taken at your passing-out parade?' The detective, to his annoyance, had been absent from the parade, nursing a client and making an important statement in court.

'Just after – a pro came along and took tons, but they were really expensive, so we just got these two and a big group picture.'

The group picture was as yet unframed. The three spent a pleasant few minutes looking at it, drinking tea, while the Toms ran their fingers along the ranks, pointing out the friends they had made, together with explanations of the different cap badges and stories of minor misdemeanours committed during the months of training.

Then Tom One's mobile rang: Ashley noticed, with amusement, that the ringing tone was an electronic version of one of the Troop's trumpet calls, which had presumably been programmed into the phone's memory in an idle but enthusiastic moment. If he remembered his calls correctly, this one ordered soldiers to pull on their boots and saddle up their horses.

In contrast to his uncle's amusement, Tom looked apprehensive. The number flashing up could mean only one thing.

'Oh dear – it's mother. What does she want?' He adopted a rabbit-in-the-headlights expression, only partly in jest.

'Shall I tell her you're mucking out?' Suggested Tom Two helpfully, as the trumpet call began for the second time. 'Or I could say that you're not feeling well and that you've gone to see the regimental vet for a worming pill. Either of those should frighten her off for a day or two.'

Tom One changed his pose to one of stoic resignation. 'No, the Patties didn't win Dunkirk by chickening out of answering their mothers' telephone calls.'

'Actually, we didn't win Dunkirk at all.' Tom Two's knowledge of history was more extensive than One's. 'And the Patties weren't even there.'

'Well, if they had been, we would have,' Tom One pronounced his cryptic verdict as though it proved he had been right all along. Finally, just as Ashley was considering throwing the phone and its electronic parping out of the window, Tom picked it up and answered. He stood to attention and adopted a blustering tone.

'Hello, Regimental Headquarters, Trooper Noad speaking.'

The booming androgynous voice that came back to him was emphatically not his mother.

'Ah! It's Tom, isn't it? You probably don't know me, but I remember you from way back – you used to wear a bobble-hat and you had mumps. Then you became very spotty when you were a teenager.'

Tom was uncertain whether to be more annoyed with the speaker, or with his uncle and Tom Two, who had heard every word and were obviously enjoying his discomfort. He blushed and replied, tersely, 'They're gone now.'

'Good thing too – make you sterile. Mumps, that is, not bobble hats or spots. *They* need fresh air and wet shaving – always works.'

By this time, Tom had worked out that the speaker was a woman. He suppressed the urge to ask if wet shaving had worked for her and simply listened on.

'Anyway, I'll get to the point – don't want to run up your mother's telephone bill. I'm Primrose Armishaw and I run the livery yard out towards Gidleigh. I'm ringing to let you know that you're coming hunting on Boxing Day.'

'*What did you say?*' Tom's eyes widened. '*Hunting?*'

'That's right – your uncle's coming too.'

An arc of tea shot across the room. Tom would have liked to pause and enjoy the sight of his uncle's discomposure, but Primrose Armishaw's commanding voice continued.

'It's your Christmas present from your Aunt – and a jolly good one as well. I hope you're grateful. Now, your mother says you're bringing a Mr Tu down with you – is he Oriental?'

'No, he's a soldier.'

'Oh, that's all right then – we've got a horse for him as well. It's all meant to be a surprise, of course, but I said that you needed to know – otherwise you might not bring your riding togs down with you. Besides, you ought to come to the yard and get to know your horses. When are you travelling?'

'On the twenty-third.'

'Right then – pop in some time on the twenty-fourth and I'll get Robert to take you up on the moor for an hour or so. Tell your uncle not to bother – we've got a nice old plodder for him – carried the rector's wife when she played Lady Godiva in the pageant – but I thought you youngsters would like something with a bit more life. Anyway – can't hang around gossiping all day – see you on the twenty-fourth. Your mother sends her love, by the way. She can't come to the phone because the central heating's on the blink and she's trying to crank it up – fat chance of getting a man out, this time on a Friday afternoon. If I were you, I'd bring some warm clothes. Bye, then.'

The phone went dead before Tom had the chance to respond. He switched it off and looked from Ashley to Tom Two and back again. All three wore the same dumbfounded expression: then, after a minute, they all began to speculate at once:

'Blimey!'

'Er – isn't hunting for the real experts?'

'Don't you have to be really good at jumping – dry stone walls and all that sort of thing? Six foot hedges with ditches on the other side?'

'I think I read somewhere that it's the most dangerous sport there is….'

'We're all going to die….'

This last was spoken by Tom Two with an air of calm resignation. The Toms looked at Ashley in the hope of advice.

'What shall we do, Uncle George?'

It was time for firm leadership and a clear decision. Ashley stood up.

'Well, I don't know about you two – but I'm going for that gin with Captain Raynham. See you at Paddington on the twenty-third.'

* * * * *

CHAPTER THREE

- CONSULTING THE ORACLE -

Fairly soon after their arrival in the troop, the Toms had come to the conclusion that Lance Bombardier Green was the source of all good advice. Once you had crossed his palm with beer, or made some tea the way he liked it, he would happily share his experiences of army life and dispense useful tips on almost any subject. Skills as varied as the fastest method of sweeping out the stable and the correct procedure for wheedling one's way into the good books of the quartermaster had been learned according to the lance bombardier's maxims and put to good use. Surely he must have something useful to tell them about hunting?

Accordingly, they changed into civilian clothes, armed themselves with several cans of Green's favourite beer and made their way to his room, a couple of floors below. Here, in the company of Trooper Sorrell, they found the lance bombardier, precariously balanced on his points on top of an inverted waste paper bin, which itself wobbled on the concave seat of a plastic chair. Sorrell held onto the chair, in the manner of a page holding his master's horse. Green had removed his tunic and tie, and slipped his braces off his shoulders, but he was still booted and spurred, giving the impression of a circus ringmaster who had condescended to demonstrate the rudiments of a new act to his team.

The cause of his extraordinary position was a series of entwined paper chains in shades of green and brown. Four twisted strands were already fastened to the corners of the room and Green was endeavouring to organise the free ends into a central gathering around the light flex. He gave a grunt of recognition as the Toms entered, performed a tottering arabesque to adjust a miswoven strand of green crepe and then sprang triumphantly to the ground, landing in the position of attention, as if he had been dismounting from a horse. The waste paper bin made a shorter but noisier descent, and was retrieved by Sorrell.

'Hello, lads – welcome to Lance's grotto. Don't worry about the mistletoe – it's not for you. What do you think?'

'Er – interesting chains, Lance.' Tom Two did his best to be tactful. 'Do you always make them into camouflage patterns?'

'No – last year I did them in regimental colours, but Captain Raynham saw them and pinched the idea for the officers' mess. Naturally, everyone thought that I had copied *him*. So this year, I thought I'd choose colours that nobody would steal.'

They all raised their eyes towards the ceiling.

'I think you're safe there, Lance,' confided Tom One, thoughtfully. 'Nobody's going to imitate that design.'

The Toms allowed their eyes to wander around the rest of the decorated room. A small, plastic model of a Household Cavalry trooper was impaled uncomfortably on the topmost strut of an artificial Christmas tree; from an otherwise unoccupied bookshelf – the nearest thing in the room to a mantelpiece – a long, green combat sock was suspended; and, twisted and turned along a bare patch of wall, Sorrell had arranged an old set of reins to spell out the words 'MERRY XMAS'. There were Christmas cards everywhere: in particular, a colony of about twenty identical regimental cards overpopulated the bedside table. Green saw their eyes resting on these cloned messages of goodwill.

'Now, it's not that I'm not grateful, chaps, but if you'll take my advice for the future, you'll just send the troop card to your relations. When it comes to mates in your own unit, send cards that convey the real message of Christmas – robins, snow and alcohol. That sort of thing.'

'Sorry Lance – we get the idea.'

'Jolly good – now, assuming that you're not just taking those four-packs of John Smiths out for a walk, sit yourselves down and chuck one over.'

They did as they were told: the troopers lounged on the bed, while Green perched on his desk and used the plastic chair for his feet. Sorrell squatted on the floor by his master: as an orphan, and the youngest soldier in the Patties, the wide-eyed trooper had adopted Green as a sort of surrogate mother, and the lance bombardier was both flattered and amused by the devotion of his honorary offspring.

Tom Two, in detective mode, diagnosed the reason for Green's idiosyncratic decorations.

'So, you're staying here for Christmas then, Lance?'

'Always do.' The lance bombardier paused for a mouthful of beer before continuing: 'I'm only missing out on the annual Green family quarrel and half a dozen vindictive games of Monopoly – New Year at home is much more fun. Besides, I'm having a room party here on Christmas Eve and Blondie Lang's bringing his lovely sister – hence the mistletoe.'

'Is she good looking, Lance?' Two was already beginning to recover from Louise Trotter.

'Well, just imagine Lang's beautiful peroxide hair cascading around a shapely pair of shoulders and coming to rest on a welcoming bosom just the right size to fit your busbies over: then you've got the idea. According to Lang, she's got a nice personality too, if you're interested in that sort of thing.'

They all took a few gulps from their cans, speculating silently on the fate of Lang's sister's honour. The phrase sounded, thought Tom One, like the title of a Victorian melodrama.

It was time to bring up the subject of hunting. As it turned out, Green's knowledge was fairly limited though, characteristically, he held firm opinions on the subject. Since hunting offended left-wingers, liberals, vegetarians and women with degrees in meaningful subjects, it was by definition a Good Thing. He also knew where real information could be found.

'Shifty Scott's your man – he helps out with his local hunt when he's on leave. If one of you pops to his room and dandles a beer in front of his nose, he'll follow it back here, looking like a Bisto kid on heat. He's two rooms down, on the left.'

Trooper Scott, post-shower and clad only in slippers and a towelling dressing gown, reacted according to Green's prediction; he was soon seated on the upturned wastepaper bin, with a pillow as a cushion, slurping noisily from the can. Framing the top of the can, and arching along the horizon of his forehead, was his single eyebrow, the evidence for his supposed shiftiness: a quality from which he was, in fact, entirely free. As he drank, the other three put him in the picture; after swallowing about half the can, Scott, temporarily satisfied, paused to take in some oxygen and to talk hunting.

'Don't worry – you'll love it. The Boxing Day meet is the biggest one of the year, so there'll be lots of people who aren't that experienced. Some of them just come along to show their support and look good; they ride for about an hour and then sneak off home. Also, a small hunt like the Gidleigh isn't going to be one of those intimidating outfits like the big Leicestershire ones – there'll be some friendly locals who'll know where all the gates are and they'll look after you.'

This was reassuring information; Tom One found himself beginning to look forward to the day. 'So we won't be expected to tackle vast jumps, or that sort of thing?'

'Not if you don't feel ready for it – the worst people to hunt with are the ones who shouldn't be jumping but have a go anyway. Nine times out of ten their horses refuse, so at the very least the whole ride gets held up and, at worst, things get dangerous. People will respect you for knowing your limitations. Anyway, I shouldn't think that Dartmoor has got that much jumping to worry about. You'll be fine – especially if you're getting to know your horses in advance.'

'If everyone's getting dressed up really smartly….' Tom Two began, but was interrupted by One, who was starting to enthuse.

'They do – I went to see them off a couple of years ago and they'd all made a real effort. Even the old toothless contingent looked as though they'd had a hose-down and put on their glad rags.'

'In which case,' Tom Two continued, 'what do we wear? We've done all our riding in uniform – we haven't got anything else.'

'No problem.' Scott looked around for a bin in which to throw his empty can, then remembered he was sitting on it: 'Wear your service dress – it's what we do if we get the chance to go out with the Artillery pack on Salisbury Plain, and that's smart enough for anyone. All the girls will love it – you'll probably come away with a huge list of telephone numbers.'

Two began purring in contemplation of the possibility: like One, he was becoming much more positive about the whole adventure. Green interrupted his thoughts:

'And if you do get a list, don't forget to pin up a copy in the NCOs' mess.'

'Are you pulling rank, Lance?'

'No, but it's worth noting that in the case of some occupants of the NCOs' mess, rank is about the only thing they've managed to pull for some time. You'd be doing them a kindness.'

* * * * *

35

The horses would all be bedded down for the night by now so, ignoring her own warning sign, which read, ambiguously, 'SLOW HORSES', Primrose Armishaw revved her ancient and battered Morris Traveller up a hill and shot through the gateway of the livery yard. The stable cat, a notoriously bad-tempered animal but a great ratter, fled for the safety of a granite mounting block, from where its green eyes, illuminated by the car's one working light, glared angrily.

'Serves you right, flea-bag.' Primrose emerged from her half-timbered crate and slammed the door, causing the whole vehicle to rattle. 'If you don't want to be taken by surprise, you shouldn't lick your privates in the middle of the drive.' She wandered over to the mounting block and gently scratched the cat behind its ears, producing from it a motorised throbbing, which sounded far healthier than the engine of the Morris.

Just after Primrose had finished her telephone call to Tom, Margery Noad had emerged from the cellar, carrying a spanner and looking utterly miserable. There had been dirt and cobwebs on her clothes and a money spider hanging from her hair. Like an inside-out Elizabeth Tudor, Primrose may have had the voice and body of a sergeant major but she had the heart of a woman: abandoning her plan to return to the stable, she pre-scribed a strong cup of tea and set about preparing it.

'And cheer up, Margery – whatever you did seems to have done the trick.'

This was true; they could hear the gurgling sound of badly-bled radiators coming to life all over the house. 'I'm impressed that you know what to do.'

'I don't, really.' Margery sipped her tea apprehensively: Primrose had made it in the chipped pint mug that was only ever used for cleaning paintbrushes. There were cups and saucers everywhere but no, this bossy woman, who smelled of horse, had to use the old meths mug. Still, the tannin was doing its trick: as she revived, Margery continued, 'I twiddled a few knobs and when that didn't work I gave the boiler a great bang with the spanner.'

'Good for you – must have cleared an air block. By the way, do you know there's a spider in your hair?'

They had chatted for half an hour and then Primrose had driven home, reflecting on Tom's mother's rather gloomy lot in life. These reflections continued as she stroked the cat. Margery was the sort of woman, she concluded, who lacked any real purpose: it was no life, stuck all alone in that house, which was obviously far too large for her to maintain. Probably, she needed a man: in fifty years of existence, Primrose had never felt the need herself, but she recognised the symptoms in others. A shame, therefore, that Tom's father had copped it under the 359 to Moretonhampstead all those years ago. Such a reliable bus in all other respects.

The cat grew tired of the attention and lunged out with a paw, before disappearing into the barn in search of a kill. Years of practice had made Primrose expert at claw-dodging; uninjured, she made her way to the stable office, where a light told her that Robert Brookes was still waiting.

The office doubled up as a snug: a couple of battered armchairs were comfortable enough, as long as you knew how to sit on them to avoid the broken springs, and a paraffin heater of the old cylindrical type was surprisingly efficient at keeping the room warm. Surrounded by the debris of stable life – grooming kits, wellingtons and vet's bills – Robert sat, leafing through the latest issue of *The Field*. He was wearing a baggy brown sweater over an old, collarless hunting shirt; on his feet, a comfortable pair of leather boating shoes, the laces long since devoured by enthusiastic puppies, served for lounging around the stable when all his duties were done. Rugby socks with red and black hoops and a sturdy pair of buff breeches completed his outfit. He stood up when Primrose entered.

'Hello, Robert, thanks for waiting.'

'No problem – Lorraine's doing the kennels tonight, so I'm in no hurry.' Robert had never quite worked out how to address Primrose, so he avoided the issue completely. "Miss Armishaw" sounded far too formal, especially with the first syllable of her surname lengthened in West Country style: on the other hand he had an uncharacteristic urge to giggle if he attempted to pronounce her Christian name. "Sir" would have felt most natural, but that was obviously out of the question.

'Got time for a whisky, then? God knows, I could do with one, after hearing Margery Noad bleating on for the last half hour. It's all fixed by the way – three more for your Boxing Day meet. The boys are coming up here on the twenty-fourth to get to know their horses.'

Robert nodded acceptance of a whisky. 'That's great – it brings us to twenty-five or twenty-six now. It'll be a good show. Will you be mounted this year?'

Primrose grunted assent; she was pretty much past riding these days but it was worth making the effort for the Boxing Day meet. 'I'll come to the Square and put in an hour's worth. Then I'll sneak off.'

She reached into a drawer for the not-so-secret key to the strong box. Inside, there were two surprisingly elegant cut-glass tumblers and a bottle of very peaty malt from a small Islay distillery. There were also the title deeds to the stable and other documents, but these were of less importance. She poured two generous measures and deposited the bottle on the desk with the cork still out, as if to imply that more would be forthcoming if needed.

'Here you go. Have a seat again – and cheers.'

'Cheers. Here's to the Boxing Day meet.'

They sipped in silence for a few moments, until a thought occurred to Primrose.

'Do you think, now that Ellen Cleghorn has turned up her toes – which, incidentally, is the only entirely popular thing she's done in over seventy years – that we'll be free of protesters? Surely old Mother Stone won't want to wield a placard all by herself. Sorry – I'm forgetting that she's your aunt.'

'*Great* aunt.' Robert was keen to keep the relationship as distant as possible. 'And as to what she's got planned, who knows? Let's face it, it wouldn't be like her to pass over the chance to make a nuisance of herself.'

'You're right there; I'm still fuming from her getting my barn conversion blocked by the council. I could have had four holiday cottages up and running by now, if she hadn't poked her nose in. Does she give you much trouble?'

Robert rolled some whisky round his tongue as he considered his reply. 'She leaves me alone, mainly. We had a blazing row when she found out that I was joining the hunt. She seemed to think I was doing it just to make her look stupid in the town.'

'I don't think she needs any help as far as that goes.'

'Now she mainly ignores me. Sometimes she'll say hello, but if I'm in riding kit, or dressed for the kennels, she'll cross the street to avoid me. I'm not complaining. Poor Evelyn has to put up with a lot more from her.'

'As you say, poor Evelyn. It would have been nice to think that after her father died she could have enjoyed a bit of freedom. I suppose there's no chance that we could get her to persuade your great aunt to stay indoors on Boxing Day?'

Robert shook his head. 'Don't even think about it. Evelyn would take fright and, as like as not, she'd tell the old girl what we'd said. You can imagine what her reaction would be then – she'd have the biggest banner ever!'

'You're probably right.' Primrose gave a sigh of symphonic proportions and reached for the whisky bottle. 'All the same it would be lovely to have a really grand meet without having to worry about that sort of thing. Another?'

But Robert had already kicked off his shoes and was reaching for his riding boots. A few minutes later, protected from the cold by a waxed jacket, woollen gloves and a tweed cap, he was heading down the hill to his cottage at the kennels. The halo around the moon provided a good light to walk by and promised a crisp day's hunting in the morning.

* * * * *

CHAPTER FOUR

- CHRISTMAS PREPARATIONS -

It is getting on for lunchtime on Monday the twenty-second. Somewhere, high above the continent, Ashley's assistant and a group of friends are making the most of Olympic Airways' in-flight hospitality, on their way to a sunny Christmas on a Greek island. Ashley himself, taking advantage of Edward's departure, is increasing his overdraft in an equestrian tailor's establishment, just off Saville Row. Frank Raynham has assured him that his hacking jacket is easily good enough for Dartmoor hunting, but Ashley has no wish to be upstaged by his nephew and is in the process of buying a black jacket with velvet collar, and a silk stock. According to the young tailor who has measured him up, the effect is stunning.

'And you'll find you've got an inside pocket for your hip flask, sir,' the youth adds, leaving Ashley feeling vaguely uneasy. Surely he doesn't smell of gin at this stage of the morning? With some regret, he decides that there is absolutely no justification for buying another pair of breeches, but he succumbs to the temptation of a pair of silver fox-head cufflinks and, after a few moments' thought, buys a further two pairs, for his nephew and Tom Two. He may as well do the job properly.

41

The Toms are just returning to the barracks with Lang, who has been giving them an extra lesson. Like Scott, he has assured them that there will be comparatively few jumps on Dartmoor and that their main hazard will be sudden dips in the ground. They have spent a useful hour riding backwards and forwards over a lumpy area of scrubland, keeping their balance while their horses negotiate the undulating terrain. As they dismount, a friendly gust of wind wafts a warm, spicy aroma towards them; evidence that the farriers have finished their work for the morning and are using the forge to mull wine. The troopers carry out their stable routines as quickly as possible, anxious to join their comrades in the illicit festivities.

In Chagford, the ladies of the parish are decorating the church. Betty Trenchard, fat and voluble, is squeezed into the pulpit, arranging large quantities of holly around the lectern and cheerfully gossiping to anybody within earshot. Evelyn Warren, diminutive distant cousin to Robert Brookes, quietly arranges chrysanthemums and greenery in a side chapel, and Mrs Farmer Crane, at the high altar, grapples with a poinsettia almost as shapeless and unattractive as herself. At the west end of the church, a Christmas tree has been decorated by the children: the rector's attempt (via a special Sunday School sermon), to have it decorated as a Jesse Tree, has been a total failure. It stands in pagan splendour, decorated with hand-coloured fairies and Father Christmases, chocolates in coloured foil, flashing lights and gold chains cut by the children into a suspiciously ivy-shaped pattern. Standing despairingly beside it, Prebendary Trevis wonders whether he needs a new Sunday School teacher. Still, at least his wife has managed to remove the mistletoe from above the crib.

Robert Brookes and the Master of the Hunt are at the kennels, discussing the fate of a bitch-hound, newly entered this season.

She has been "skirting": cutting corners and running around the edge of the pack, upsetting the flow of the hunt. Worse, on the previous Saturday, while splitting off from the pack, she had picked up a false scent and made off on her own: Robert had been forced to leave the hunt and chase after her for some way before discipline was restored.

They debate the necessity of having her destroyed, knowing that an errant hound is poor for sport and useless for breeding, yet both hoping that Saturday's adventure was an isolated incident. In the end, they come to an English compromise: they will rest her tomorrow, then hunt her on Boxing Day, making a final decision afterwards. Both feel vaguely dissatisfied by this conclusion, realising that they have probably only delayed an unpleasant task. They decide that a visit to the Buller Arms is in order and the Master drives them both into town in his Range Rover.

In Meldon Dene, a large granite house on the edge of the moor, Katherine Stone puts the finishing touches to her anti-hunting placard. The old one had been stored in Ellen Cleghorn's garden shed, and Katherine rightly assumes that Ellen's other executor has destroyed it. The new poster is made from a length of old wallpaper, which she has stuck onto hardboard with parcel tape. Red letters vividly, if unevenly, proclaim the message: KILLING A FOX IS AN EVIL WAY TO CELEBRATE THE BIRTH OF CHRIST. The sentiment is not original: she had been watching a television programme about hunt protesters and had seen a similar message being waved about by an unwashed-looking woman from a Christian pacifist organisation.

In truth, Katherine cares very little about the birth of Christ. She does not even particularly care about foxes but she is roused to passionate anger by the sight of huntsmen, her own great-nephew among them, in their scarlet coats, rampaging across the countryside, blowing those silly horns and followed by the whole ridiculous Chagford "establishment" of landowners, farmers, rich "in-comers" and pushy teenage girls on ponies.

Contemplation of this scene has turned Katherine's face a livid red: almost, in fact, to the shade of her great-nephew's hunting coat. She sits down and rests until the slight dizziness passes and her blood pressure sinks back down again. It wouldn't do for her nose to bleed all over the new poster. Perhaps she will even lie on her bed for a while; Mrs Trenchard can clear up the table when she comes to clean.

* * * * *

'So, Robert, do you feel settled in?' Colonel Hargreaves placed a pint of ale in front of his whipper-in.

'Thank you, sir. Yes, I think so. The kennel cottage is comfortable and handy for the livery yard, and I like the work with the hounds.'

'They're not a bad pack, are they? I suppose some would call them a bit under-sized, but they've got stamina, and on the whole they go well together. We've got some good breeding lines there. How are you getting on with John?' John was the other huntsman with the Gidleigh; approaching sixty, he was Robert's immediate superior.

'Fine, sir; I've learned a lot from him that I hadn't been taught at college. He puts in a day at the kennels as well, so that I can get a bit of time off.'

'Yes, he's always been good like that. You know he's thinking of retiring?'

Robert raised his eyebrows in surprise. 'No, sir, that's news to me.'

'Well it's going to be news to the committee soon, so keep it to yourself for a bit. His back's not too good these days and he's feeling the strain of being in the saddle for long stretches of time. He'd rather quit while he's still doing a good job, than linger on and gradually become a liability.'

'I suppose we'd all rather do it that way, sir, but I should have thought he had another season or two in him. I'll be happy to help him out in any way that I can.'

'I'm glad to hear you say that.' The Master paused, to allow a barmaid to place a generous plate of sandwiches between them. They devoured one each in silence before he continued:

'Of course, if John goes at the end of this season, we'll be advertising for a new huntsman. On the other hand, if he'll agree to stay on for another year, I think I could persuade the committee that you were ready to take over from him and we'd be looking for a new whipper-in instead. What do you think?'

Robert found himself thinking about a number of things. Naturally, he wanted to climb the ladder of his chosen profession, but he was not long out of his Equestrian Studies course at Newton Abbott: for which, he reminded himself, the Master had paid. Ideally, he would like to make a proper go of the kennels and learning his art as a whipper-in but if he passed over this opportunity, who knew when another might come along?

He was spared the necessity of replying immediately by the arrival of Stephen Trevis. After saying polite nothings to the ladies of the church – or, in the case of Mrs Trenchard, having nothings said to him at great length – the Rector felt the need of a drink. Seeing Colonel Hargreaves, who was also one of his churchwardens, he approached. The Master held up a finger to Robert to indicate that their conversation was temporarily closed, and pushed the sandwiches in the direction of the clergyman.

'Plenty here for three, Padre, and what'll it be to drink? A pint?'

It was, and while the Master went to the bar to buy it, the Rector chatted to Robert. The whipper-in wasn't exactly a regular member of the congregation, but he was well-known and popular in the town. Besides, Trevis mused, if he only so-cialised with regular members of his congregation, life would become very dull.

'All set for Boxing Day, Robert?'

'Well, there's about a thousand things to do, Padre, but otherwise, I hope so – there'll be nearly thirty of us mounted and I shouldn't be surprised if a few more turn up on the day. The Master says that the *Western Morning News* might be putting us on their front cover this year and the *Okehampton Times* is sending a photographer as well. I hope you'll be there to see us off.'

'I shall be there willingly; if I ever missed, I think that some of the congregation would do to me what your hounds are hoping to do to the fox.'

Robert smiled at the thought. 'I'm sure you'd manage to go to ground in time, Padre.'

The Master returned with the Rector's drink, catching the last part of the conversation. 'Not likely – he'd be chopped before he reached the Rectory. How's the church looking, Padre?'

'All set for Saturnalia, as far as I can see. I've done my best to retain a few remnants of the Christian faith, but it's a losing battle: the good ladies are probably dancing naked on the altar, even as we speak. Are you coming to the mince pie and mulled wine orgy tonight?'

'I'll be there – jacket and tie, is it?'

'Just a loincloth, I should think.' The Rector continued in cynical vein, 'And a few strands of ivy in your hair. What about you, Robert – would you like to come to the parish party?'

Robert grinned: 'I'm not sure they make loincloths in my size, Padre.'

* * * * *

Having announced that 'she has no appetite at all these

days', Aunt Lavinia has put herself outside of the better part of a stilton and broccoli quiche and is now absent-mindedly emptying the top layer of a box of crystallised fruits. Margery had bought the fruits to pass around after the Queen's speech: Aunt Lavinia is washing them down with the remnant of a bottle of *Amoretto*, which had been earmarked for the Boxing Day trifle. Having put up with her aunt for an hour and a half, Margery is already longing to send her back to her geriatric remand home on the south coast, but Aunt Lavinia's parole lasts into the New Year – and she is clearly determined to make the most of it. At the moment, she is eulogising Tom.

'Honestly, Margery dear, he's done the right thing. Nobody respects academic qualifications these days – everybody's a Doctor in some silly study or other, and none of them has an ounce of common sense. The army will do wonders for him – a soldier is always so *handsome*, don't you think? Oh – have I eaten all those fruits? I only meant to have one or two. We may as well finish that bottle, dear, there's only a dribble left….'

Margery grinds down her fillings as she tops up the liqueur glass for the third time. Why Lavinia has decided to put the first person pronoun in the plural is beyond her, since the disposal of the *Amoretto* has been, like the drawings of a pavement artist, all her own work.

Aunt Lavinia is, of course, unreasonably rich; otherwise Margery would never let her past the letterbox. Even with her retirement home gobbling up hundreds of pounds each week, her investments are secure and what she loses at bridge every Thursday ('Such unlucky cards, dear – you'd never believe it') would go a good way towards maintaining the Chagford house. Margery puts the kettle on and, not for the first time, finds herself speculating as to the contents of Lavinia's will. She hopes it contains some more satisfactory clauses than her father-in-law's.

* * * * *

'You ought to take more care, Mrs Stone – you let things work you up too much and with your high blood pressure, it's asking for trouble. Remember that nasty nose bleed you had the other day – you wouldn't want another one like that, would you?' Betty Trenchard places a cup of hot, sweet tea in front of Katherine and then pops a couple of artificial sweeteners into her own. 'Look at me….'

It was, thought Katherine, sourly, difficult not to: there was so much of her.

'…If I didn't think about what I was eating all the time, I'd spend half my life out cold and what good would that be? Folk don't want to be picking me up off the floor every other minute.'

This is certainly true. Betty had had a 'turn' in the hardware store about a month ago and it had taken a couple of strong farmers and half a visiting bell ringing team to raise her to a seat. Katherine, thin and brittle, could have been lifted by a Boy Scout. She takes a sip of sickly tea and decides that it is time for her cleaner to get on with her job.

'Well, I'm all right now, so that's all that matters. Perhaps you could make a start by clearing the kitchen table, Mrs Trenchard. I'll take my tea into the sitting room.'

Betty waddles around the table, clearing scraps of wallpaper and tape. Once Katherine has left her, she allows herself a dis-approving cluck at the red, poster-paint motto: she has no truck with the sentiment and, besides, it seems wrong to drag Christianity into the argument. She knows perfectly well that Katherine will be tucking into a turkey on Christmas day; so it was all right to kill a bird, but not a fox, was it? And what about all those fur coats in her wardrobe? The problem with Katherine Stone, reflects Betty, is that she has too much time on her hands: if she had any proper interests, she wouldn't have to spend her time meddling and making herself a nuisance. Perhaps now that horrid old Ellen Cleghorn is dead, Katherine will find some nicer friends: though Betty has to admit that this seems unlikely. Katherine will probably just make more and more demands of Evelyn Warren. What that poor little woman has to put up with….

* * * * *

Evelyn Warren is wondering what to do with Ellen Cleghorn's Christmas pudding. It has been sitting, in its little bowl, at the end of the larder shelf since Stir-up Sunday. Now that Ellen has gone to a place where Christmas puddings flame of their own accord, the compact amalgam of suet, plums and spices has become redundant.

Evelyn had trained as a cook before her father became ill, when she had given up everything to nurse him. She is particularly famous for her cakes and puddings; every year, ready for distribution around the town, there is a shelf full of bowls tied up with muslin turbans and a collection of inverted biscuit tins containing snow-white cakes. The profits pay for her own meagre celebrations. She runs her eye along the row: a large pudding for the Rectory and one of similar size for Margery Noad; a diminutive offering for Katherine Stone and three enormous specimens for the Colonel, one for his own table, the other two for the hunt staff. Perhaps Betty Trenchard would like the spare pudding? It will be much tastier than the factory-made example that Evelyn had seen her put in her wire basket the other day. But, of course – Betty Trenchard has a gluten allergy.

The problem admitting no immediate solution, Evelyn closes the door on the larder and returns to her kitchen.

* * * * *

CHAPTER FIVE

- CHRISTMAS EVE -

Tom Two had assumed that the first full day of his Christmas leave would begin with a lazy snuggling down into his sheets, safe from the twin authorities of bombardiers or trumpet calls. No actual time for rising had been discussed, but some time around nine o'clock would have seemed right; that being almost the middle of the morning, as far as a mounted soldier is concerned.

The reality was rather different. In the first place, his body, accustomed to the routine of early rising, sprang to instant life at *reveille* time, bypassing the pleasant half-dreaming slumber to which he had been looking forward; in the second place, it was freezing cold. Even inside the bed the sheets had no warmth in them and, outside them, his nose felt moist and his ears tingled numbly. The pillow was frozen and damp and, at the foot of the bed, a rubber hot water bottle gave a remarkably good impression of a slab of refrigerated raw offal.

Tom stuck his head under the bedclothes, kicked out the hot water bottle and wriggled all his limbs vigorously, until a small amount of warmth had been generated. Then he massaged his ears with the palms of his hands; finally, he cupped his hands over his mouth and nostrils and blew warm air into the hollow until his nose came back to life. He wasn't exactly comfortable, but at least he felt human again. After a while, he felt ready to peer out from his cotton womb.

The room was completely dark. Back at the barracks, where there were always a few lights on outside and where the curtains were unlined, his room never got beyond a murky twilight: even when sleeping out on night exercise, the moon and stars had ensured a certain level of visibility. Here, half a mile from the nearest street light and with thick, efficient curtains, all was black as Erebus. After waiting a minute to allow his pupils to dilate to owl-like proportions, he could still make out nothing beyond a few vague outlines. He gave up the attempt and retreated back into foetal security.

The last twenty-four hours, he thought, had been rather good, at least, once the packing had been done. What with needing smart clothes for church and drinks parties, and scruffy clothes for other occasions; everyday riding boots for today's hack and best riding boots and service dress for the hunt itself, it soon became clear that their tubular green kit bags were not up to the job. Eventually, feeling rather foolish until they got used to it, the troopers had worn their breeches and best boots under their smartest civilian trousers. This meant that there was just enough space for the rest of their clothing if Tom One packed an enormous military rucksack instead of his kit bag and if Two, by way of return, carried their service uniforms in suit covers on coat hangers. As they hovered on the Paddington forecourt, displaying their artillery ties under blazers and wax jackets, nobody could have mistaken them for anything other than soldiers on leave.

Tom One's uncle had arrived with about ten minutes to spare and about ten tons of luggage. This included a fan heater, an electric blanket and two litres of gin, in case of emergencies; it was quite clear that the troopers were going to earn their drinks in the buffet car. The journey itself had been cheerful; alcoholic enough to inspire jokes and anecdotes, but not so much as to render them unsteady on arrival at Exeter. Shortly after Westbury, Ashley had abandoned his first-class seat, and did indeed end up squatting on Two's kit bag by the telephone in the buffet car.

Tom paused in his thoughts to re-heat the bed with another vigorous scramble. He wondered if similar athletic feats were going on all over the house, and tried to picture Mrs Noad and her Aunt Lavinia squirming in their nightdresses, frantically keeping the frostbite at bay. Mr Ashley, of course, had come prepared for the arctic conditions: how cold would it have to get before the electric blanket was declared common property and all five of them attempted to squeeze into bed with it?

They had been met at Exeter St. David's by Tom's mother. As Ashley had foreseen, Margery had been studiously polite, so that Two found himself wondering why Tom One and his uncle portrayed her as such a dragon. Aunt Lavinia had been even more welcoming: having taken advantage of her niece's absence by making a start on the Bristol Cream, she had greeted them with sherry-laden kisses on arrival and had then fussed around the two soldiers for the rest of the evening. She delighted in calling them by their numbers rather than their names and listened avidly to their tales of barrack life. Eventually, Margery had decided that the old lady was feeling tired, had frog-marched her up the stairs, and barricaded her into the best spare bedroom for the night. So, all in all, it had been a successful day.

Tom ventured another inspection of the room. Just enough dull light was now struggling around the edge of the curtains for him to be able to make out individual pieces of furniture and to identify the corpse on the hearthrug as his kit bag. It was a well-proportioned room, sufficiently large to retain a good amount of floor space even after allowing for a substantial

Victorian wardrobe and chest of drawers, a couple of armchairs and, of course, the double bed which Tom had converted into a fortress against hypothermia. If only there had been a fire crackling in the grate, he would have regarded it as a very comfortable apartment.

There was a dull thumping knock at the door, obviously made by a slippered foot rather than by knuckles, and Tom One manoeuvred his way in. In his hands, he carried mugs of tea; slung over one forearm was an old, stretched sweater, and nestled in the pit of the other arm was a fresh hot water bottle. On his feet, he wore a hideous pair of furry slippers; another oversized sweater was visible between his dressing gown and pyjama top, and his legs were encased in an olive green material, which Tom Two found worryingly familiar.

Two groaned: 'Before you come any closer, One, promise me that you're not wearing a pair of army long johns under your dressing gown.'

Grinning from ear to ear, Tom One continued advancing: 'One regulation pair of Passion Killers – Men's, Green. I knew they'd be just the thing for home when we were issued with them. My thighs and my manhood have stayed as warm as toast all night, in spite of the central heating conking out again.'

'Thanks, One, I really needed to know that, first thing in the morning.'

'Happy to oblige. Now, if you put on this old jumper, and stick the hot water bottle in your bed, I'll hand over your tea.'

Two seized both articles eagerly. He was soon sitting up, enveloped in thick cable stitching, drinking tea and warming his feet. 'Thanks One – this is making a big difference.'

'Hang on to your mug – I'm coming on board.' Tom One clambered onto the far end of the bed, crossed his legs, and leaned against the oak frame. 'Sorry about the central heating. Uncle George is doing his best to light a fire in the sitting room, and he's turned the oven on full blast in the kitchen, so it should be warm enough to go downstairs in about half an hour.'

'That's good, but I assumed that your uncle would be hiding under his electric blanket.'

A contented smile stretched itself across Tom One's face: 'I dare say he would be, if Aunt Lav wasn't occupying the only spare bedroom with three-pin sockets. You should have heard him swearing this morning – he's obviously picked up bad habits from his visits to the barracks.'

'Well, what can you expect, mixing with all those officers?

* * * * *

The hounds have had a cold night as well. When Robert peers through the iron bars of the gate to the dog-hound quarters he sees them piled together for warmth, one on another, in a great tangled heap of legs, ears and tails. He turns the key in the lock and instantly the furry mountain tears apart and a joyful ululation of anticipatory crying and barking begins. The gate is opened and the hounds escape to the compound beyond, giving Robert the opportunity to rake out their bedding and hose down the lower walls and the concrete floor.

As the water splashes around, Robert considers the possible routes for his hack with the Toms. The standard ride for new clients is up to the top of Meldon Tor: this offers a spectacular view of Chagford, and the round trip takes little more than an hour. On the other hand, two mounted soldiers probably have a bit more stamina and sense of adventure than most new customers: perhaps they should head across Chagford Common up to Kestor Rock and maybe even beyond that, to the stone circle at Scorhill? Or they could ride south to the reservoir at Fernworthy, enjoying a good gallop over Thornworthy Down. Whichever they choose, the dawn sky promises a fine morning.

Robert tries to picture Tom Noad, but cannot recall a face to go with the name. He calculates that Tom must have started at the primary school at about the time Robert himself was going up to Okehampton College; maybe they overlapped by a year. After that, according to Primrose Armishaw, Tom went off to boarding school, so although they have both been based in Chagford for most of their lives, they have never met, as far as Robert knows. Probably they will recognise each other when Tom arrives at the stable this morning.

The dog-hounds' quarters are clean; fresh bedding is laid in one end and Robert moves across to the bitch-hounds' compound. The bitches, woken by the howling of the dogs, are already clamouring at their iron gate. Robert opens it and they stream past him, a sniffing, wagging, chaotic muddle of curiosity and enthusiasm. They surround him, breathing in his familiar scent, acknowledging him, with the instinct of the pack animal, as their leader. He makes much of the nearest few, calling them by their names, rumpling ears and giving hearty smacks to rib cages, before pushing the bitches aside and entering their quarters to repeat his work with the rake and the hosepipe.

Half an hour later, he is walking along a footpath, dog-hounds and bitch-hounds clustering around him, young hounds coupled to older ones, learning his commands and understanding the intonations of his voice through the example given by their more experienced partners. The skirter is doing her best to shake off her colleague but the double collar is close fitting and the older bitch-hound is wise and authoritative. Robert hopes that the coupling will work and that the skirter will begin to learn her trade. He tries hard not to contemplate the alternative: why spoil the atmosphere of this magical morning exercise?

* * * * *

The Toms emerged from the house just after eight o'clock and walked up the drive to the road. When they reached the gate, Tom Two turned back to get his first daylight view of his friend's house.

'It's pretty big, One – it must be fun living here.'

'It is, but we can't really afford it. My grandfather-to-the-power-of-about-six bought it back in Queen Boadicea's time, or thereabouts, and my great-grandfather added all the bits to the south of the main entrance. Now guess which chunk is falling down.'

Tom Two could see what his friend meant. The sturdy, timeless granite of the old building was massive and immovable, whereas the brickwork of the inter-war years was crumbling and the roof sagged. After a quick architectural calculation, Two realised that he was sleeping exactly under the most dangerous-looking section. Tom One continued: 'Mother hates it, of course – it's too big for her to clean all by herself and she can't manage the garden, but we haven't got enough money for a cleaner. Someone comes to do the lawn every so often, but that's about it. One of the reasons she's so cross about me joining the army is that I'm never going to make enough money to pay for the work that needs doing.'

They leaned against the gate for a while. Now that he knew to look for signs of dilapidation, Two began to see them everywhere. Paint was peeling from woodwork; in the garden, shrubs were scruffy and misshapen. A length of guttering threatened to detach itself during the next good wind and, even during the middle of winter, it was easy to see that the flowerbeds had been neglected for many months.

'I know it's not my business – but why doesn't your mother sell it?'

Tom One perked up; there was a malicious streak in his smile as he replied, 'She can't – it's mine.'

'Wow! Really?'

'Yes – you know my father died when I was quite young? We all lived here with my grandfather and he left the house directly to me. Mother holds it in trust until I'm twenty-five, at which time, she's convinced that I'm going to chuck her out on the streets.'

'You wouldn't, would you?'

One considered and sighed wistfully. 'I suppose not – but there's a shed at the bottom of the garden which would make a lovely granny flat.'

They turned into the lane and began the walk up to the livery yard. It felt strange to be wearing their army boots and breeches with civilian shirts and sweaters and to walk bareheaded, swinging their hard hats in their hands, without fear of being assailed by the nearest NCO. In fact, they soon began to feel the lack of a headdress, their short haircuts affording no protection against the cold. By the time they were half way to the stable, they had resolved to buy themselves caps in the Moorland Clothing store that afternoon.

'Un' than uz'll be parsing forra real cuppola country voke.' One lapsed into an entirely artificial dialect.

'Does that mean that we'll be expected to take advantage of the local ovine population?'

'Only on Toosdays an' Thursdays, my luvver. The rest of the week, 'tis incest in these parrts.'

'That's all right then – my family's a couple of hundred miles away.'

Tom One gave up the silly voice and offered to lend Two his Aunt Lavinia for the purpose; an offer that was politely declined.

The livery yard was about a mile from Tom's house. There was a moment of recognition as the two walked into the office and found Robert Brookes in the process of kicking off his wellingtons and pulling on a riding boot. He paused to look up and stood awkwardly, a boothook in each hand and his right foot halfway down the leather shaft. Then he gave a big grin and said: 'So you're Tom – I thought I'd know you when I saw you.' He gave a good tug on the boothooks and his foot thrust itself down into position. Standing upright, he shook hands with Tom One, who then introduced Two: 'I remember you as well. This is another Tom, just to be confusing.'

'I'm Two, he's One, if that helps.' Tom Two clarified the situation, holding out his hand.

'I think I can just about cope with that.' Robert's soft Devon drawl was sufficiently related to One's ridiculous farmyard impression to make Two smile: fortunately, it was the sort of occasion where smiles were expected.

'Your horses are all tacked up and ready. If you want to go and find them, I'll be along in a minute.' Robert reached for his left boot. 'They're a grey mare and a chestnut gelding – it doesn't matter who rides which.'

They wandered outside and along the stalls. Primrose Armishaw's yard was spotlessly clean and efficiently run; nonetheless, to the Toms, used to the rigid lines and uniform appearance of a military stable block, it had an attractive ramshackle and rustic appearance. Stalls, created from huge, irregular beams and planks sunk into a granite outer wall, were of uneven height and size. The roof along one line was an ageing thatch; along another, the occupants were protected from the weather by slate tiles, pleasingly muddled and misshapen. The large barn, in which feed and bedding were stored, was roofed less picturesquely, but more practically, in corrugated iron. The complex was obviously a result of architectural evolution rather than deliberate design.

The horses, too, were more varied. Far from the regulation height and appearance of the Troop's magnificent collection, the Toms found themselves the latest objects of interest to a selection of hunters and ponies, which seemed to represent every possible equestrian breed and shade. A surly-looking piebald made a lunge for one of Tom Two's tempting ears as he walked past, while One exchanged affectionate clucking greetings with a fat and complacent Welsh Cob.

Their mounts were at the far end of the yard, with saddles loosely in place and reins tied up and tucked into the bridles. Both animals were a good hand higher than the compact troop horses: it was going to be a longer way down than usual, Tom Two observed, stoically. He bagged the grey, on the grounds that that was what state trumpeters rode, and they entered the stalls, slipping the reins over the horses' heads before leading them out into the yard. Robert, now booted and spurred and with his hard hat on, came out of the office in time to see two well-practised examples of the army 'quickest and best' mounting technique: gripping the saddle, each soldier gave two preparatory bounces and then vaulted directly onto their horses' backs. It made a pleasant change from watching riders teetering nervously on the mounting block.

'Well you two obviously know what you're doing.' He led his own black mare out, put his left foot into the nearside stirrup and jumped into the saddle. 'I guess that means we can go for the challenging ride rather than the beginner's plod. Are you up for it?'

They were. It was the work of a minute to adjust the stirrups and tighten girths another notch or two and then they rode their three horses towards the moor.

* * * * *

CHAPTER SIX

- LUNCHTIME IN CHAGFORD -

Ashley had planned a pleasant morning in Chagford. He would potter into the town and exchange news and gossip with any acquaintance he happened to meet; he would spend a civilised half hour in the Godolphin Gallery admiring the Widgerys and Brittans on sale; then he would chew the cud with his old friend, the vintner, before buying a copy of the *Telegraph* and heading for the Ring O'Bells pub.

Margery had different ideas. If George was going into town, he could pick up half a dozen essential bits and pieces; drop a Christmas card through Evelyn Warren's letterbox (a late response to an unexpected arrival), and call in at the church to see if the flower arrangers needed more greenery.

It was not surprising, therefore, that Ashley felt rather grumpy as he joined a long queue in Norah Dyer's corner shop and listened to her exchanging symptoms and intimacies with a succession of late Christmas shoppers. By the time he reached the front of the queue, Ashley felt that he knew considerably more than he wished about Ellen Cleghorn's heart problems (which had come to such a satisfactory and spectacular conclusion), Mrs Farmer Crane's cystitis (less satisfactory, but occasionally just as spectacu-

60

lar) and Mrs Dyer's own rheumatism (a failure on both counts). He had also heard that Katherine Stone had written to the Bishop to complain about the planned peal of Grandsire Triples after Midnight Mass and that the Bishop had telephoned Stephen Trevis to insist that the peal be limited to half an hour. This last piece of gossip came via Mrs Trevis, who had complained bitterly to Mrs Hargreaves, the master's wife; their conversation had been overheard by Betty Trenchard, who had passed the information on in the corner shop and thence to the world.

Eventually, Ashley was in a position to place his wire basket on the counter. Mrs Dyer rummaged nosily through the contents, passing a verdict on each purchase as she tapped its price into the till.

'Crystallised fruits – very nice. My Arthur always likes a box of those on the sideboard at Christmas…. Toilet paper – I think that's the last couple of rolls of the extra soft – Mrs Crane bought a whole basketful yesterday…. Flour – oh….'

Mrs Dyer's pause punctured Ashley's vision of the farmer's wife stockpiling lavatory paper in the outside privy.

'Did you realise, my dear, that you've got gluten-free flour here? It says on the front of the packet, here.' She pointed out the information, making Ashley feel about five years old.

'No, I hadn't realised – does it make any difference?'

'Well, you wouldn't want to use it if you didn't have to. It makes horrible pastry, all chewy, just like cardboard. Hang on a minute, I'll get you some of the proper stuff.' She eased herself off her stool and ambled over to the appropriate shelf, continuing her monologue all the time. 'We get the gluten-free in for Betty Trenchard. She has a dreadful allergy, poor thing – she's a coelacanth according to the Rector's wife, and now they think it's all linked in with diabetes.'

'Terrible thing that is,' contributed a wizened spinster with a packet of dried peas. 'We had a cat with it once – we got the vet to put her to sleep.'

61

'Well, it's kinder in the long run, though I shouldn't tell Betty that, she might not thank you....'

Five minutes later, feeling like an aristocrat who had just made a lucky escape from the Bastille, Ashley stood on the pavement outside the shop. According to Margery's list of imperatives, he should now cross over to the church: a more persuasive voice in his left ear told him that he needed a drink. He was hovering indecisively at the crossroads of things Godly and things alcoholic – which, he reflected dryly, summarised much of his life so far – when he heard a familiar voice. It reinforced the tempting eloquence of the devil on his shoulder.

'Hello George, I thought I might bump into you at some point. I'm just popping into the Ring O'Bells; have you time for a drink?'

It was entirely appropriate, thought Ashley, that this summons to the bar should come from Peter Masters, the Chagford solicitor. They turned in the direction of the pub: the flower-arranging Mafia would just have to eke out their greenery as best they could.

Chagford boasts four public houses, all on, or nearly on, the Square. The Buller Arms and the Globe cater for the younger farming and hunting set; the Three Crowns, scene of historic murder and Civil War drama, takes up most of the tourists; and the Ring O' Bells is ideal for those who like their pint in peace. It is the sort of pub that feels empty if there is not a Labrador or retriever snoozing in front of the fire. The bar staff will happily chat with you if you are in a sociable mood, and the landlady will enlist your help with difficult crossword clues or leave you undisturbed in a corner, if that is your wish. Peter Masters ordered two pints of ale and the two retreated to a bench near the fire. They shared the heat with the Rector's dog which, more sensible than its owner, was hiding from the world and minding its own business in peace.

'Cheers Peter. You're looking well; life in Devon obviously suits you.'

'If by that, you mean that I'm putting on weight, you're all too accurate. There's an excess of clotted cream in the bloodstream: it will be your fault if I die from a dairy produce-induced thrombosis.'

Ashley had known Peter in London. When they were both setting out on their careers, each had been able to put some work in the way of the other. From the very start, the solicitor had hoped to move to the West Country and Ashley had recommended the Chagford practice warmly when it came up. He was a few years younger than Ashley but dressed a few years older: there was a mustard waistcoat under his tweed suit, with a substantial gold chain threaded through a buttonhole and leading, presumably, to an expensive watch in the left-hand pocket. His round spectacles were metal framed, matching the watch chain; his hair was just beginning to show signs of receding. He was far from fat, but he had certainly added to his figure since his London days, and his waistcoat was fully occupied. He had been spending an unpleasant morning tying up the details of Ellen Cleghorn's will.

'Is it a complicated document?'

'No, that's the most annoying thing about it: just a few simple bequests and the residue of her estate to some ridiculous animal charity. She lived in rented accommodation and was nowhere near the inheritance tax bracket, so it ought to have been really simple.'

'And the snag?'

'The snag, as you say, is that she appointed Katherine Stone as joint executor and I've just spent two hours in the company of that pestilential woman, going through it clause by clause. Because she was married to a New York attorney, she fancies herself as a home lawyer – in fact, she helped draw up the will in the first place. I think I was only put down as an executor because Cleghorn didn't fully trust her.' Peter paused to refresh himself from his glass, then added, 'Apart from actually dying, it's one of the few sensible things Cleghorn ever did. Mother Stone spent quite a lot of time trying to persuade me that all the china had been intended for her, even though only a tea service was specified. I'm sure that if I'd let her get away with it, she'd have moved on to other demands.'

Ashley wondered why he had never come across this unpleasant-sounding woman. It was easy enough for decent people to remain anonymous: nasty people tended to make themselves known. Peter filled him in on some details.

'She's only been here for a couple of years – or, rather, she only returned a couple of years ago. Her family was very much Old Chagford, if you know what I mean. Apparently, she met a lawyer attached to the American Air Force after the Second World War and married him. He died not so long ago, leaving her very comfortably off. There were no children, and she'd offended all her American in-laws, so she came back home, where she has been making herself a nuisance to Chagford in general and to me in particular.'

Ashley took in this potted history appreciatively. 'It sounds as though your, "in particular" embraces more than just one morning.'

'Well, I'm sure you can imagine the sort of thing, George. Because she thinks she knows about law, she'll start something, make a mess of it and then expect to be bailed out. When she bought her house here, she wanted to close a bridle path at the bottom of her land and caused one hell of a stink about it – she wouldn't believe me when I told her that if it went to court, she'd lose. Then, when she did lose, she tried to wriggle out of paying me, claiming that it was a "no win, no fee" case!'

'I'm getting the idea. I hope that when she finally did pay up, the fee was substantial?'

Peter looked pleased with himself. 'Enough to buy a second

hunter and to afford the livery fees for a year or so. I take particular pleasure in riding it along her stretch of bridle path – she has very high blood pressure, so with any luck the sight will bring on an attack one day.'

'And then you'll have the pleasure of proving her will?'

'A keenly awaited event, I can assure you.'

* * * * *

A broad track runs from the foot of Meldon Tor all the way to the granite outcrop at the peak. Robert had no need to suggest a run to the top; he simply spurred his horse on and left the Toms to follow his example. The gallop would form a spectacular end to a superb morning's riding over open moorland. They had been out even further than the stone circle at Scorhill; to the iron age huts beyond and to Throwleigh Common, galloping back via the steady rise to the top of Kennon Hill and then, on a long rein, walking the descent to the clapper bridge over the Teign. Troopers Scott and Lang had been right when they said that unexpected dips in the ground would probably be the most common hazard on Dartmoor. At first it had produced a strange lurching effect in the stomach when the horses had treated these as small jumps, but the Toms soon became used to the sensation: realising that the horses knew the ground better than they did, they trusted to their mounts and gave them enough rein to do the job.

They had reached the turning to the livery yard about half an hour ago, but instead of finishing then, Robert had suggested this final run to the top of Meldon so that Tom Two could enjoy the panoramic view of Chagford.

Tom One let his friend take the second place; for a moment he held back his gelding and briefly enjoyed the sight of the two horses in front of him taking the rising path as quickly as they could. Then he too brought his spurs into contact and thrilled to the sound of the thudding hoofs below him and the snorting breaths from his horse's flared nostrils; keeping his aching calves firmly in contact to maintain the pace, he absorbed the motion of the stride into his own body, willing the horse along with every muscle.

All too soon, it was over. Even as Tom closed the gap between himself and the grey, Robert was slowing down the pace. They reached the great stones at the top at a steady canter and transposed rapidly down to a halt. Relaxing, they and the horses gulped in oxygen, the hot breath of both humans and animals condensing in the December air.

Behind them lay views across the moor; in front were the wooded slopes of the Teign gorge, dominated by the bleak mass of Castle Drogo; and below lay Chagford itself, white and compact. Tom Two gasped with astonishment at the landscape; he gave four successive turns on the forehand and admired the scenery through a full circle. Even Tom One, to whom the view was familiar, felt that he was seeing it anew from his position on the chestnut hunter. Why had he wasted so many years, living on the moor, yet never learning to ride?

They lingered for about ten minutes, then took a steeper path down the eastern slope of the tor, sitting back in the saddle and trusting to the horses to maintain balance. The route took them along a bridle path and then down a narrow lane, which led into the town. As they turned into the square, Ashley and Peter Masters emerged from the Ring O'Bells. Tom One greeted his uncle, while Robert touched the brim of his hat to one of the wealthier patrons of the hunt.

'Morning, Mr Masters – we've been giving her a good go, as you can probably tell.'

'Jolly good – I see she's still got all four shoes.'

The grey mare was Peter Masters' new hunter. He turned to Tom Two.

'How was she?'

'She was fine, sir – she really looked after me when I needed it. Thank you for letting me ride her.'

'Not at all, I'm delighted that there's someone good to go with her on Boxing Day. Just keep an eye out for her nearside rear shoe: she's got into the habit of casting it. How much have I spent on the farrier in the last six months, Robert?'

'I wouldn't like to say, sir, but I know he's taking a holiday in the Seychelles next summer.'

'Well, I hope he sends me a postcard – I feel I've earned it. You've just come along the devil's bridle path, I suppose?' Peter Masters raised an eyebrow to Ashley, then, suddenly remembering that Katherine Stone was distantly related to the whipper-in, he blushed and quickly changed the subject. 'Anyway, I'll see you all up at the yard on Friday. Have a good Christmas, Robert.'

'You too, sir. And thank you for the box. Very generous of you.'

The solicitor gave a deprecating wave of the hand and disappeared in the direction of his office. Ashley looked at his watch and calculated that his friend, the vintner, would probably be conducting an informal and solitary tasting session in the flat over the shop.

'I'll see you back at the house, lads. Luncheon can be at any old time – there are sandwiches in the kitchen whenever you want them.'

* * * * *

Clutching her Christmas pudding possessively, Katherine Stone approached the Square from Southcombe Street, the corner furthest from the riding party. She glared venomously at a scene which represented all she hated most: horses which had undoubted been riding on *her* land – a hunter bought with *her* money – a lawyer whom she disliked, who had just outwitted her – and a great-nephew who worked for an organisation devoted to killing animals and lording it arrogantly all over the countryside. Her cheeks infused with blood; she took deep breaths and stood still to ward off another attack of high pressure.

The party broke up. Katherine watched the lawyer take his leave and then sniffed disapprovingly as Ashley went into the vintner's shop. The three riders clopped gently along the road: how stupid of all the locals to smile at them, as if they were doing something good just by being on top of a horse!

The sound of hoofs on tarmac grew fainter as the group headed down Mill Lane and out of sight. Gradually, Katherine's cheeks faded to a shade of pink, which would have looked attractive on a face accustomed to smiling. Deeming it safe to continue walking, she turned to her left and headed towards the gallery: Ellen Cleghorn had owned a pair of watercolours by George Oysten, and Katherine wanted to find out how much they were worth.

* * * * *

CHAPTER SEVEN

- THE KENNELS -

Robert was impressed with his two young horsemen. They had displayed increasing confidence out on the moor; although their technique was by no means very advanced, it was clear that they had mastered fundamental skills thoroughly. They were intelligent enough to be aware of their limitations but, within them, they were adventurous and energetic. Finally, and most importantly, they treated their mounts with respect, knowing when to encourage, but also when to leave the horses to find their own pace and route through the irregular terrain.

Just as the best parties end up in the kitchen, so the best rides conclude sociably in the harness room. After grooming was finished, the Toms had assumed that a cleaning of saddles and bridles was part of the morning's programme, so Robert, carrying in his own tack, was entertained to find them in the whitewashed room, stripped to the waist and systematically working saddle soap into leather.

'This makes a pleasant change,' he rinsed his bit and then hung up the bridle. 'I normally end up doing the kit myself at the end of the week. Whether it needs it or not,' he added, ironically. 'I suppose you spend a lot of time doing this sort of thing in the army?'

Now it was Tom One's turn to be ironic. 'Just the odd minute, here and there,' he replied blithely. 'We've been missing it since we came down.'

'So we may as well get our fix now.' Tom Two continued the subject while One paused to activate his salivary glands. There was a satisfying smacking sound as a small globule of projected fluid spattered against the seat. Tom One took up the conversation as he gently massaged the leather: 'Tell you what, Robert – if that's the saddle you're going to be riding on Boxing Day, we'll do it for you, won't we, Two?'

'Sure – it's the least we can do after that ride. We'll do your boots at the same time if you like: we may as well do the job properly.'

This was not the sort of offer to be turned down: the two saddles were already the brightest objects in the harness room. 'Thanks, I appreciate that. My hunting boots are back at the kennels though. Why not come down there for a drink after you've finished here? I can show you the hounds, if you like.'

'That'd be great. We're in no hurry to get back, are we, One?'

'Not unless you want to get to the sherry before Aunt Lav drains the last glass. We've got about half an hour's work here, Robert; shall we head down after that?'

Robert looked at his watch. 'There's a chap coming to look at a horse in a few minutes. My guess is, he'll want to try her out in the field, and perhaps a quick run on the moor as well. Why don't you just head down to the kennels when you're ready? The front door of the cottage is always open and there's beer in the fridge, or some scrumpy under the sink, if you're feeling brave. I'll join you as soon as I can.'

'Sounds good – what do you think, Two?'

'Let's go for it, One – if it's under the sink, Robert, will we be able to work out which is the scrumpy and which is the lavatory cleaner?'

'Not from the flavour, I shouldn't think.' The homemade cider was produced by John, Robert's fellow huntsman. He aimed for effect rather than subtlety. 'But the scrumpy is the one in the four-litre plastic container. Sip it delicately, if you want to remain conscious.'

* * * * *

Ashley and Mark Overland, the vintner, were comparing two vintages from the same vineyard in Meursault, when Stephen Trevis arrived, searching for his dog. Having established that the animal was warming its stomach in the Ring O'Bells, he gratefully accepted the pair of goblets that was placed in front of him. After a Crib Service for children, the Burgundian wines were particularly acceptable. For a while, conversation was limited to details of *terroire, bouquet* and the qualities of the *Pinot Noir*. The Rector held up his first glass and tilted it.

'Lovely legs.'

'Oh, but not nearly as good as yours, Rector.'

'Please, Mark – we're in civilised company here.'

They agreed in preferring the 1995 wine to its companion from the previous year, then Trevis and Overland began eulogising the 1978 vintage; alas, long since consumed. Ashley, who had not had the pleasure of experiencing that particular wine, gave his attention to those that were at hand. After a couple of glasses apiece, talk turned to matters of more general interest. The Rector had seen Robert and the Toms ride into town as he entered the church, steeling himself for the full awfulness of infantile devotion.

'Was that your nephew I saw on one of the Colonel's hunters as I came out of church? With Robert and another young lad?'

'It was, though I didn't realise the horse belonged to the Colonel. The other chap was from his regiment, taking refuge from a family Christmas.'

'One can only sympathise. They seemed to be hitting it off with Robert: he's a good lad. The Master thinks highly of him, I know. He's been very generous to the boy.'

Ashley's curiosity was aroused; he knew nothing of Robert, and said so. The Rector and Mark Overland exchanged glances.

'You've been in Chagford longer than I have, Mark. You know more of the people.'

'I think you'll know more of the details, though, Rector.'

In they end, they told the story between them, filling in each other's pauses; this made for a rather muddled version of events, but Ashley was able to sift out the important details in order to get a good idea of Robert's history.

Through his father's mother – the side of the family on which he was related to Katherine Stone – Robert came from a line of yeomen by the name of Freston who had been farming Chagford land for many generations. Over the last century, the land had been divided several times, so that the portion inherited by Robert's father was barely sufficient to provide a livelihood for James Brookes, his wife and a young son. Nor was James a farmer of any great skill: he had consistently made poor decisions, and his farm became more and more of a liability. Finally, after a season in which his herd was decimated by tuberculosis, he had shot himself.

'Was that 1987, Mark? I know it was late in the eighties, and that Robert had just started at school. We could check in the churchyard, of course.'

"87 or '88, Rector – I'm not sure which. I know the school sent the children home for the day. He was a popular man, James, and lots of the children came from families who were friendly with him.'

Ashley co-ordinated the dates with those of his own family. Tom had been born in 1985 and his father had been killed in the winter of 1987. Margery had her own worries at that time: it was hardly surprising that she had failed to pass on this sad story.

Robert's mother had sold the land to Colonel Hargreaves and returned to her people at Tavistock. The Colonel, who had been a good friend of Robert's father and grandparents, continued to take an interest in the widow and her son; perhaps the more so after his own son was killed by 'friendly fire' in the first Gulf War. He sent money regularly and, in recent years, had financed Robert's course in equestrian studies at an agricultural college. At the end of the course, he had used his influence with the committee to have Robert appointed kennelman and whipper-in to the Gidleigh Hunt.

'And, in brief, that's the story,' the Rector summed up. 'Two sad deaths which, I suppose, have led to good actions and, therefore, one must give thanks.'

Ashley and Overland nodded solemnly: the detective added the story to the ever-increasing collection of tragedies with which life and work had brought him into contact.

* * * * *

Robert's tied cottage was a four-roomed bungalow, its front door opening directly onto the Gidleigh road. The high walls of the kennels were built into the side and back of the building, giving the effect of a cloister or, as Tom Two observed, a small barracks. A large wrought-iron double gate was set in the front wall and through this they could see the hounds in their two compounds. Tom One foolishly bid them a good morning, setting off a chorus of barks and howls, and causing several of the more inquisitive animals to stand on their hind legs and force their noses through the wire mesh which enclosed them.

'I think you've made about forty friends, there, One,' said Two, heading rapidly for the cottage door. 'No wonder he never bothers locking the place – that lot would frighten off any thief, I should think.'

They shot into a small hallway and shut the door. The clamour of the hounds became muffled and gradually subsided of its own accord, leaving the Toms in peace to make themselves at home.

It was quite clear that Robert's priorities in life were his hounds and his horses. Some way behind them were his own bodily requirements and the necessity of looking smart for his job; right at the bottom of the list was housework. The sitting room was a superb clutter of old furniture, hunting equipment and memorabilia, and the remains of meals enjoyed in front of the television. Around the fireplace, the ash of ages spilled onto the hearthrug and a scruffy collection of newspapers, kindling wood and logs overflowed a large wicker basket. Above, two foxes leered angrily from wooden mounts, not at all pleased with the dubious immortality conferred upon them by the taxidermist. Tom Two took up a small hunting horn from a table and produced a few buzzing sounds, before giving it up as a bad job.

In the kitchen, the washing up appeared to have been accumulating since the first day of the hunting season; and an illicit glance into Robert's bedroom revealed an unmade bed, a chest with permanently open drawers and the twin of the fire basket, bursting with laundry. Contrasting with this evidence of domestic neglect were Robert's best white breeches and scarlet hunting coat, wrapped in thin transparent plastic, obviously just back from the dry cleaners. They hung from the open door of a wardrobe; the Toms observed and approved the coat's shining buttons with the raised letters G and H entwined in cipher, and the velvet collar of the hunt's colour; a green so dark, it might easily be mistaken for a blue.

Back in the kitchen, they discovered the scrumpy, compared

its bouquet unfavourably with that of the lavatory cleaner and returned to the sitting room with a glass each. They fell into a pair of elderly club armchairs. Two swung himself sideways, so that his back leaned against the threadbare fabric of one arm, and his legs hooked over the other. His spurs clashed with each other as he made the movement and, enjoying the metallic sound, he clicked his heels together two or three times as he surveyed the room once more.

'You know, One, if it weren't for the tyranny of regular room inspections, we could live in agreeable squalor like this. Can you imagine what our inspecting sergeants on basic training would have said, if they'd come across this on their rounds?'

'I think their Tourette's syndromes might have suffered a relapse – if they didn't burst a few blood vessels first. Have you tried your cider yet?'

'I was waiting for you to go first.'

'Coward.' Tom One took a good mouthful. His eyes bulged with horror as the rough alcohol burned his taste buds and scoured his throat as he swallowed: 'Wow!'

'Was it good?' Tom Two adopted an air of innocent inquiry.

'Let's put it this way – I think we've found the alcoholic equivalent of the lance bomber's tea. Have a go.'

Two shared the corrosive sensation in his mouth and on the lining of his oesophagus. He spluttered and gulped for air: 'We must take some of this wonderful drink back for him – he'll love it!'

After a few more mouthfuls, the initial violence of the brew faded. They were even beginning to acquire a taste for it, when they heard the hounds yelping and barking once more.

'That'll be Robert.' Two craned his neck towards the window: 'No – it's some little biddy. She's heading this way: do you think one of us ought to go to the door? She'll think it odd if she just sees us through the window, slouching about in somebody else's house.'

One, who was nearer the hallway, stood up and headed for the front door, opening it before Evelyn Warren had the chance to knock. Surprised, she gave a little shriek, which sounded like a genteel version of the babble coming from the hounds' compounds. The trooper gabbled an apology: 'I'm terribly sorry – I didn't mean to take you by surprise. We saw you coming, so I opened the door.'

Evelyn took a moment or two to get her breath back, holding a small hand against a vestigial bosom.

'That's quite all right – so silly of me. I was expecting to see Robert, of course: you must be a friend of his.'

Tom Two joined One in the doorway. 'We've just been riding with him – he'll be along any minute. Would you like to come in?'

Evelyn seemed intimidated at the thought of entering a shrine to youthful masculinity. 'No, no, I only came to give him a Christmas card. Perhaps you would be so kind….' She reached into an ample shopping bag and brought out an envelope, handing it to Tom One. 'And if you could tell him that his cousin Evelyn called, I'd be very grateful.'

Tom accepted the card and Evelyn scuttled back in the direction of Chagford. The soldiers returned to the sitting room and reoccupied their armchairs.

'Well, we frightened her off, poor dear.' Tom Two began clicking his spurs again. 'Did you know her at all?'

'Not really – I think mother comes across her at Church. There's a whole posse of them. I just keep out of the way, really.'

'Very sensible.'

Robert arrived a few minutes later. He gave them a short tour of the kennels and took them into the compounds, where they were enthused over by the hounds, excited at the arrival of two new smells. They saw the night quarters, the separate accommodation for sick and lame hounds and a heated room with blankets for whelping bitches. A truck, new that season, for transporting hounds and the horses of the hunt staff, was admired, and the whole business of kennel routine, both summer and winter, was briefly explained. It was too early for feeding time, but Robert gave them a gory introduction to another of his regular tasks as they approached the stores.

'If any of the local farmers has an animal die on him, we bring it back here, skin it and feed it to the hounds. It's not pleasant work but it's a good source of raw meat for them, and I can sell the hides and fleeces and keep the money.'

In a corner of the stores, a small pile of hides, salted and ready for the tanner gave evidence of this source of income. A larger collection of fleeces nestled under a table. In a separate room, with a concrete floor and prominent drainage system, a pair of meathooks, suspended on adjustable chains, provided the means for hanging carcasses prior to skinning them. The Toms exchanged glances, secretly relieved that no farm animal had died unexpectedly in the last couple of days.

Robert observed their expressions and shrugged: 'If there'd been a carcass hanging here, I wouldn't have brought you in. But you get used to it.'

The Toms returned to the cottage with their heads full of new vocabulary and the impression that Robert worked for at least twenty-three hours every day. Robert poured more scrumpy and confirmed the latter observation.

'You're not far wrong,' he gave wry grin, 'but it's a good life. If we were a large hunt, we'd have four or five full-time staff, but the Gidleigh's always been small, so we have to do a bit of everything. John puts in one day a week here and there's a girl in the town who comes down as well: that gives me some free time and it means I can put in a few hours up at the livery yard, which brings in a bit of extra cash.'

Back in the sitting room, Tom Two pointed out Evelyn's card, which was added to a small collection above the chimney.

'She's one of my few relations: as you can see, I don't have many.' He paused for thought, then added, sourly, 'And I'm not expecting one from my other Chagford relative.'

The Toms exchanged glances. It was the first indication of any anger or bitterness they had observed in Robert.

* * * * *

CHAPTER EIGHT

- THE BOXING DAY MEET -

Half past seven on Boxing Day morning. Christmas has passed; mainly agreeable, frequently dull and, in some houses, occasionally malevolent. Today, many of the inhabitants of Chagford enjoy the rare chance to lie in on a weekday: others have already been up for some time, preparing for the events to come.

Prebendary Stephen Trevis gives a gigantic snore and rolls over, stealing most of the duvet in the process. Mrs Trevis, woken simultaneously by the porcine grunting and the sudden sensation of cold, makes an attempt to reclaim her own, but her husband, even asleep, is a strong and determined man. After a few depressing moments looking down the length of her body, and wondering if a new nightdress would improve matters, she decides that a cup of tea by the Aga will provide more stimulation and warmth than her present position. As she rises from the bed, the dog leaps to take her place and breathes last night's tin of pet food into the Rector's face. Mrs Trevis goes to grab the dog's collar but, before she can reach it, her husband rolls over again, and embraces the animal, snuggling up and producing little humming sounds. The dog, in ecstasy, licks her master's ear and beats her tail against the mattress: Mrs Trevis decides to leave them to it.

Descending the stairs, she tries to remember when she had last come in for a display of affection like that. What had the dog to offer that she hadn't? Silky ears, and a wet nose? Perhaps it was the extra dugs: Stephen had always liked that sort of thing.

She spilt some water on the hot plate of the Aga; it formed into little droplets, which shot in all directions across the surface before evaporating. Waiting for the kettle to boil, she reviewed her Christmas. Midnight Mass, of course, had been packed. Stephen had preached very cleverly, comparing the pealing bells to the singing of the angels on the first Christmas night: 'Let us all pray that tonight's peal – though, sadly, only a short one – will be carried by the wind across the moor, bringing the true message of Christmas into the homes and hearts of all.' It was all beautifully expressed and everybody had smiled piously, realising that the subtext was a wish that the clamour would be wafted across to Meldon Dene and wake up that old witch, Katherine Stone.

Robert has been up since before six o'clock; together with John, the old huntsman, he has selected the hounds to be hunted and separated them from those being rested. In a few minutes, Lorraine will be along to assist with the morning routines and then Robert can wander up to the livery yard to tend to his horse. Perhaps the two Toms will already be there? Robert is grateful to them for saving him at least an hour's work on this busy morning, and makes a mental note to repay them by taking a large flask of tea up to the stable.

Fresh bedding is distributed; the whipper-in rolls up his hosepipe and wanders into the yard. Lorraine is already there dressed, like him, in old clothes and wellingtons, surrounded by excited, noisy hounds. Climbing over her colleagues in an attempt to pick up the new scent more fully, Robert sees the "skirter". Slipping back to the ground, she runs round and round the other animals, looking for an opening.

Robert clenches his teeth and wills the animal to run straight that day.

He has never shot a hound before.

Katherine Stone is sitting up in bed, her lips pursed against the rim of a teacup. Like Mrs Trevis, she is reviewing Christmas: she had fully intended to be woken by the wretched pealing of those ghastly bells and is now, happily, in a position to write a further letter of complaint. There is a whole folder of such letters in the top drawer of her bureau, marked "Bishop". His Lordship, presumably, has a similar file marked "Mrs Katherine Stone". He might not like her letters, but each one has to have a response; beautifully polite documents, printed on parchment-coloured, thick writing paper, with the coat of arms of the diocese at the top. Lesser complaints receive replies that begin, 'The bishop has asked me…' and are signed by some minor clergyman; lately, she has become more clever in the wording of her letters and the Bishop's own signature ornaments the foot of the page. He had even been spurred to action by her last one….

Katherine drains her cup and places it on the bedside table next to the tea-making machine. The Bishop will have to wait until tomorrow: today, she has other business.

* * * * *

'It wasn't bad, yesterday, was it, Two?'

'It was good fun. Thanks again for inviting me.'

'No problem – as I said, it's been great having somebody of my own age here. The presents went down well, didn't they? Aunt Lav loves her regimental brooch.'

'Yes, it seems that everybody loves military tat – you can't go wrong. The troop shop is going to keep us in gifts for years.'

The Toms, as scruffily dressed as everybody else, were nearing the livery yard, their grooming kits slung over their shoulders, and their new tweed caps (Christmas presents to each other) helping to keep out the cold. Even at this early hour, the yard was a busy place: all the outside lights were on, two stable girls were in the process of mucking stalls, and Primrose Armishaw trundled uncertainly behind a full wheelbarrow, her buttocks chewing the cud in a conversational manner. She looked over her shoulder and shouted a greeting.

'Hello, chaps – harness room's open, and the stove's on. Just kick the cat out of the way.'

They did as instructed and were duly hissed at. The cat, disturbed from his doormat, stalked angrily into the room and settled down on an old saddle blanket near the paraffin stove, where he continued his methodical ablutions. The soldiers each dismantled a bridle, stretched out the separate lengths of leather, and got down to work.

The routines of the harness room demand thoroughness rather than concentration and are conducive to philosophical speculation or gossip. After church on Christmas Day, the Toms had telephoned Lance Bombardier Green and their conversation had given them much to talk about, now that they were away from the curious ears of the older generation. They had huddled around the Bakelite headset of the elderly telephone and heard the lance bombardier's hung-over account of his party, the events of which he had been piecing together with Troopers Sorrell and Scott over multiple mugs of strong black coffee.

'Yes lads, the bits we can remember went well, and the bits we can't remember must have done. The duty officer popped in for five minutes, just to show goodwill, and was found this morning, in full mess dress, asleep on the straw in an empty stall. Scotty lost most of the forfeits in the drinking games, so he'll probably have to apply for a transfer to the Household Cavalry after what we made him do. Oh yes – and the reins which said "Merry Xmas" have now been arranged to say something I shan't repeat over the telephone.'

'What about Lang's sister, Lance?'

'Yes – did you get anywhere?'

'Wrong question, lads. Lang's sister was last seen heading in the direction of the gun park with the whole of number three team. There's been a lot of speculation concerning the range and velocity of the weapons she was called upon to inspect.'

So, what with one thing and another, the Toms had plenty to discuss. On the whole, they were relieved to have been two hundred miles from the party. As Tom Two observed, it didn't sound like the sort of gathering for young, impressionable troopers.

Robert, carrying a vast thermos flask, appeared at about eight o'clock and admired their work. They took a break, passing the single plastic mug from the top of the flask between the three of them.

'So, Robert, any final bits of advice for us?'

'Only what I said the other day, really. Keep with the crowd rather than running up to the hounds – you'll only get in the way and mess things up if you're too far forward. If you're not sure what to do, let your horses look after you; they know the moor better than any of us. Oh, yes – when we're in the town square, I'll introduce you to a nice old chap who'll look after you. He's a good rider, but his horse is a bit past jumping, so he knows where to find the gates when necessary. You'll be fine – there's going to be a lot worse riders out than you two today.'

This was reassuring news, though they had heard it several times already. They continued with their work, while Robert went to prepare horses for himself, John and the Master. By nine o'clock, four sets of saddles and bridles were prepared for the day's sport; by a quarter to ten, their horses and Ashley's now groomed and loosely tacked up, they were running, as fast as their wellingtons would allow, down the hill in order to get themselves ready in time. In the bathroom, Tom One shaved while Two bathed, then – pausing for one second to be disgusted by what he was about to do – plunged into Two's old water to wash himself.

'I hope you realise how appalling that is, One.' In the mirror, Tom Two saw his friend leap into the bath, while he massaged foam onto his face with a shaving brush. 'Suppose I had a disease?'

Tom One stuck his head under the grimy water, came up for air, and began massaging in shampoo.

'Judging by the taste of it, you've got several – and most of them socially unacceptable. Still, in moments of crisis, the British Army has to perform logistic miracles.'

The British Army, as represented by Toms One and Two, performed another small miracle. By half past ten, immaculately turned out in service dress, their boots and leathers gleaming in the frosty sun, they were mounted on their hunters, walking down the hill to the town square.

* * * * *

And now it is nearly eleven o'clock. For the last forty minutes, spectators have been arriving in the Square; now, they number nearly four hundred, and the four pubs are doing a roaring outdoor trade. Two barmen from the Buller Arms have dressed themselves up in black waistcoats and bow ties; they carry large silver trays of some hot and potent stirrup cup, which they offer to riders as they arrive. Since most of them have been up for hours, this stimulant is very welcome. Ashley and Peter Masters accept second cups from a proffered salver, and survey the crowd.

In the saddle, every age and class is represented: young girls on bulging ponies, invariably either too large or too small for them; two or three smart young men on holiday from boarding school, one of them looking particularly jealous as his girlfriend's horse gravitates towards the swarm of females around Tom Two. There are farmers of all shapes and sizes, from the fresh-faced to the weather-beaten; and expensive-looking city businessmen and their wives, who have weekend country houses and have spent more on their turn-out today than a working huntsman earns in a season. Ashley speculates on whether any of them can actually ride, then reminds himself that he is hardly in a position to sit in judgement on this matter: he will be happy if he can just stay on his horse for the duration.

Peter, whose black jacket is rendered more distinguished by the hunt's buttons and collar, nods in the direction of the Toms, obviously amused. 'I think your nephew's friend is doing slightly better in the glamour stakes this morning. It must be the ears – they have a certain elephantine charm, I suppose.'

Charm or not, Two's ears are glowing red with cold. Their size is enhanced by the service cap, which both soldiers wear, fastened under the chin with a leather strap. Ashley notes his sister hovering nearby with their hard hats, for which the caps will be exchanged once the hunting begins. He also notes that Tom One is doing his best to look politely interested in the conversation of an elderly gentleman with a florid complexion, a moustache and bulging eyes.

'I think the old boy who is hanging on to Tom's bridle might have more to do with it. He seems to have a deterrent effect on the young ladies.'

'Oh yes; Major Staunton doesn't get out much these days. I shouldn't worry, look – Mrs Staunton's on her way to the rescue.'

A capable-looking woman muscles her way through the crowd and leads the old soldier firmly away. A few girls from the outer rings of Two's solar system turn their attention towards One, who colours as red as his friend's ears.

Ashley turns to survey the spectators. Photographers move among the riders taking both individual shots and group scenes; the Rector, with wife and dog, chats to members of his congregation. Mark Overland hovers outside the open door of his shop, knowing that when the hunt has moved on, many people will take the opportunity to buy a bottle of wine for their Boxing Day luncheon; Mrs Dyer, similarly predatory, gossips with Betty Trenchard by the door of her stores. Parked in one corner of the square, a police car from Okehampton acts as an apparently unnecessary symbol of law and order. Its driver, who seems no older than the Toms, leans against the roof and chats genially to an older Special Constable, who has put on his uniform for the morning. Neither of them expects any trouble.

Finally, with her placard aloft, Katherine Stone stands a few yards from the police car. With her, Evelyn Warren looks as though she is longing to lose herself in the crowd, but the people of Chagford are not obliging: an imaginary *cordon sanitaire* cuts off Katherine and her relative from the rest of the world, and the space around them represents the only section of free pavement in the square.

Ashley's observations are interrupted by the distinctive sound of an approaching pack of hounds and the clopping of trotting horses. A few seconds later hounds and huntsmen enter the square, to cheers and applause from the crowd. The regular huntsmen have been joined by two extras, so the array of scarlet coats is a fine one: the Toms are upstaged momentarily and begin to lose their admirers to the magnetic pull of Robert and one of his young colleagues. The Master raises his hat to the spectators, acknowledging their support, and one of the auxiliary huntsmen dismounts, passing through the crowd with his hard hat functioning as a collecting bowl, which fills rapidly. Meanwhile, the bar staff from the Buller Arms bring out fresh supplies of hot punch. Robert rides around the hounds, his long whip trailing behind him, then hands over charge to the second volunteer huntsman. He walks his horse over to the Toms, looking their uniforms up and down, approvingly.

'Very smart, lads.' He grins knowingly; 'I bet the girls fancy you something rotten in those outfits.'

'Well, they did until you arrived.' Two feigns jealousy. 'Another time you can do your own kit.'

Robert looks down at his highly polished tack and boots. 'Yes, thanks for all that work, I'm really grateful. The Master is wildly impressed – and he's pleased with the turn-out today as well. That's Farmer Crane over there, by the way. He'll keep an eye out for you, but he won't get in your way. It's a good crowd, isn't it?'

'It's great – and only one protester in the whole lot.'

A frown appears on the whipper-in's face.

'Yes, Great Aunt Katherine up to her mischief once more. The Master wants me to go over and say a few polite things to her. He says that if we're seen to be decent about it, it'll look good, especially with the press being here.' He grits his teeth and gathers up his reins. 'And I suppose I may as well get it over with. Back in a second.'

The Toms watch as Robert heads towards the old lady. He is wearing an old-fashioned, strapless hat, which he removes as he nears her, taking both reins into his left hand as he does so. This turns out to be a mistake: affronted by the sight of her relative in his scarlet coat, Katherine waves her placard violently.

Everything happens very suddenly – the horse rears and whinnies – Robert's hat flies from his hand – he leans forward, trying desperately to recover control of the reins. The front hoofs clatter back down on the road and the panic-stricken black mare manoeuvres noisily backwards; the crowd does its best to separate and make room. Robert tries to calm the horse with his voice, but the furious waving of the placard continues, until the whipper-in makes matters worse by shouting abuse at the angry woman. She replies in kind and continues waving.

There is a sickening metallic thud; the horse's rear hoof has lashed out and a great dent appears in the bodywork of the police car. The horse swivels and kicks out again. A front light shatters noisily.

The dismounted huntsman, abandoning his collection and passing the overflowing hat to a bystander, runs across and takes hold of the bridle. Robert, who, by a superb instinct for balance, has avoided being thrown, is able to sit back in the saddle and collect his mare. Evelyn, with the help of Betty Trenchard, is leading a triumphant Katherine Stone towards a bench, where her livid red face will gradually return to normal. The Master has dismounted and is walking over to the police constable. On the way, he retrieves Robert's hat and returns it to the bare-headed whipper-in. He pats the hunter's neck, reassuring both horse and rider.

Tom Two relaxes enough to begin conversation once more; he adds his voice to the indignant buzzing of the crowd.

'Blimey, One – that was a bit too dramatic. What did that silly cow think she was doing?'

'Causing maximum disruption, I suppose. I'm glad *we* were nowhere near her bloody placard – I doubt if I could have stayed on in those circumstances. When it reared right up, I was sure he was going to come off backwards. And did you see her face? I thought she was going to burst a blood vessel.'

'Shame she didn't, really. Here comes the Master again.'

The Master, having promised to have the police car repaired at the hunt's expense, returns to his horse, which he mounts with surprising agility, using the kerb to give him a few extra inches of height. He is near enough to John for the Toms to overhear their conversation and to catch the angry tone in the Colonel's voice.

'Come, on, John – let's get going as soon as possible. Where did you say we'd draw?'

'Out by Thorn was what we spoke of last night, sir.'

'Well, we're changing plan – we'll head to Meldon. That way she has the whole hunt going down her blasted bridle path and, with any luck, she'll have a stroke when she sees us all out on the Common. Are you ready?'

'I'm ready, sir, and here comes Robert now. James has finished taking his collection.'

'Let's go, then.'

John pulls a short hunting horn from his tunic and begins a rhythmic calling. The Master indicates the new direction to his team, and hounds and huntsmen head off in the direction of Meldon Common. The applause of the crowd sounds sympathetic.

The Toms exchange their caps for hard hats and take a moment to adjust them. Margery, who has felt slightly foolish nursing two riding hats, now feels even odder as custodian of military headwear.

'Thanks, Mum – you're a star.'

'Thank you, Mrs Noad. We'll bring you back a brush!'

And Margery watches as the soldiers follow on with the main body of riders.

* * * * *

CHAPTER NINE

- RETURNING HOME -

If Katherine Stone was pleased with her stand on behalf of the fox, the four landlords of Chagford were delighted. Indignant conversations buzzed in crowded bars as the episode was reviewed from every possible angle. In the Buller, the two waistcoated barmen caught detached sentences as they drew pint after pint:

'So she claims to care about the blasted foxes, but she don't think twice about endangering an 'orse, do she?'

'Did you see the look on her face? She was really enjoying it all; 'specially when the door of the police car got kicked in. Pint?'

'Well, I think several of us enjoyed that…. Yeah, another one'd be great, thanks.'

'Carole?'

'Bacardi Breezer please. And I felt sorry for the policeman – he's only a youngster. He was ever so good-looking, don't you think?'

'Hey, everyone – Carole fancied the copper!'

'Oh, you just shut up, Matthew. Anyway, she soon had the smile wiped off her face – did you see how she looked when they all rode off?'

'Well they were off down her bridle path, weren't they? Good for them, I say! Cheers everyone.'

Outside, Police Constable Harry Sefton, crouching down by the side of his car, took a philosophical approach to the damage. There was nothing, after all, that couldn't be put right fairly quickly. On the other hand, his report would take a bit of time.

'I suppose I should have taken lots of notes, and all their names and addresses, and that sort of thing. I was so taken aback, that before I thought about it, they'd set off.'

'Don't you worry about that – I know all their names, all right.' Ernest Yeo, when not serving as a Special Constable, worked as a part-time plumber in Chagford. He also rang bells and dug graves. 'I know what you mean though – when you're not expecting any trouble, it's easy to forget all the routine drills. Especially when you're still new on the job. Get your notebook out, and I'll fill you in on the details. If we sit in the car, it'll be more private and we can warm up a bit too.'

Harry straightened himself up and walked round the car to the driver's door. Climbing inside, he turned on the heating and pulled out his notebook.

'All right – so the old girl – who's she?'

Yeo paused to rummage for a packet of Mint Imperials, and popped one in his mouth. 'Mrs Katherine Stone, Chagford's Bloody Nuisance in Residence – if you can fiddle the evidence so that she's liable for the repairs to the car, the whole town will love you. Been living up at Meldon Dene for about four years now and causing as much trouble as she can. Mint?'

'Thanks. Trouble such as…?'

'Such as buggering up the Christmas bells – writing to the Bishop and threatening to take the church to Court. Don't get me going on the subject, unless your notebook has asbestos pages.' He crunched his mint viciously.

'I get the idea – give me a moment.' Harry wrote: "On Friday, 26th December, a breach of the peace was caused by Mrs Katherine Stone (86) of Meldon Dene, Chagford." Grinning, he handed the notebook to the special constable. 'How about that to begin? I made up the age, but it looked about right.'

'That's just lovely – mind you, she'll have you through every court in the land if you actually submit any of that: she's a litigious cow.' He passed the notebook back. 'Next?'

'The hunting chap? The one on the horse, that is.'

'Yes, and only just on his horse as well, at one point. Robert Brookes – lives at the kennels out on the Gidleigh road. Good lad – born and brought up in Chagford. Ironically, he's a relative of the old lady. You might put something in your report to the effect that, had he not had such good control of his horse, the damage could have been far worse.'

'I like that.' Harry wrote a few laborious sentences. 'And the old boy, who came over?'

'Colonel Christopher Hargreaves, Respected Member of the Community: write that down. He's the MFH.'

'Which stands for?'

'My Fanny Hurts – no, that was a joke. Tear that page out, before it gets into your report. Master of Foxhounds. It may not mean much to a townie, but in the country, it means a lot. He lives in one of the big places at Gidleigh….' Ernest paused, unable to recall the exact house. 'Oh, just call it "The Old Rectory". That sort of address always goes down well with the magistrates.'

Harry wrote down the details and added, "….who witnessed the episode, testified to the good character of Robert Brookes and, without admitting liability, offered to make good the damage to police property."

'How's that?'

'You're learning, Harry, my boy. Have they put you up for the Masons yet?'

* * * * *

Tom Two's mare cast a shoe at just about the right time; had she lost it an hour earlier, the troopers would have felt cheated of their sport. By three o'clock, however, they were becoming tired, the weather was growing ever colder and the night clouds were already gathering. They were not sorry to have an excuse to leave the field; besides, for a while, the fox had doubled back on himself, so they were probably considerably nearer home than they would be in thirty minutes' time. Giving their horses a long rein, they walked along a moorland road, Tom One clopping along the metal track and Two, for the sake of his horse, taking the soft verge.

From a technical point of view, perhaps, it had not been the best day's hunting, but the Toms were largely unaware of this. Only the fact that Robert had obviously had a vexatious time of it prevented them from regarding the exercise as wholly successful.

The Master's change of plan, though understandable, was probably not a good idea. They had enjoyed trotting along the disputed bridle path, but the hounds had been a long time in drawing the common, and there had been a lot of hanging around. As Tom Two said, after their rush earlier on, it had been a typical army situation of "hurry up and wait". Still, after a while, they heard a cry of, 'Gone away!' and the distinctive sound of John's horn. There was a thrill of excitement as they caught sight of the fox itself, streaking across open moorland, and heard the hounds give tongue as they sped in pursuit. Within seconds, the whole field was galloping across the rough terrain.

It was then that Robert's second annoying event of the day took place. A hound detached herself from the pack as they broke cover and, instead of heading after the fox, followed some other scent which led back towards the bridle path. Robert called after her, but the wind blew his cry of 'No riot!' back in his face, and he was forced to leave the hunt to fetch her back.

The Master made the decision not to wait for him, and it was a good half hour before he rejoined the field, accompanied by a very chastened bitch. He galloped past the Toms on his way to the front, and slowed down for a few yards to put them in the picture.

'Only after a bloody cat! It took me ages to catch up with her, and then the stupid thing wouldn't come. I knew she skirted – now she's started rioting as well.'

Tom One struggled to recall the relevant vocabulary from their conversation on Christmas Eve. 'Did you give her a good sterning?'

'Not much point now – I'm going to have to shoot her this evening.'

With that, Robert had spurred on his black mare and galloped up to the front of the field.

Thereafter, things had gone more smoothly. After the initial chase across Meldon Common, the fox had headed west across farmland. Some brave souls had jumped hedges at every opportunity, but gates were ready to hand and the majority of the field made use of them. Crossing one farm, where the hedges were very high and the queue for the gates correspondingly long, they found themselves alongside Ashley, who was beginning to tire.

'What do you think of it, Uncle George? We're having a great time.'

'Good – me too, but I'm running out of steam. I'm keeping an eye out for all the townies – I'm determined not to drop out before they do. Some of them are flagging quite badly, I think.'

Tom One looked about him; the general rule seemed to be, the more expensive the hunting costume, the more exhausted the rider. 'I think you can probably sneak off with honour in about half an hour, Uncle George. Two and I are hoping to stick it for the whole day.'

'Quite right too.' They passed through the gate together. 'Don't wait around for me, boys. This old faithful is happier at the back of the field – you go ahead.'

'All right, Uncle George.'

'Thanks Mr Ashley, sir – see you at the next bottle neck.'

The Toms cantered along the perimeter of the field.

The fox applied his cunning in crossing the South Teign and there was much debate as to whether he had run upstream towards Fernworthy or downstream to the wooded territory at Yeo. The pack searched for the scent in both directions, and Robert dismounted in order to hold up the hound with the best nose. Several of the expensive-looking members of the field took advantage of this delay to make their way back to Chagford; Tom One, remembering his hack across the moor from two days before, persuaded his Uncle that it was worth hanging on for the chance of a run across some spectacular country. Ashley, who had used the pause to gain his second wind, agreed.

Eventually, the Master made an educated guess and cast the hounds upstream, on the assumption that, the wind being in that direction, their noses would have regained the line if the fox had gone any other way. It was a happy choice: after a few minutes, the music of hounds on the scent echoed around; they broke out into open country, and from Frenchbeer Rock, over to Middle Tor and across Chagford Common, the remaining riders galloped at full pelt. The wind was rushing in their faces now; the scent was stronger, and the sound of the hounds an ecstatic cry. Again and again, the Toms found their horses jumping minor dips in the ground, but they were used to this now and enjoyed the sensation: if they had not held their horses back, they could easily have found themselves at the front of the field, their khaki uniforms interrupting the thin red line of scarlet ahead of them.

They decided to run to the top of Kestor and pause for breath there, where they could see the hunt continuing and wait for Ashley. The detective saw them shooting up the hill and guessed their purpose; he managed to keep his horse going almost to the top, but took the final hundred yards at a slow trot and then a walk. Together, the three admired the sight of the hunt continuing below, and congratulated themselves on the privilege of being part of it.

'Good old Aunt Lav! And to think that we were all so nervous about it. It's been fantastic, hasn't it, Uncle George?'

Ashley agreed. 'Yes, it's been wonderful, but I'm all in now. Do you know the way back from here?'

The Toms were uncertain, but Two noticed a rider gradually slowing his horse down and turning it away from the setting sun.

'I reckon if we go down to meet him, Mr Ashley, he'll be able to point you in the right direction – he looks as if he's heading home himself. Are you up to a steady trot downhill, sir?'

It was about an hour after Ashley's departure that Farmer Crane pointed out the missing shoe to Tom Two. The fox had doubled back towards Thornworthy in order to run with the wind rather than against it, and the farmer advised the soldiers to head east until they hit the road.

'It'll take you back towards Meldon, and then I guess you'll know your way back from there.'

They thanked him, and took his advice, bidding him goodnight, in the traditional manner. For a while they walked in silence; then, regaining some energy, devoted themselves to eulogising the day's sport and anticipating hot baths ('I hope you're going to run yourself fresh water this time, One'), followed by a lazy evening in front of the fire, reliving the day to an admiring Aunt Lavinia.

After a mile and a half, the road reached Meldon Common,

and they skirted round the edge until they came to the famous bridle path that led back to Chagford. The overhanging trees plunged them into temporary darkness and low branches, so easy to avoid earlier, seemed to leap out at them, forcing them to bend low over the necks of their horses. Laughing, they concluded that these hazards were Katherine Stone's revenge.

Perhaps they had acquired the habit of looking down by the time they emerged from the path and out onto the road beyond; otherwise, in the twilight, they might have missed the awkward, huddled figure that lay, face downwards, in the ditch beside the road. Even when they saw her, they mistook the caked blood in her hair for mud.

But there was no mistaking the broken placard that shared the ditch with her.

* * * * *

CHAPTER TEN

- TABLEAUX OF DEATH -

Five o'clock. Vehicles jamming up the single-track lane, their headlights on, white and penetrating. Other lights, blue and orange, rotating and flashing, distorting shapes and colours. Harry Sefton, unexpectedly still on duty, taping off the area around the ditch, his face bleached and spectral, his fluorescent jacket an eerie, luminous green. Cameras flashing; radios bleeping and issuing metallic instructions. Policemen, uniformed and plain clothed; ambulance men; a doctor. A handful of spectators, stamping their feet and blowing air into their hands to keep warm.

Through the middle of everything, Primrose Armishaw, leading the grey mare to a horse box, parked way down the lane.

In the back of a police car, Tom Two, huddled in a blanket, answering questions through chattering teeth. A police sergeant taking notes.

In the lane, farther down, Ashley and Tom One, anxious for their friend, restrained from approaching more closely by the special constable and another length of tape.

In the ditch, Katherine Stone, the centre of attention for the second time that day.

The kennels. Washing and feeding; tired hounds scrabbling around raw meat; hounds being checked for cuts; hounds being brushed down. Huntsmen removing scarlet coats and changing into drab country clothes. In the kitchen, on an old newspaper, the fox's mask, glaring and bloody.

In a back yard, Robert stroking a hound, speaking to her softly.

Sitting her down on her haunches, facing away from him.

Standing astride her.

Staring momentarily into her eyes as the click of the humane killer causes her to look around.

Shooting her in the back of the head.

A policewoman in plain clothes and a uniformed constable, both driven out from Exeter. Evelyn Warren, unexpectedly summoned, opening the door of her cottage. Suddenly, light from the hallway streaking across the dark street. The tiny woman, looking apprehensively from one official face to the other. Confirming her identity.

'May we come in? I'm afraid we've got some bad news.'

Entering the cottage; closing the door.

Darkness again.

A quarter to six. More onlookers gathering in the lane, held in order by the special constable. A local reporter, moving among them, gathering information; a photographer, taking pictures with a huge lens and a powerful flash. Beyond the tape, Tom Two, still in his blanket cloak, standing with Ashley and taking a drink from a flask. Tom One, in the back of the police car, giving his evidence.

Ambulance men lifting Katherine Stone onto a stretcher, raising her awkwardly into the ambulance.

Scattering the crowd as vehicle after vehicle reverses down the lane until a turning point can be found.

Driving to the mortuary in Exeter.

Robert, alone, an old, thick sweater over his hunting shirt, drinking scrumpy and staring into the eyes of the fox. Looking down at his boots; seeing the dull patches where contact with his horse has scuffed the polish; examining the splashes of mud and a scratch from a thorn bush.

Other splashes. He runs a finger along the leather.

Blood. Fox blood? Hound blood?

He pulls his boots off, clears the sink of plates and dishes, and runs a bowl full of hot, soapy water.

* * * * *

It occurred to Betty Trenchard that the last time she had made a therapeutic cup of hot sweet tea, it had been for Katherine Stone herself. She remarked on the coincidence, then apologised.

'Oh, I'm sorry, Miss Warren – that wasn't very tactful of me, was it? It was the spooning the sugar in that reminded me, what with so few people taking it these days.'

'Don't worry, Betty, it doesn't matter. And thank you for the tea – you're very kind. You too, Rector; it's very good of you to come round.'

Stephen Trevis stirred his own tea and muttered something appropriate. The three were sitting at the kitchen table in Evelyn Warren's cottage. Built of oak and taking up most of the room, it dominated her culinary life and most of her social life as well. Two hours earlier, Evelyn had sat there with the policewoman and the constable as they broke the news of Katherine's death. They had used expressions like 'accident' and 'incident' awkwardly, almost theologically, avoiding any reference to murder. But the word had hovered silently over the conversation. Strangely, Evelyn had found the presence of the uniformed constable more comforting than the plain-clothed female officer. She speculated on why this was so.

'Perhaps it was because he didn't say anything. The woman did all the talking. She was very good; I suppose it's the sort of thing she's done before.'

'Well, she came out from Exeter, didn't she?' Betty seemed to imply that the genial county town was the world capital of violence and murder. 'I dare say they always send out a woman on these occasions; they probably think it seems a more caring way of doing it. I agree with you, though – a strong, quiet man can be wonderfully reassuring. Especially in uniform. What do you think, Rector?'

Two thoughts occurred to Stephen, both of which would have amused him at any other time. The first was that Betty's husband, long since placed beyond the reach of her incessant voice, had probably been of the silent type, simply because it was impossible to get a word in. The second was that, never having been in a position to be comforted by a strong, quiet man in uniform, he was hardly qualified to give an opinion. For about the tenth time in the last twenty minutes, he responded with a bland, all-purpose answer: it seemed to do the trick. He decided to turn the conversation to practicalities.

'Did the policewoman give you any idea of what will be happening over the next few days, Evelyn?'

Evelyn took another sip of tea and nodded.

'They want me to go into Exeter tomorrow to do a formal identification of….' She hesitated. How should she refer to her relation? Aunt Katherine? The *remains*? 'Well, the body, I suppose. They're going to send a car round in the morning.'

'Would you like someone to come with you? I can, or my wife, if you like.'

'Or I could, no trouble.' Betty managed to sound both caring and curious. 'Mind you, I'd have thought they'd have asked Robert to do any identifying. He's her nearest relative, isn't he?'

Evelyn nodded again. 'Yes, he is – was. They were going to see him after they'd been with me. The policewoman said that they would ask him to do the identification if I didn't feel that I could. But Robert and Aunt Katherine didn't get on, did they? I thought that she would rather I saw her there, though perhaps that's just being silly. And no, I don't think I need someone to be with me – it's not as if I've got to get there all by myself. But thank you for thinking of it.'

Probably, thought Stephen, riding all the way to Exeter and back in a car with a young policeman was about as exciting as things could get for Evelyn. Who was he to tear away the silver lining from her cloud? As ever, correct platitudes fell from his tongue.

'Well, you're being very brave, Evelyn. If you change your mind, just say, and someone will come with you.'

'Thank you, Rector. The woman said that, if I felt up to it, they'd like to ask me a few, well, what they called 'routine questions' at the same time. What sort of things do you think they'll want to know? I hope it won't be an interrogation?'

Stephen had looked after people in trouble a number of times, and was able to put her mind at rest.

'Don't worry Evelyn – they're interested in Katherine, not you. They'll need to know all the usual things about her; her age, when she came back to Chagford, and that kind of thing. They'll probably ask about that incident with Robert as well, and Katherine's movements afterwards. She had luncheon with you, didn't she?'

'Yes, if you can call it luncheon. I'd prepared such nice food, and she ate hardly anything; she was so worked up about Robert and the hunt. She wanted to leave quite early: she was sure that all those hounds and horses going along her bridle path would have caused some damage, and she was going to get her camera and take photographs. I walked with her to the outskirts of the town, but then I came back here.'

Evelyn paused to reflect on the events.

'If I'd gone another half mile with her, she'd probably be alive now.'

* * * * *

Urgent and desperate, Tom Two is struggling to preserve his life. He is trying to scramble up the side of the ditch but the smooth soles of his boots are slipping in the mud and he can make no progress. If only he can get a grip with his hands – a tuft of grass, the root of a tree, a thorn bush…. But no, even now, he is being sucked back down into the ditch, his hands lacerated by the thorns. He kicks out with his feet, but bony fingers are locked around his spurs and his body is dragged down the slope, into the dirty water – water in his mouth, muddy liquid in his throat….

Splashing and fighting, forcing his body around to keep his mouth above the water line – the calcified hand again, on his shoulder, pushing him down – the leering, trepanned skull laughing at him.

'No, please, no!' Ossified fingers forcing themselves between his thighs – his mouth prised open to receive a rotting tongue – filth from the ditch flooding into his lungs – his body invaded – 'Please, no, not there, not….'

He is woken by his own scream.

'Tom! It's me – it's all right.'

There is light from a torch. Tom One is in the room with him; staring, where the skull was, but with concern, not with…. Well, not with anything else. His right hand rests on Two's shoulder, reassuring, not compelling; soft, not skeletal. He is wearing the same comfortable, ridiculous outfit that Tom Two had seen on their first morning in Chagford.

'Oh, God.' Tom Two breathes deeply, sinks back into the

damp pillow and tries to relax. 'Sorry Tom – did I wake everyone up?'

'No, only me I should think. Mother and Aunt Lav are at the other end of the house, and I could hear Uncle George still snoring. Are you all right now?'

'Yes thanks, I think so. I dreamt that the old woman was trying to drag me into the ditch with her, and that....'

He pauses, and concludes lamely: 'No, you don't want to know the details.... What time is it?'

'About two o'clock, I think. Shall I make some tea?'

'No, I'm all right thanks, but....'

'Yes?'

'This sounds really stupid, One – but will you hang on here for a bit? I could do with some company.'

'No problem – give me a second.' Tom One places the torch on a table, pointing the light towards the door. He disappears from the room, returning a moment later with the pillows from his own bed.

'You take this one – yours looks as though it's soaked through. Budge over, it's freezing out here, even with my army issue willy warmers on. There's tons of room for both of us.'

Two does as instructed and Tom One climbs in. They lie on their sides, facing each other. The torchlight forms a corona around One's head, giving him an unnaturally saintly appearance.

'I'm sorry, Two – I shouldn't have left you with her.'

'Don't be silly; one of us had to stay, and you could trot with your horse. It made sense.'

'I know; but all the while, I found myself thinking, well, if it *is* murder, suppose the person who did it was still hanging around? I was really worried.'

'*Do* you think it's murder, One? Isn't there any way it could just be an accident?'

'I don't know – the police seemed to be treating it like a

murder. At least, there were lots of them and they wouldn't have got all those people out for an accident, surely. Uncle George thinks it's the real thing. I can tell from the way he's gone all silent.'

They discuss the death and its implications. They compare their interviews with the police and speculate on the significance of the questions. At length, they grow tired again: their conversation becomes slower; sentences fail to conclude, or drift from the point….

Tom One watches his friend as Two's voice fades and his eyelids become heavy. At length, he slides from consciousness. His deep, regular breathing implies that this rest will be calmer than the last. One waits for a few minutes, then rolls over to turn off the torch.

Within seconds, he is also asleep.

* * * * *

'Wake up, Harry – it's your turn to take over.'

The police constable yawns and stretches uncomfortably. 'What time is it?'

'Three o'clock – which means that we've been on duty for eighteen hours now, on and off. While you were having your wet dreams, the station called; some wild party in Okehampton went wrong about an hour ago, so the chaps who were meant to be relieving us have had to go and sort it out. Isn't life wonderful?'

'Bloody fantastic.'

'They will, of course, be expecting us to report for duty tomorrow, as fresh as daisies and if we want time off in lieu, we can whistle for it. Not that it makes any difference to me, being just a Special…. Who is Sally, by the way? You mentioned her while you were asleep.'

'Sally? She's my dog.'

'In that case, you should be ashamed of yourself. Right, I'm going to get some kip. Wake me up in an hour.'

The special constable pulls the reclining lever of his seat and lowers himself into a comfortable position. Harry Sefton yawns again, sniffs his armpits distastefully and then checks his stubble in the car mirror. He decides to bring himself back to life by wandering up and down the lane for a while.

As he walks, shining his torch into the ditch every so often, he contemplates his first murder case. Of course, it wasn't definitely murder until the pathologist had taken a look at those wounds, but everyone seems to be assuming that they were inflicted deliberately. He tries to picture the scene: the old lady walking along the lane by herself, perhaps greeting her killer – or was she ambushed from behind? Then the blow, or maybe blows, on the head and the falling into the ditch….

Harry has stopped at the white tape around the place where Katherine's body lay. He shines his torch around, hoping to find some scrap of evidence, some clue which more experienced colleagues had missed. After all, they had only carried out a preliminary search in the dark. More detailed work would be done tomorrow – no, later today.

The scene does not choose to reveal its secrets. Harry continues his walk up and down the lane.

* * * * *

Six o'clock. At some point, Tom Two must have rolled over in his sleep. Tom One wakes to the pressure of a head resting on his rib cage and an arm entwined around his torso. Gradually, he becomes aware that his own left arm curls around Two's back, the hand resting on his friend's shoulder.

Tom's first instinct is to shove his friend back onto his own side of the bed, but then he remembers why he is sharing it with him; far better to let Two continue in his sleep, undisturbed.

106

So he lies there, smelling the scent of a wood fire in Two's hair; conscious of the contrast between the warmth of Two's body and the coldness of the room; between the sound and motion of Two's breathing and the surrounding stillness; between the friendship that binds them together and the hatred that has led to a murder.

He has known Two for only six months, but it has been a time of such intense commitment and activity that they have been drawn together more closely than any relationship Tom has ever experienced. As young cadets, they arrived at the barracks of Prince Albert's Troop together, and together they were drawn into an arcane world of horses and traditions, of back-breaking hard work and chivalric glamour. By the end of their three weeks' experience, they had both decided to throw over their final year at school, and to sign up for the army at once. It was so much easier making the decision knowing that they would not be alone.

And they had needed each other. Basic training at Pirbright had been a world away from the civilised atmosphere of Prince Albert's Troop. For three relentless months they had marched and exercised, patrolled and attacked, submitting themselves to the pitiless regime of bawling sergeants and the tedious routines of sentry duties and kit inspections. They had discovered together that the army's method of building a soldier is to break a civilian; and there had been times when they had felt themselves broken, without being able to picture the reconstruction that lay ahead. They had seen other recruits leave the course early; without each other, they might well have done the same.

At first, the pack mentality of their fellow soldiers had been difficult for them too. Both Toms were from public schools (though very minor ones) and had chosen the unusual route of joining the army in the ranks. In Prince Albert's Troop, this was an unimportant detail: their urge to work with and

107

around horses, and to be part of an elite unit with a proud history, was all that mattered. There was no denying, though, that at Pirbright, their accents and manners made them stand out and, at first, they had come in for a large share of sarcasm and inverted snobbery. They had, Tom reflects, a lot of corners rubbed off them. Fortunately, in a course so devoted to the military art of 'bulling,' their head start in everything to do with cleaning kit gained them a grudging respect: when One had been awarded an early commendation for shooting on the range and Two had been consistently top in every exercise that involved written work, that respect had increased. In many cases, it had gradually developed into friendship, so that now, lying in bed with Two still embracing him, Tom can look back on the three months almost fondly. It had been a time of huge personal growth, naturally, but also a time of great camaraderie, when strong relationships were forged and when, for the first time, he had begun to realise how much he could achieve, working as part of a team, striving for excellence.

It must be about half past six now, because Tom can just begin to make out shapes and silhouettes. He can now see Tom Two, as well as sense his warmth and hear his breathing. In black outline, he sees Two's left ear sticking out from the side of his head, and imagines the other, squashed between skull and ribcage, crumpled and deaf. For a moment, he has the urge to take his hand from Two's shoulder and run his fingers against the lie of his hair, releasing more of the gentle ash wood aroma. But no – better not.

After Pirbright, they had enjoyed a weekend in London and then returned straight to the Troop, picking up duties and friendships where they had left off. Tom thinks of his horse, being tended over the Christmas leave by Trooper Scott; of the stark barrack buildings and the soldiers, particularly Lance Bombardier Green, who make up their world; of the room which he and Two share.

And now Two is awake. Tom can tell, because the slow breathing has changed its pace, stopping momentarily and then continuing irregularly, as Two becomes aware of his situation. The flattened ear must be listening to Tom's heartbeat: as this thought occurs to Tom, he is embarrassed to feel the pace of the beat increasing.

'It's all right, I'm awake as well. I didn't want to disturb you.'

'Thanks One, that's really decent.' Two untwines himself and rolls his body through forty-five degrees, so that he is lying on his side, still close by his friend, unaware that Tom One's left arm is now trapped between his neck and the pillow. 'I had a really good sleep that time around.'

'I could tell. At one point, I thought you were dreaming that I was that nice girl on the piebald pony from yesterday.'

'No – your breasts are bigger.'

'Ungrateful bastard!'

'I know. Any idea what the time is?'

'I don't think it can be seven yet. The police won't be round till after nine, so there's no need to get up for an hour or so.'

'That's good, I'm still pretty flaked. Do you mind if I try to go back to sleep?'

'Of course not – go ahead.'

On impulse, Two returns to his former position and gives One a big bear hug: 'You're a real pal, One.'

Tom One allows his freed arm to curl around his friend again and, this time, he does rest his hand on Two's head, disturbing the short, soft hair and dispersing the smoky perfume.

'You too – Two.'

His hand drops back onto Two's shoulder and they return to sleep.

* * * * *

CHAPTER ELEVEN

- PRELIMINARY ENQUIRIES -

In spite of Special Constable Yeo's prediction, Harry Sefton *was* given the chance to spend the morning in bed, but turned it down. This was his first murder case and he didn't want to miss out on anything. Detective Inspector Alan Simkin looked up from his mug of coffee with amusement and approval, and exchanged glances with his sergeant.

'We've got a keen rookie on our hands, Sergeant Craggs. Do you think we can cope with him?'

'I think we might just manage, sir – we were all young once.'

'Well I was; I'm not so sure about you.' Simkin turned again to Harry. 'All right, Constable, you've got yourself a job, and a jolly boring one too, in all probability. Do you live far from here?'

'Five minutes' walk, sir.'

'So then, nip back home, get yourself a shower and a shave, and change into clean togs. Grab half an hour's sleep as well – the sergeant and I have got enough routine stuff here to keep us going until about nine o'clock. Then you can drive us out to Chagford, preferably in a car with all its lights working and without hoof-shaped dents in the bodywork. Okay?'

Harry beamed. 'That's great, sir – thank you. I'll be waiting in the car park ready for nine o'clock.' He scuttled out of the door and Simkin watched him run up the path which led from the police station to the main road.

'You won't regret that, sir.' The policeman manning the main desk had been listening in to the conversation. 'He's a good lad.'

'I can see that, Constable. Nice set up you've got here. Old school building, isn't it?'

'That's right, sir – it converted into a police station quite well. We've got a big car park where the playground was, and tons of cell space in the old science labs – not that we get to use them much. The occasional occupant after closing time on Fridays and Saturdays, that's all.' He gave a regretful sigh. 'Okehampton's never been a great centre of crime – not like you must be used to in Exeter.'

Craggs drained his mug. 'You never know, perhaps we can put a few people behind bars for you over the next few days. In the meantime, I gather a room has been set aside for us. Could you take us to it? And thanks for the coffee by the way, much appreciated.'

'No problem, sir. If you'd like to come this way?'

Simkin and Craggs were led along a corridor and deposited in an old classroom, which was to act as their headquarters for the foreseeable future. The original slate blackboard was still on the wall opposite the door and hessian notice boards ran around the rest of the room. Simkin looked around him, approvingly.

'They were going to take the blackboard away, sir, but in fact it's come in very handy over the years. There's chalk and dusters in the cupboard if you need them. Shall I leave you to it, sir?'

'Thank you, Constable. We'll give you a buzz if we need anything.' Simkin nodded in the direction of the telephone.

'Right you are, sir. Just press zero for the switchboard, nine if you want an outside line. The key to the room is in the door, sir, and I've got a spare behind my desk if you need it.'

He left them alone. The two detectives removed their coats and sat down at a large desk. Simkin pulled some blank paper from his briefcase and they began to plan their movements for the day.

Simkin and Craggs had worked together for many years: between them, they were responsible for the early termination of a good number of criminal careers. Simkin's carefree manner masked a formidable intellect, to which Craggs' thoroughness and attention to detail were the ideal foil. If nature had been doing its job properly, they would have had markedly different appearances to match their contrasting personalities: as it was, they were both balding slightly and prone to middle-aged spread. Craggs' stomach protruded over the top of his trouser belt; an unattractive feature which Simkin avoided by wearing a waistcoat. Being unmarried, the inspector's clothing budget was significantly larger than that of his sergeant, who had already bred four future policemen by two separate women. Simkin's grey pin-stripe suit, made up by his tailor in the Cathedral Close at Exeter, was altogether more successful in concealing the expanding march of time than Craggs' blue two-piece from a department store.

Their current work centred around drawing up a list of names and addresses for the day's visits. This sort of task was Craggs' department.

'So, we may as well start with the two chaps who found the body.' He consulted a notebook. 'Troopers Thomas Noad and Thomas Marsh, both staying at Waye Lodge, just outside Chagford.'

'Cavalrymen?'

Craggs checked his notes again. 'Horse Artillery, apparently. Is there a difference?'

'Probably enough of a difference for them to be annoyed if we get it wrong.' Simkin paused for thought. 'There are going to be a lot of horses in this case: do you know anything about them?'

'I was kicked by one once, if that's what you mean. I had a bruise the size of a dinner plate.'

'Really? I hope you found someone to kiss it better?'

'No one my wife need ever know about. Apart from that, I've lost a bit of money on horses from time to time, and that's about the limit of my knowledge. You?'

'I rode as a kid: never hunted though. The dear departed was very much an "anti", wasn't she? A rare breed in this part of the world.'

'Even rarer now. If Special Constable Ernest Yeo is to be relied on, she was pretty much anti-everything. He reckons the Chagford bell-ringers are going to offer to play a muffled peal for her funeral – and then forget to muffle it.'

'Any idea what that means?'

'No, but it sounds creatively vindictive.' Craggs smiled his approval.

The police car drew up outside Waye Lodge about an hour later. Margery, who was convinced that the whole of Chagford would think her son was about to be arrested, showed Simkin and Craggs into the sitting room, before retiring to her bedroom for a minor species of nervous breakdown. Ashley brought the Toms in for the interview, obtaining permission to remain, while Aunt Lavinia fussed around Harry Sefton in the kitchen.

It was very straightforward. Sergeant Craggs confirmed that the Toms had left the hunt at about three o'clock and found the body about forty-five minutes later.

Simkin butted in. 'Could you be a bit more precise than that?'

'Not really, sir – watches aren't worn with service dress. It was getting quite dark, though.'

'Which would fit in with about a quarter to four,' Craggs observed. He pulled out an Ordnance Survey map of the area. A large cross already marked the place where the body had been discovered. 'Any good at maps?'

'We looked at a few on our basic training, didn't we, One?'

'Just a few,' One's voice was heavy with sarcasm. Cartography had not been his speciality. Sensing this, Craggs handed the map to Tom Two.

'If you could just show us the route you were taking. Not the whole day's hunt, of course.'

Tom Two worked backwards from the cross, tracing their route through the bridle path and then back along the lane.

'We must have joined the road somewhere about here.' He indicated a grid square. 'Though I can't really be exact about that.'

'That's not a problem – this will do nicely for us to be going along with. Now, when you found the body, did you touch anything?'

Tom One took over. 'No – we knew that we weren't supposed to, and she was obviously dead. We didn't even dismount, though we walked our horses right up to the edge of the ditch. Perhaps we shouldn't have done that?'

'Don't worry about that. Just carry on.'

'Well, then we discussed what to do. In the end, I came into Chagford, while Two stood guard....'

'I had to walk my horse up and down to keep her warm, sir, so there'll be tons of hoof prints. On the verge, too, because she'd thrown a shoe, and I was trying to keep her off the tarmac.'

Simkin nodded. 'I examined the area with a torch last night: it looked as if the Charge of the Light Brigade had taken place there. I wondered about the less well-defined marks – they must be from the hoof with no shoe. And then?' He turned back to Tom One.

'And then, sir, I trotted up to the livery yard and rang the police from there. I thought it would be quicker if I did that and returned my horse at the same time. That way we could get a horse box out to pick up Trooper Marsh's horse as soon as possible. I had to hang around a bit before the stable owner came back, and then we drove out as quickly as we could.'

Craggs wrote down Tom One's story in his notebook, then looked up at Simkin, who shook his head. 'That's it then, lads – thank you for your help. Will you be here for the next few days?'

'We're on leave until the 30th and then we have to go back to London.'

'That's fine. We've already got your contact details at the barracks.'

Ashley had enjoyed sitting in on the interview and was impressed with the civilised way in which the inspector and his sergeant had conducted it. He assumed that the policemen would now take their leave, but Simkin showed no signs of rising from the sofa. In fact, the inspector was raising an eyebrow in his direction.

'I think, chaps, the inspector might like a few words with me now. Judging by the smells wafting from the kitchen, Aunt Lavinia is producing a full English Breakfast for Constable Sefton....'

Craggs wrote the words, 'Jammy bugger' in his book and left it in the middle of the sofa, where Simkin could see it.

'If you're lucky, she might do the same for you.'

'All right, Uncle George, we get the hint. Shall we bring tea or coffee through?'

They made arrangements for refreshments and took their leave. When the door was closed, Craggs remarked: 'Nice lads. Good to see young people like that opting for the services – I wish more did.'

Ashley agreed: 'And you seem to have a good example in

the constable, whom my aunt is trying to seduce with eggs, bacon and saucy gossip from the nineteen-fifties. But I assume, Inspector, that you didn't want to speak to me just to compliment me on my nephew and his comrade in arms?'

'That's right, Mr Ashley and, by the way, I'm sorry I didn't come over to say hello last night. I was rather busy, as I'm sure you'll appreciate.'

'I could see – unexpected bodies make for a lot of work, don't they?'

'Precisely. Anyway, to cut a long story short, Mr Ashley, the special constable told me that you were a private detective in London. It occurred to me that you might be the George Ashley who had worked on a recent case with a former colleague of mine. An Inspector Cowan?'

Ashley felt rather awkward. He had not so much worked with Cowan, as against him. He remembered the hard-bitten inspector as one of the less pleasant characters his work had brought him into contact with. He was trying to think of something polite to say, when Craggs saved him the necessity:

'Evil bastard, isn't he?'

Ashley smiled. 'Thank you, Sergeant Craggs: I couldn't have put it better myself.'

Simkin nodded agreement. 'There were a lot of happy policemen when you got the better of him, Mr Ashley, I just thought you might like to know that. We were at Police College together and he was one of those officers who thought you could solve every case by bullying the truth out of people. Of course, sometimes it works, and he had a lot of early successes; but I can't say I like his methods.'

'Nor I – but I'll grant you that, in London, it's sometimes necessary.'

'Anyway, Mr Ashley, I thought I'd show that not all of us at CID hate private detectives by asking if you had formed any opinions on the case, as you see it?'

The Toms knocked on the door and brought tea and coffee. Ashley used the interlude to organise his thoughts, though he noticed, in amusement, that his aunt's finely-tuned sense of class distinction had provided china cups and saucers for his tea and the inspector's, and the paintbrush mug for the sergeant's coffee. He went through the rituals of handing out refreshments.

'In the first place, I presume that there's no doubt now that it was murder? Tom thought she might have fallen into the ditch by accident, and I didn't get near enough to have a look. But you wouldn't be here if it was just an accident, would you?'

'That's right, Mr Ashley. We haven't had the full medical report yet, but we're sure it's homicide.'

'Pesticide, by the sounds of it,' suggested Craggs.

'Thank you, Sergeant Craggs, that's really helpful. When he saw her, the doctor was pretty sure her neck was broken, which could have been as a result of slipping, but the wound – or wounds – on the back of the head must have been inflicted deliberately, especially given that she was lying face downwards.'

Ashley took a mouthful of tea and considered the implications of this.

'So, if an intelligent murderer had wanted to make it look like an accident, he or she might have tried to turn the body over and place an appropriate stone in the ditch where she fell. But then that's a lot of work: it would leave too many traces.'

Simkin nodded. 'Traces on the murderer himself, as well as at the scene of the crime.'

'That's right. There's no point in organising the perfect setting, if you're going to wander back into town covered in mud and God knows what else. So, granted – as you assure me – that murder is certain, and that we can't go into forensic details until the post-mortem report is back, the natural first question to ask is, who gains from her death?'

'Apart from the whole of Chagford, you mean?' Craggs interrupted his note-taking to make the cynical remark. He had never met Katherine Stone, but he had heard enough to decide that he disliked her. Ashley continued:

'As the Americans say, Sergeant, I hear what you're saying. But, assuming for a moment that the whole of Chagford didn't queue up to bash her on the head, we come back to the more usual sort of suspects: those who benefit financially from her death, and those who wanted her out of the way for other reasons, as yet unknown. I know that she didn't have many surviving blood relations – do we know the contents of the will?'

'It's our next task, Mr Ashley. A couple of our chaps are going through her house at the moment.'

'In that case, I think I can save you some time. I was chatting to Peter Masters the other day – he's the Chagford solicitor – and, from what he said, I gained the impression that he had the will in his office.'

Simkin was visibly surprised. 'Really? I rather thought that Katherine Stone would have hated lawyers.'

'I'm not so sure about lawyers generally – she married one, after all – but she certainly disliked Peter. On the other hand, she needed him. Lawyers are like clergymen and doctors in that respect: every so often, you require their services, whether you like them or not. Would you like me to telephone him?'

Simkin consulted his watch, but to gain time, rather than to check it. He decided that he would enjoy working alongside Ashley, if the detective were willing to help out.

'That would be very kind of you. Perhaps, if he's in and he has the document, you'd like to come over with us? It would be much more civilised to have a proper introduction, and I'm sure your input would be valuable.'

The policemen wandered back into the kitchen while Ashley put the call through. There they found a contented Constable Sefton staring placidly at a plate edged with bacon rinds and streaked with egg yolk. The Toms were wolfing down the last mouthfuls of similar plates, and Aunt Lavinia was topping up the teapot. Harry sprang to his feet and blushed guiltily as his superiors viewed the table jealously. There was a bitter tone in Craggs' voice as he addressed the young policeman:

'So, Constable Sefton, having conducted an in-depth investigation into the quality of the local eggs and bacon, are you ready to drive us back into Chagford? Not forgetting to thank this kind lady, who has kept you and your tapeworm sustained and nourished.'

'It was no trouble, Sergeant, no trouble at all.' Aunt Lavinia had thoroughly enjoyed cooking for, and flirting with, the young man in uniform. 'I'd offer to fry some more but the boys have finished everything up.'

Craggs gave a resigned sigh. 'Not to worry, madam – the Inspector and I are used to going hungry in the course of duty. If we're lucky, Constable Sefton might bring along one of those bacon rinds, so that we can chew on it in the car.'

Ashley came into the kitchen while Harry Sefton was still trying to work out whether Craggs was being serious. He pulled on an overcoat as he gave the news from the solicitor:

'Peter said that he thought there'd be a call today, so he's already at his office, with the will in front of him. He suggests we wander over as soon as we're ready.'

The policemen said their goodbyes: Simkin and Craggs were polite and formal; Sefton, bashful and grateful. Ashley noticed that the Toms were also getting to their feet. He had a good idea of where they were off to.

'Do you two have any plans for the day?'

Tom One answered. 'We thought we'd head down to the kennels, Uncle George and say, "Hi" to Robert.'

Ashley shook his head. 'Not today – he'll have enough on his plate. You'll only be in the way, trust me. Bye, Aunt Lavinia – see you later.'

The Toms stared as Ashley left the room with the policemen.

'What did your uncle mean, One?'

'No idea. I thought we were being helpful.'

Aunt Lavinia contributed the suggestion that Ashley usually knew what he was talking about; in the morning, at any rate.

'I know, Aunt Lav – the last time I disobeyed an instruction like that, I got myself into the most enormous mess.'

The Toms hung around, feeling vacant and functionless, until Aunt Lavinia came up with the happy suggestion that they should go into the garden to chop some wood. It seemed an appropriately violent and cathartic exercise.

'Come on, Two – let's do it. Last one into the garden has to play Charles the First.'

* * * * *

CHAPTER TWELVE

- THE WILL -

Harry Sefton dropped off the inspector and Ashley in the town square: Simkin had decided that his colleagues could be more usefully employed driving up to Katherine Stone's house.

'Tell the chaps there that they can stop will-hunting, but that they should still keep their eyes open for anything that might be of interest. After that, you can check up on progress at the scene. Harry, I'll need you back here in an hour or so.'

'Right you are, sir.'

The car drove off in the direction of Meldon Dene. Ashley rang the solicitor's doorbell.

Peter Masters' office, like Peter himself, was splendidly old-fashioned. From his predecessor, he had inherited a panelled room, cracked leather armchairs, a vast, antique desk, and piles of legal boxes inscribed with the names of living and dead clients. He had also inherited a vast, antique secretary, who took notes in erratic and illegible shorthand and punched out letters on an indestructible Remington. During her lunch break, Peter would retype these on an up-to-date laptop, which he kept concealed in a box marked 'Estate of Mrs Nelstrop (decsd.)'. Today, however, being the Saturday after Christmas,

Peter was alone. He ran an appreciative eye over the inspector's suit, and served dry sherry from a decanter with half a dozen chillies at the bottom.

'It was a tip I got from Mr Justice Anstruther – the last of the great hanging judges. They give it a bit of a kick; it's amazing what clients will sign away after a couple of glasses.'

'Their lives, by the sound of it, in Judge Anstruther's case.' The inspector's tone was approving. 'I suppose after a few sips of this at eight o'clock in the morning, the noose and the trapdoor would hold no fears.'

Ashley and Simkin deposited themselves in armchairs and Peter Masters placed himself behind his desk. A large, unopened envelope lay in front of him. Flowing, copperplate letters spelled out, 'The last Will and Testament of Katherine Laetitia Stone'. Peter passed the envelope across to the inspector, turning it over so that he could see the seal.

'I thought, in the circumstances, you'd like to be here when it was opened. Mrs Stone drew up her own will, so I have no idea of its contents other than that I am the executor, jointly with the late Ellen Cleghorn. That much, Mrs Stone told me herself.'

Simkin analysed the envelope, noting the crisp, expensive quality of the paper and the firm handwriting, which was obviously the combined product of a valuable fountain pen and a strong personality. The red wax seal on the reverse side was a pretentious touch, giving the document a bogus veneer of legal authority.

'Isn't it a little odd that she should appoint you joint executor, but not employ you to draw up the will?'

'Very odd: but entirely in character. Katherine Stone would have considered it a waste of money to have an easy task like a will done professionally. It'll serve her right, if she's made a mess of it, though it doesn't weigh much, so my guess is that she kept it simple. Shall we?'

The inspector handed back the envelope, which Peter sliced open with a knife. He drew out a single sheet of paper, the same heavy parchment as the thick envelope, and read the contents, his eyebrows ascending gradually towards the ceiling. When he had finished, he handed it over to the inspector. 'See what you make of that.'

Simkin held the document so that Ashley could read it at the same time. It was written by the same hand as the envelope:

The last Will and Testament of me Katherine Laetitia Stone (nee Freston) of Meldon Dene in the Town of Chagford in the County of Devon which I make on this twelfth day of July Two Thousand and Three and whereby revoke all previous Wills and Dispositions.

To my First Cousin Twice Removed Miss Evelyn Margaret Warren also of Chagford I bequeath the Oil Painting of Kestor Rock by William Widgery presently hanging in the Entrance Hall at Meldon Dene. This is in gratitude for the kindness which she has shown me since my return to Chagford.

To Miss Ellen Alice Cleghorn also of Chagford I bequeath the Set of Six Silver Apostle Spoons in Token of our friendship.

The remainder of my Goods Chattels and other Possessions including my House and Furniture I instruct to be sold and the whole of the Money resulting together with the Residue of my Estate I bequeath to the Charity Women Against Needless Killing based in Golden Square in Bloomsbury in London.

I appoint as my Executors the aforementioned Ellen Cleghorn and Peter Henry Masters also of Chagford.

Signed: Katherine Laetitia Stone

Witnessed: Ellen Alice Cleghorn
  Mill Road
  Chagford

Elizabeth Alexandra Trenchard
Thimble Cottage
Lamb Park
Chagford

The detectives spent some time taking in the contents of the document. On one level it was very simple; but it raised some interesting questions. Also, Ashley guessed, Katherine Stone's do-it-yourself legal language might suggest a few things to Peter Masters. He sat back in his chair while the inspector placed the will back on the desk.

'So: lucky animal rights charity, unlucky Robert and Evelyn.'

The solicitor nodded. 'That's about it: how utterly typical of her. Any detective's thoughts before I give my legal commentary?'

Inspector Simkin made them pause for a moment, while he rummaged around in his briefcase for a notebook. When he was ready, he looked up at Ashley:

'All right – fire away.'

'I think I've got three things to mention.' Ashley sipped his sherry carefully, organising his thoughts. 'In the first place, the will is dated quite recently and she takes care to revoke any previous wills. Now, I know that's quite standard, but then she's missed out other bits that ought to be standard – I'll leave those to you, Peter. Question number one, therefore, is what made her draw up a new will? The second question follows on from that: what was in the old will? The third question is then obvious: how many people were told of this new will and, if they knew of its existence, were they aware of the contents?'

Peter Masters also made a note of Ashley's questions. 'I can give you some information about all that, and I can have a good guess about other bits. Katherine Stone made a will when

124

she first came back to England. She drew it up herself and left it with me, exactly as she did with this one: I have no idea of the contents, nor of who witnessed it. When she brought in the new will, she tore up the old one in my presence, without opening it. The pieces went into my wastepaper basket and, when she left the office, I fed them through a paper shredder.

'As for the date of the new will, I can tell you that it coincides with Robert's return from his Equestrian Studies course at college and his employment with the hunt. It's presumably no great leap to infer that Robert was mentioned in the previous will, whereas, of course, he doesn't appear in the present one. It's probably also worth pointing out that the late Ellen Cleghorn's will was drawn up at about the same time as this one, and that the same animal rights charity was the main beneficiary.

'Finally, as far as your questions are concerned, George, I don't know whether anyone knew the contents of either will. Betty Trenchard and Ellen Cleghorn must have known what they were witnessing, because the laws concerning the signing of a will are so specific, but they need not have seen the contents. Betty is the biggest gossip in Chagford, but she was quite intimidated by Mother Stone, so she might have been frightened into keeping her mouth shut. Needless to say, I haven't told anybody apart from yourselves about the existence of either will, and I wouldn't have been in a position to let out the contents, because I didn't know them. Anything else, or shall I go on to a few legal observations?'

Simkin was writing frantically: he held up his free hand to request a pause.

'Hang on a minute. I should have brought Craggs along after all – he's much better at taking notes than I am.'

He took a minute to catch up and then rested his pen. 'Before we get onto the legal observations, I have a couple of questions. In the first place, you referred to "the late Ellen Cleghorn".

Since she witnessed the will in July, she presumably died fairly recently?'

Peter Masters nodded. 'About three weeks ago.'

'All above board?'

'Above the chemist's shop, to be precise. She had a sudden heart attack in her flat: there's been no suggestion that it was anything other than a natural death, though the doctor will be able to tell you more about that than I can.'

'All right, I'll get Craggs to call on him, just in case. One other thing: just how much money are we talking about here? I can tell that Meldon Dene must be worth about half a million pounds. What else was there?'

The solicitor shrugged his shoulders. 'I shan't know that until I get hold of the relevant documents. I think you're right in your estimate of half a million for the house, and the contents are probably worth another hundred thousand: say a hundred and twenty once you've included her jewellery – she had some good pieces. My guess is that she had at least as much again in the bank and in investments: Katherine Stone wasn't the sort of person to put more than half her fortune into buying a house. So, in all probability, somewhere between a million and a million and a half. Quite a nice sum.'

'People have killed for less,' Ashley observed.

'Significantly less,' agreed Simkin. 'Oh yes – what about this oil painting by Widgery? Are we talking thousands of pounds there?'

'You'd know more about that than I should, George.' Peter Masters had a guess anyway: 'Two or three thousand, do you think?'

Ashley agreed. 'He's a good painter, but we're not in the serious league. You can pick up a good watercolour by him for about a thousand pounds. An oil would be less than five thousand.'

Simkin got the idea: 'So you'd have to be pretty desperate

to murder for a Widgery.' He jotted a few more notes, then looked up again. 'Okay, Mr Masters, give us your legal observations. Preferably slowly.'

Peter gave his first grin of the day. 'All right, as slowly as I can. Point One: the document is written in what a layman thinks legal language is like. She seems to think that all nouns should begin with a capital letter, and she's obviously read somewhere that punctuation has no legal function. She apes official language, but clearly doesn't understand any of its implications: she'd have done far better to write the whole thing in plain English.'

'Point Two: George, you're quite right to observe that she's careful to revoke previous wills, but leaves out other usual things. Most importantly, the conclusion is all wrong: she doesn't make it clear that she has signed the will in the presence of the witnesses, and that's a big mistake. Wills have been contested over that sort of thing.'

The inspector's eyes lit up: 'Are you saying that there are grounds for disputing the will?'

Peter Masters adopted a professional attitude and sat firmly on the fence. 'Well, maybe, but there probably wouldn't be that much of a case. Not with Betty Trenchard still alive to give evidence.'

Simkin was crestfallen. 'A shame – it was a nice idea. Anything else?'

'Just a small point: a properly drawn-up will wouldn't have left anything to one of the witnesses, and we try to avoid using an executor as a witness – things like that muddy the legal waters too much. It doesn't make any difference here, because Ellen Cleghorn is dead and the spoons can't be worth more than a couple of hundred pounds at the most; but it's indicative of Katherine Stone's vague grasp of legal matters. I've already told George that she drew up Ellen Cleghorn's will for her and the same problems occur there. It took a lot of extra work to sort out the details.'

Ashley smiled wryly: 'And presumably your bill was correspondingly large?'

Peter beamed in response.

'Well, Ellen didn't leave very much money, as you know: but I did feel it my responsibility to make sure that as little of it as possible went to that silly charity.'

* * * * *

The Toms had chopped enough wood to keep the Noad fires burning for some time to come: in the woodshed there was now a pile of large, slow-burning logs and several baskets of kindling. During a childish interlude, they had re-enacted the execution of Charles I: Tom One, having lost the race to the garden, made a tasteful and tragic speech ('Tell my horse I loved her'), then knelt down and rested his head on the chopping block, while Two wielded the axe sadistically. There was, thought One, something oddly exciting about the passive kneeling position, staring into an empty basket, aware of Two's actions from the movement of his shadow. Standing with his feet well apart, Two extended the axe over Tom One's neck, bringing it so close that One could feel the blade brushing the short hairs that grew there; then it was raised aloft and brought back down in slow motion, coming to a halt about an inch away. Two made a splatting sound with his mouth, approximating the noise made by contact between blade and spinal cord, and Tom One slumped sideways, shedding imaginary blood over Two's wellingtons. They swapped roles, but Two got a large splinter in his Adam's apple and decided that the game was over.

Dragging in one basket of logs and another of kindling wood, they built up the fire in the sitting room, which had been dying down since Ashley and the policemen had left. Once there was a good blaze going, they lounged around on the hearth rug, cracking walnuts, and debating what to do next.

'I suppose we could watch a video?'

'Dull.'

'Or raid the drinks cabinet?'

'A bit early.'

They found temporary distraction from their boredom in throwing fragments of walnut shell on the fire.

'The problem is,' Two philosophised, 'that the police and your Uncle George are having all the fun. We're not allowed to go to the kennels and see Robert, but they haven't given us anything else to do instead. We want to be hunting for clues, or re-enacting the crime, or something.'

Tom One had a bright idea.

'That's it, Two – we'll re-enact the crime!'

'You mean you want me to bash you over the head this time and chuck you in a ditch?'

'No, not like the Charles I nonsense – that was just fooling around. What I mean, is reconstruct things here, as best we can, with my old toy soldiers and the scenery from my railway set. We can draw up a list of times and movements and see who was where, when. What do you think?'

'It sounds good. You never know, we might even have solved the crime by the time your uncle gets back.'

Tom One doubted it: he was more aware than Two of the amount of work that went into solving a crime. 'Still, we might come up with something useful. Let's go upstairs and get all the stuff.'

* * * * *

CHAPTER THIRTEEN

- BETTY TRENCHARD'S EVIDENCE -

It was clear to Ashley and his companions that their best course of action was to interview Betty Trenchard.

'Though when we say "interview",' observed Peter, 'what we mean is, listen to a series of rambling monologues, in which there might just be one or two useful pieces of information. She's the gossiping champion of Chagford.'

'A hotly-contested title, I should imagine.' The inspector had met many Betty Trenchards over the years. Peter and Ashley nodded vigorously. The solicitor consulted his watch and continued:

'But if we go now, she might start to crave her lunch after about half an hour. Then she'll have to get to the point. She's recently developed diabetes, so I imagine she has to be quite precise about meal times.'

'How very convenient.' Simkin also looked at his watch. 'And then, perhaps we can get something for ourselves in one of the pubs. Do we drive?'

The cottage was within walking distance, which was just as well for Harry Sefton, who was fast asleep in the driving seat of the police car. His right cheek was pressed against the window, which had the effect of puffing out his lips, making him look like a chubby and contented *putto*. With difficulty, Simkin resisted the temptation to open the car door and send the constable flying into the Square.

'Up all night, poor kid, then volunteered to stay on duty. We'll let him sleep while he can.'

They turned eastwards out of the Square and ambled down to Lamb Park. The houses here were comparatively modern, built at a time when all the old properties in the area had become so expensive that only rich outsiders could afford them. It was an irony that some of the oldest Chagford families now lived in the newest houses, many of them having taken the opportunity to sell off their crumbling ancestral cottages for a ludicrous profit.

Betty Trenchard's pudgy hands were covered in dough when she answered the door. Forgetting this, she gave a little scream at the sight of the three official-looking gentlemen, raising her palms to her cheeks and daubing her face liberally with flour.

'Oh, there, how stupid of me – I was that surprised, I didn't think.' She lifted her apron and gave herself a vigorous rubbing, leaving her face looking even redder than usual. 'Do come along in – you won't mind if we go into the kitchen, will you – I'm just in the middle of making bread, and if I don't carry on kneading, it won't rise – I'm sure you know how it is….'

She eased herself round and plodded off, talking all the time. The men exchanged glances and followed in her wake.

The kitchen was a comfortably untidy muddle of cooking utensils, recipe books and pot plants. On the table, Ashley noticed a new and glossy book with the revolting title *Deliciously Diabetic!*; he recognised the packet of flour as the gluten-free type he had nearly purchased in the shop.

There being no point in waiting for Betty to pause in her rambling, he interrupted her: 'I nearly bought some of this flour by accident the other day.'

Betty shot off effortlessly on a conversational tangent: 'Then you had a lucky escape, my dear – do sit down wherever you can, I'll put the kettle on…. No? Well, just as you please – yes, I suppose I've got used to the taste now after all these years, but it's not the same – still, what can you do, you have to make the best of things, I always think – look at poor Mrs Stone, now, if she'd had a more cheerful outlook on life, she'd have had a lot more friends and a nicer time of it. What I say, is….'

'It was about Mrs Stone that we called.' Peter raised his voice and spoke slowly, as if he was speaking to a foreigner on the telephone. 'And specifically about her will.'

There is something about a will which arouses curiosity in all of us. Betty Trenchard stopped in her tracks and stared at the solicitor. He took full advantage of her temporary silence.

'Katherine Stone drew up a will about six months ago and she appointed me and Mrs Cleghorn her joint executors….'

'But, surely….'

Peter stared over the top of his spectacles and continued talking, giving her no chance to interrupt. Ashley and the inspector exchanged amused glances, impressed with his technique.

'I know exactly what you're going to tell me: that Mrs Cleghorn, of course, predeceased Mrs Stone. Naturally that leaves me as sole executor. Now, what I have to say concerns you very closely, so please listen carefully….'

Ashley wondered if poor Mrs Trenchard might, at this point, think she had inherited a large sum of money, in which case, she was in for a disappointment. If the thought had occurred to her, she showed no sign of it; her expression displayed only the unnatural concentration of a talker who was, for once, forced to listen.

'You will be aware, of course, that Mrs Stone was a wealthy woman. Given the unfortunate circumstances of her death, the contents of her will naturally acquire a great importance.'

Betty was nodding slowly and repeating significant words under her breath: 'Importance, yes....'

'The inspector here needs to establish the extent to which Mrs Stone's intentions for the distribution of her property were generally known, and we thought that you might be able to assist us in this matter.'

Again, a strange silence filled the kitchen, as Betty Trenchard translated the solicitor's English into her own, more rudimentary native speech. Eventually, she asked:

'Wouldn't you be better asking Miss Warren, or Robert Brookes? I certainly didn't know anything about her will – I don't know why you might think I would.'

'Well, it occurred to us that, as one of the witnesses of the document....'

Peter stopped. Betty Trenchard's expression had changed from curiosity to surprise. She was so shocked, Ashley noticed, that, for once in her life, she uttered a short, complete sentence:

'I never witnessed a will for Mrs Stone.'

* * * * *

With the aid of a map and a tape measure, the Toms had transformed a large portion of the sitting room into a model of Chagford and the moor. Underneath an expanse of green baize, two shoeboxes represented Kestor Rock and Meldon Tor, with a few building blocks from an old construction set taking the place of the granite outcrops. Sections of railway track served as roads, and the troopers had used their regimental ties for the river Teign. Tom's railway set had been well provided with buildings and accessories: Meldon Dene was a signal box; the kennels proclaimed themselves to be the Watford Junction ticket office and Primrose Armishaw's livery yard, complete with horses from a farmyard set, was a railway warehouse. Tom had reserved the model of a public lavatory for his own house, knowing that it would annoy his mother excessively if she came in to find out what they were up to. The farmyard set had provided hedges for fields, and Chagford itself was a jumble of plastic houses arranged around yet more railway track.

They paused for mutual congratulations and a magisterial survey of their kingdom: it was easily as good as any of the models they had used, during their basic training, for patrolling or battle plans.

'Now for the characters.' Tom One up-ended a large box, producing a jumble of toy soldiers of every description: Viking warriors with horned helmets, Roman gladiators, Napoleonic cavalry, and even an alarming selection of Red Indians, waving tomahawks and obviously well tanked up with fire water. They separated out the mounted soldiers from the infantry.

'So, these five Life Guards with their red tunics can be the huntsmen, and Napoleon's Imperial Guard in blue can be all the posh people. Blue's almost black, after all: let's have about fifteen of those.' Tom One organised a pile of Imperial Guards and a smaller pile of Life Guards. Tom Two picked out two Horse Artillery models and held them up triumphantly:

'Hey, One, I've just found us!'

'Great! Now, what about a dozen Red Indians for all the local farmers?'

They had almost completed the casting process. Ashley would have been pleased to be represented by a model of the Duke of Wellington, whereas Primrose Armishaw would probably not have been so flattered had she seen herself as Boadicea, complete with knives extending from the wheels of her chariot. Katherine Stone was General Custer. After all, as Tom Two pointed out, it was her last stand.

'Okay, shall we put them all in the Square to start with?' Tom One began to fill a cupped palm with models.'

'I think I've got a better idea, One. When the police showed me that map, with the cross marking the place where we found her, it was much easier to trace our route by working backwards. Why don't we do it that way?'

'Good thinking, Batman.' The presence of all his old toys had caused Tom One to revert to a pre-pubescent state of mind. Tom Two decided that it would be better for both of them if he took charge.

'So, time: approximately fifteen forty-five hours. Position of victim: face down in ditch. Position of Troopers Noad and Marsh, ditto.'

'Well, we weren't actually in the ditch.'

'Stop quibbling – you know what I mean.' Two placed General Custer and the two Horse Artillery soldiers by a section of railway track. 'Position of your Uncle George?'

Tom One moved the Duke of Wellington to the model representing Waye Lodge.

'In the Watford Junction public lavatories, warming his feet by the fire.'

'You have a very strange family, One. All posh hunters, i.e., the Napoleonic Guard, similarly buggered off home. Red Indians and Life Guards somewhere on the moor, probably about….' Two arranged the incongruous battle party a few miles south-east of Kestor Rock, somewhere near the drinks cabinet: 'Here. Is that it?'

'Not quite – what about Primrose Armishaw?' One held up the menacing Queen of the Iceni.

'Oh yes, she didn't hang around long, did she? Back at the stables, do you think?'

Tom One shook his head. 'She wasn't there when I got back at about a quarter past four.' A brilliant idea occurred to him. 'Hey! Does that mean we've got suspect number one?'

'I wonder if it does? What time did she leave the field? And was her horse back at the yard when you arrived?'

One paused for thought. 'Pass to both questions. I didn't look to see if her horse was back, and I'm not sure when she left the field – though I remember her saying at some point that she was only there to fly the flag and that she'd head off once she'd had a good run for the horse's sake.'

'Let's make a note of that.' Two reached for the old maths book which Tom One had brought downstairs for the purpose. It was largely blank, though a few blotched and inaccurate calculations were sprawled across the opening pages, and an obscene geometric doodle of a maths master and a pair of compasses was tucked away on the inside back cover. Two found a clean page and wrote:

EXERCISE 'TOM ONE'S TRAIN SET'
1. Observations Arising:
a) For some time prior to 1615 hours, the movements of Miss Primrose Armishaw were unaccounted for.

* * * * *

The party in Lamb Park was gathered around the dining room table. It had changed slightly in content, Harry Sefton having taken the place of Inspector Simkin. The presence of the uniformed constable lent an air of officialdom to the occasion and Betty Trenchard was awed into comparative silence as Peter Masters drew up a statement for her to sign.

After he had got over the initial surprise of her announcement concerning the will, the solicitor had questioned Betty Trenchard quite closely.

'Let me get this quite clear: you are certain that at no time you witnessed a will for Katherine Stone?'

'Absolutely certain. I've witnessed many documents for the people I clean for and I know that a will is different.'

'Very well, I'll come back to that point in a moment. Did you ever witness any other documents for Katherine Stone? Specifically, did you witness one on or about the twelfth of July this year?'

'Well, I've witnessed a number of things for her – and there certainly were one or two about six months ago.'

'And can you tell me how these occasions were arranged?'

'Easily – there was always a piece of paper over whatever it was, so that just Mrs Stone's signature was visible. I then signed my name where she'd pencilled a cross. Sometimes I had to write my name and address in block letters as well.'

'Did you ever see Mrs Stone sign a document?'

'No – it was always signed already.'

'And were other witnesses ever present?'

'No, not that I can ever remember.'

Peter had remained remarkably calm during this cross-examination, although he had exchanged several glances with Ashley. He continued:

'That's been very helpful, so far, Mrs Trenchard. Now, you say that you have witnessed wills at other times for some of your employers. Can you tell me what procedure was followed when you did so? You might find it easier to use a specific example.'

Betty proved to have a remarkably accurate notion of what was required. 'When Mrs Dyer – not that I've every cleaned for her, mind you – wanted to sign her will, Mrs Farmer Crane and I were both in the shop. She asked if we'd mind coming through to the back room for a moment. We went in and her daughter made us a cup of tea, I remember – of course, she couldn't be a witness, because she was the main beneficiary. Anyway, the will was there on the table, waiting to be signed, with another sheet of paper covering up the top half. We both watched Mrs Dyer sign, and then we signed as well, and added our addresses. She popped a packet of chocolate ginger into my shopping basket as a thank-you afterwards. That was before I developed my diabetes, of course.'

'That all sounds very correct. Tell me, Mrs Trenchard, was this procedure followed on all other occasions when you witnessed a will?'

137

'Yes, of course. No, wait a moment! Years ago, when old Mr Russell was making his will, he asked the meals on wheels lady and me to be witnesses, but he'd already signed himself – and the meals on wheels lady said we couldn't witness it like that. That's how I first learned about it. Ever so cross he was – I thought he has going to drop down dead then, which would have left his estate in a nice old pickle…'

It was at this point that Peter Masters had suggested the importance of drawing up a statement for Mrs Trenchard to sign and they had moved through to the dining room. Having supplied the solicitor with paper, Betty retreated to the kitchen for five minutes in order to eat a sandwich: 'Otherwise I might get one of those hypos or hypers like I had in the shop the other week – that's how they came to diagnose me….'

Left alone, the three men were free to express restrained surprise.

'How very interesting.'

'So the millions appear to be redistributing themselves.'

'They do indeed. My goodness, I knew that Katherine Stone was an incompetent lawyer, but I thought she would know enough to get the witnessing right. By the sounds of it, she'd have done better to let Mother Trenchard draw up the whole thing for her – at least she seems to know what she's doing.'

Given that the next stage of the business was going to be a straightforward legal process, Simkin had begged to be excused. 'I think I can probably be of more use up at the house with Craggs. If I go and kiss the sleeping beauty and send him here, there'll still be a police presence.'

A few minutes later, therefore, Harry was sitting among them, feeling very important as the Official Representative of the Law. The change-over had proved to be quite useful, since Peter Masters had been able to give the inspector the keys to his office and the police constable had appeared with the will itself.

This he had tucked inside his jacket: he felt that a briefcase handcuffed to his wrist would have been a more appropriate method of carriage but, alas, no briefcase was to hand.

Peter Masters placed the will on the table and covered up the main body of the document in the manner described by Betty Trenchard. When she reappeared, he asked her if the signature was hers. She hesitated.

'It certainly looks like it. Would that be the will itself, Mr Masters?'

'It would.' Peter dextrously withdrew the document and folded it back into its envelope. He spent some minutes drawing up a carefully-worded statement which testified that Elizabeth Alexandra Trenchard, of Lamb Park, Chagford, denied having witnessed the signing of a will by Katherine Laetitita Stone, of Meldon Dene, Chagford: that she did not deny the signature on the document was her own, but that she had not fulfilled the legal requirements necessary for the valid witnessing of such a document. There was another paragraph concerning the absence of a second witness on any possible occasion, and a third stating that Elizabeth Alexandra Trenchard was fully aware of the laws concerning the witnessing of wills and that had she been informed of the nature of the document to which she was appending her signature, she would have pointed out the irregularity of the proceedings.

When he had completed his task, the solicitor read the contents aloud, then passed the paper to Mrs Trenchard for her to read at her own speed. She followed the words with her finger as she read and mouthed them slowly and silently. Eventually, she reached the end and looked up.

'That's about the long and the short of it, Mr Masters. I'll happily sign that, and say the same in court if necessary.'

The solicitor watched her sign and then, in succession, the document was witnessed by: Peter Henry Masters of the Square,

139

Chagford; George Frederick Thomas Ashley, of London, N1; and Police Constable Henry Christopher Sefton, of Exeter Road, Okehampton.

As Peter said, walking back towards the town centre, no-one was going to be in a position to question the legality of *this* document.

* * * * *

CHAPTER FOURTEEN

- A GAME OF SOLDIERS -

Peter Masters declined Ashley's suggestion of luncheon in the Ring O' Bells: he was going to buy a sandwich at Norah Dyer's stores and spend an hour or so rummaging through case histories and legal textbooks.

'I just want to make sure of something: I'm worried that a court just might decide that, because Stone actually handed it to me, her action could be taken as meaning the will reflected her true intentions, even if it wasn't properly valid. I need to check up on my facts. I'll ring you if I find anything out, and perhaps, Constable, you could tell Inspector Simkin the same.'

'Very good, sir, I'll make sure he gets that information.'

By this time, they were back in the Square. The solicitor took his leave and headed off to the stores. Ashley decided that the young policeman would probably make quite a good lunchtime companion.

'What about you, Constable Sefton? Are you up for a bite to eat?'

'I wouldn't say no, sir. Just something light though – that was a big breakfast the old lady gave me. The inspector can get me on the radio if he needs me.'

141

Ashley enjoyed the slight *frisson* that Sefton's entrance caused among the drinkers and bar staff, and was similarly amused by their obvious feelings of anticlimax when it became clear that he was only there for a drink and some food. The silence which had fallen at their arrival was gradually replaced by the low-pitched rumbling sound of multiple conversations. They ordered ploughman's lunches and Ashley convinced Harry that a pint of shandy did not constitute drinking on duty. Some way off from other customers was a window seat with a good view of the police car, so they occupied it and made themselves comfortable.

'So, Constable Sefton, are you enjoying your first murder?'

Harry weighed up the interesting duties and offset them against the dull ones.

'On balance, yes, sir – so far. It wasn't much fun being up all night guarding the scene of the crime, a bit creepy, in fact, but it was interesting listening to all that will stuff. And the inspector seems a good sort to work for – a real gent. I'm not so sure about Sergeant Craggs. What about you, sir? How does this compare with other cases you've been on?'

The ploughman's lunches arrived; Ashley bit into a slab of cheese while he considered his answer.

'I suppose a murder case is always rather entertaining at first, if you're convinced that the victim was a thoroughly unpleasant person who deserved what he or she got. It starts getting difficult when you realise that the person who committed the crime is a decent and likeable person. On the other hand, there's an enormous satisfaction in tracking down a real villain who has murdered some poor, inoffensive creature.'

'From what I've heard about the victim, sir, I guess that this case is one of first type.'

'Absolutely – so enjoy it while you can, Constable. There are going to be grim times ahead.'

* * * * *

The Duke of Wellington sat astride his horse, regally perched amongst the toy building blocks at the top of the shoebox. Two Horse Artillery troopers acted as his bodyguard, while he surveyed an unlikely battle between the Life Guards and the Sioux for control of the fire irons.

Tom's exercise book was filling up with diagrams, lists of timings and an increasing number of general observations. Two, as scribe, lay on his stomach on the hearth rug with the book and a scattering of coloured pencils in front of him. He had lifted his feet off the floor and was knocking his heels together again, though this time producing only a dull thud, rather than the satisfying metallic click of spurs. One moved around the model, trying not to tread on any of the characters.

'So, that's done the diagram for approximately fourteen hundred hours.' Two put down his pencil and turned to a new page. 'What were we doing before then?'

'We'd galloped like crazy all the way from the river, I think. Fifteen minutes?'

'That sounds about right – I remember now – that's when the hounds found the line again, at about….' He consulted the map: 'Grid six-seven-three, eight-four-seven, give or take a few thousand miles.' He jotted down the reference, and began a new diagram, headed "c.13.45HRS".

'Where's that in terms of the model?'

Two looked up. 'Let's say, your tie, just to the south of the second zigzag. Do we need to bring on any of the Imperial Guard?'

'I don't think so.' Tom One began placing the model soldiers by the blue and purple silk. 'They'd mainly melted away when we lost the scent, I think.'

'Oh, yes – up by about the seventh zigzag. We'll do that next. What's the time, by the way?'

'Thirteen forty-five. You've just written it down.'

'No, twit, the real time. I was wondering if your earlier suggestion of the drinks cabinet had reached maturity?'

Tom One looked at his watch and beamed. 'It's well past midday. Since we're being high-powered detectives, shall I sneak some of Uncle George's emergency gin? It's his fault we're stuck here, after all.'

'Well, it seems only fair, as long as you don't think he'll mind. Where is it? In the fridge?'

'As good as – it's in his bedroom, which has been like Ice Station Zebra since the heating packed up. Let's do a quick sneaky-beaky patrol up the back stairs and raid the enemy supplies.'

'Good idea. Rendezvous points at the top and bottom of the stairs?'

'Yes, then kitten crawl along the landing.'

'Action on being challenged by a sentry?'

'Mother or Aunt Lav? Shoot to kill.'

* * * * *

Harry Sefton's radio came to life just as he was finishing his meal. Conversation in the pub dried up, and the constable felt awkwardly aware of being the centre of attention once more.

'I'll take this in the car, sir, if you'll excuse me.'

'Of course.' Ashley smiled again at the almost palpable disappointment of the other drinkers. 'If it's an emergency, don't feel you have to come back – I can settle up here.'

Harry did come back, with a message from Simkin.

'The inspector wants me to pick him up and drive out to the kennels and the stable now, sir. He says, if you'd like to join us, you'd be very welcome.'

Ashley did some quick thinking. He had a hunch that this could be one of those grim moments that he had referred to earlier. There was also another trail he wanted to follow.

'Perhaps you could thank the inspector from me, but say that I'm going to try another line of inquiry.'

The constable grinned. 'That'll keep him guessing, sir. One second.'

He withdrew again, returning a minute later, with the grin still in place. 'He says all the very best with your lead, sir and he's so desperate to know what the hell it is that he asks if you would care to satisfy his curiosity back at the station at about five o'clock. By that time, he hopes to have the doctor's report, if that tempts you, sir. He'll send a driver to pick you up – which means me, of course.'

'That sounds excellent. Tell him we've arranged to meet outside the churchyard. That should really get him wondering. See you later, Constable Sefton.'

'Harry, sir, if you like – and thanks for lunch. Shall we say half past four at the churchyard?'

'That will be fine. Thanks, Harry.'

* * * * *

'Hey, One – it's no wonder your uncle is such a brilliant detective. We've been getting on really quickly since we had that gin.'

The Toms were sitting cross-legged on the green baize: their glasses stood empty on top of the Kestor shoebox. Tom One looked around the model with satisfaction. The models were now significantly closer to Meldon Common, where the hounds had originally flushed out the fox.

'It's looking good. We've done all that boring gate work through the fields; there's not much left, now.'

'Okay,' Tom Two took up his pen once more. 'Sometime about twelve-fifty. That must be when Robert caught up with us after he'd been looking for that hound.' Two became serious. 'He said he was going to have to shoot her. Do you think he has done? I'm not sure I could shoot a dog, unless it was attacking something. Could you?'

'I don't know – perhaps it's different with fox hounds. They're not pets, after all, and if one is no good at its job, what do you do? He was in quite a temper about it, wasn't he?'

'Wouldn't you be, if you knew you were going to have to kill something?'

Tom Two began drawing yet another diagram, marking the northing and easting lines 69 and 86 respectively. He was drawing rough contours for Meldon Tor, when an idea occurred to him. He put down the pencil, paused to think, and then said quietly, 'Oh, shit.'

One looked up from his task of moving the soldiers out of the farmyard hedges. 'What?'

Two gestured at the model. 'It all fits, doesn't it? Robert rejoined us about *here*.' He picked up one of the Life Guards and placed it at the edge of Meldon Common. 'He'd left us about half an hour beforehand when the hounds had picked up the scent – *here*.' Again, he moved the toy soldier. 'Look how close he is to the place where we found the body. How long would it take to gallop there? Three minutes?'

Tom One followed the movements of the model, a look of bewilderment on his face. Tom Two continued:

'So he rides off, kills the old bag, takes time to do anything he might have to and then catches up with us half an hour later. It's simple, isn't it?'

It was frighteningly simple. Tom One did his best to find objections.

'But hang on – he surely can't have known that she was going to be there at that time? He couldn't have arranged to meet her.'

'Perhaps he waited for her, knowing that she would be on her way home. Or perhaps he really did chase after the hound and bumped into her by accident – after all, we don't know that the murder was planned in advance.'

'That would make it manslaughter.' Tom One had picked

up some legal information from his uncle. Tom Two took the word over enthusiastically.

'All right – *manslaughter*. Suppose he met her in the course of chasing the hound and she cut up rough again. The horse spooked, she fell back into the ditch – and died. Then – I don't know – perhaps he took a bit of time to calm his horse down, found the hound, if he hadn't already, and rejoined us. What do you think?'

One was still muddled. 'Well, I see that it *could* have happened like that. But, surely, if it was an accident, he'd have dismounted and tried to help – or, if she was dead, done what I did and ridden into Chagford to summon assistance. Surely he wouldn't just have left her there?'

'Perhaps he panicked?'

'I don't think Robert would panic at an accident like that – only if he really had done something dreadful. If he'd hit her over the head with his whip, or ridden his horse at her.'

They both stared gloomily at the toy cavalryman. Two was the first to speak.

'However it happened, he's in a lot of trouble. I suppose this is why your Uncle George didn't want us to go down to the kennels: he'd worked it out already.'

'Yes – but surely he didn't think we'd be in any danger from Robert?'

'Who knows? Supposing we found him destroying some evidence? Burning the whip he'd hit her with, for instance. Or perhaps he just didn't want us to be there when the police came for him.'

There was another morose lull. Tom Two rolled back onto his stomach and began throwing walnut shells on the fire. 'Do you think they've already been?'

'Maybe. Perhaps they're round there now. Weird to think that they were such a good bunch when they were here this morning, and yet now they could be doing something really unpleasant. I reckon Robert would put up quite a struggle as well.'

'I think you're right: I don't see him going with quiet dignity.' Two smiled bleakly, 'Not like your impression of Charles the First.'

Tom One rested his chin on his fists. He felt uncomfortable.

'I rather wish we hadn't done that now. It was in pretty poor taste, wasn't it?'

'Oh, come on, One, it was just a bit of fun – and it gave us the idea to do all this. Do we leave it out to show your uncle?'

Tom One had been wondering the same thing. He stared into the fire for a while, then made up his mind.

'No. If they want to find Robert guilty of murder, or manslaughter, or whatever – well, that's their job. But they can do it without our help. Let's get all these things back in the boxes and upstairs before Uncle George comes home. And as for this….'

He picked up the exercise book and threw it on the fire.

* * * * *

CHAPTER FIFTEEN

- CHAGFORD CHURCHYARD -

The military grave was not Ashley's objective, but its slender white headstone and its understated quiet dignity drew his eye. Beneath it lay Lieutenant James Edward Charles Hargreaves, aged, as the stone announced, twenty-two years. There was a carving of the young officer's regimental crest and, beneath that, a cross. Chrysanthemums were arranged in a wreath at the foot of the stone.

Ashley found himself trying to visualise the body below. He remembered seeing pictures of battlefield excavations after the First World War, when skeletons in tin helmets and boots were dug up for identification and reburial. Perhaps James Hargreaves looked like that now: the perishable parts of his body and uniform eaten away or rotted, and just bone, metal and leather remaining, with buttons and belt caught amongst the white ribs. Then again, the coffin might be airtight and, by one of those strange suspensions of the laws of nature, the body perfectly preserved. A final, awful thought came to mind: if the poor boy had been killed by so-called 'friendly fire', perhaps there was never that much of him in the coffin in the first place.

Then Ashley thought of Tom. His nephew was in a ceremonial unit, but Prince Albert's Troop was part of the Royal Artillery, and soldiers sometimes moved across for a few years. It would be typical of Tom to volunteer to do so if the present war escalated. Perhaps, in another twelve months, there would be a second slim war grave, with a carving of a field gun and Tom's age chiselled into the stone: and under it, Tom himself – amusing, enthusiastic, headstrong Tom; intensely loyal, handsome Tom – returning to the earth from which he came.

He became aware of Stephen Trevis at his side.

'It is very moving, isn't it? There are always fresh flowers, not just at Christmas and anniversaries: that means that the grief is still fresh as well.'

Ashley felt slightly ashamed of himself: he had allowed an imagined, potential loss to push aside the actual, living anguish of others. Perhaps worse was the fact that the clergyman had mistaken his self-indulgent emotions for genuine concern. Still, there was no point in a long-winded explanation: instead, he shrugged himself back to normality.

'I'd seen the name on the War Memorial inside the church, but this is the first time I've come across the grave. I've not had cause to be on the north side of the church before.'

'And in contrast, I am on the north side far more than on any other: it's the only part of the churchyard where there is still room for new graves. If you're searching for deceased Noads, they're round the other side, in a large family tomb. There's enough room left in it for your sister.'

Somehow, this thought appealed to Ashley's sense of humour and he cheered up. 'She's been wanting to move out of Waye Lodge for years – this is probably the only way she could do it that is both legal and affordable. But no, I wasn't Noad hunting, Rector – I came here to search out Brookeses and Frestons and Warrens. I assumed I'd find the more recent ones here and then have to hunt around for the older generations.'

'That's about right. Robert's father is just over here.' They moved along the line of graves. 'A hundred years ago, of course, they wouldn't have allowed him in the churchyard – he'd have been out on the moor somewhere, at a crossroads.' The Rector halted by a simple monument in black marble. 'Which makes one realise that, however much we moan about modern times, some real progress has been made.'

Ashley nodded and pulled out a notebook. James Brookes had been born in 1960 and had killed himself (though the headstone, naturally, was silent on that matter) in 1987. The 'much loved only son of John and Emily Brookes' had the grave all to himself: there was room on the stone for a further inscription and, presumably, room for another occupant one day.

'And John and Emily Brookes? Are they nearby?'

'Yes, we're still talking in terms of north side graves. Let me see....'

The Rector looked around. 'Over near the church wall itself – the granite one.'

Successively, they found Robert's ancestors all the way back to Elias Freston, who lay to the east of the church, beneath a slate headstone. The carving on the slate was curved and ornate:

HERE LIETH THE BODY
of
ELIAS FRESTON
of
RAYBARROW FARM, CHAGFORD
Who was Born the 17th Day of September 1826
And entered into Rest the 14th Day of January 1892

Stranger behold! What you now see
That am I and you shall be;
What you are now, was once I so:
God's Will be done on Earth below

The rustic doggerel, which appeared beneath a distinctly piratical *momento mori*, had a pleasing solidity of faith about it. Ashley imagined Elias sitting upright in his pew on Sundays, taking his religion like a man; then returning to his land and farming it with the same dogmatic assurance, year after year. As an afterthought, 'Also his wife, Susan', had died two years later. She lacked an age and had never, it seemed, been born: nor did she qualify for a poem of her own. As Stephen remarked, she sounded altogether insignificant.

'Though perhaps that isn't fair. After all, she would have been the one responsible for getting her husband's monument made: perhaps she even wrote the poem herself?'

'In which case, it rather sounds as though she was relieved to be rid of the old boy.'

'Well, they were an awkward lot, the Frestons, by all accounts. Raybarrow was a big farm when it was all one property, but it's a bleak stretch of moorland. I should think they had to be fairly bloody-minded to keep it as a going concern. That's probably why poor James Brookes was so unsuccessful: the land was only a third of the original and he didn't have that hard-bitten, determined quality in him. I think Robert's got some of it, and Katherine Stone….'

'Who was born a Freston, I seem to remember?'

'That's right. Well, she had it in spades, as they say.'

There was a particular intensity in the Rector's voice; Ashley's curiosity was aroused. 'Do you speak as one who was trumped by them at any stage?'

'Well, there was the Christmas peal, for a start. That was a real trump, because she won. With other things she was on fairly dodgy ground because she wasn't a regular churchgoer, so the Bishop just filed the letters away – but she still kept on writing them.'

'Any motive?'

Stephen leaned against a granite obelisk and put his hands in his pockets.

'I'm not sure that people like Katherine Stone ever need a motive. Did you ever study *Othello*?'

'Not at school – we did *Troilus* and *The Tempest* – but I've seen it at the Globe. Why do you ask?'

Because when I studied it for my A-levels – it was part of the 'contemporary literature' paper in those days, of course – we had to do a lot of background reading and trawl through everything the Shakespearean authorities had said over the years. Well, to a man, they all had problems with the character of Iago, who enjoys mischief-making for its own sake and who works Othello into such a jealous frenzy that he commits murder. According to all these essayists, this is an unconvincing aspect of the plot, because a character needs to have a cause for such evil actions. I believed it all then and churned it out for the exam – but now, I'm not so sure. There are some people who really do enjoy causing trouble for the fun of it and who gain pleasure from the distress of others.

'Take that incident yesterday – Katherine loved every minute of it. She had a marvellous old time, upsetting everyone and making Robert's horse kick in the door of the police car. And yet I know perfectly well that she couldn't care less about foxes: according to Betty Trenchard, she's got a wardrobe full of fur coats from her days on the New York social register. If everyone in Chagford was *against* hunting, she'd have been up on her horse, chasing every fox in sight. Shakespeare was right.'

It was, Ashley felt, an accurate piece of character analysis.

* * * * *

The Toms were half way up an oak tree at the farthest end of the garden. Two had straddled a fat and knobbly branch, interlocked his ankles underneath and leaned backwards. Resting his shoulders on a fork in the bough, he had allowed his head to hang loosely among twigs and remnants of dead leaves, and

153

was enjoying an upside-down view of Waye Lodge.

Tom One, on a higher level, was riding side-saddle and tapping numbers into his mobile telephone. Extensive experimentation a few summers ago had taught him that the oak tree was the only place for half a mile around where a good signal could be obtained.

'It's probably something to do with the fact that the moor is radioactive,' observed Two, simultaneously extending his arms out to the side. 'I remember our Geography teacher banging on about it once. Hey – it feels really weightless like this. You should try it when we've finished telephoning.'

'Hang on, it's ringing.' Tom One looked down towards his friend, who appeared headless and impaled. He was reminded of a drawing by Goya that he had seen in a history textbook, illustrating the horrors of war: it was a strangely disturbing association of ideas.

His contemplation was interrupted by the reassuring sound of Lance Bombardier Green's voice.

'Hi, Lance, it's me, Tom One. Two's here as well. Have we 'phoned at a good time?'

'Sure – I'm just perched on a saddle in the harness room and Scotty's making some tea. Hang on a second....' Green broke off to address his companion: 'Here, Shifty, don't take the teabags out yet and I want another spoonful of sugar in there.' He returned to the receiver: 'Honestly, Tom One, you don't expect much from a mutant with one eyebrow, but you'd think he could count to five.... Oh, God – he's just stirred it with a dirty hoofpick. You're an animal, Shifty! Anyway, Tom, what can I do you for?'

'There's been a murder, Lance – Two and I found a body yesterday.'

'Blimey!' Apart from a passing interest in the women who sometimes hung around them, Green was mainly unconcerned with the world beyond the barrack gates. A murder, however, commands interest. 'Who got done in?'

'A horrible old lady, who was protesting against the hunt. It hadn't made the newspapers this morning – Uncle George reckons it'll be in tomorrow and Monday. But listen, Lance, Two and I are worried….'

Tom retold the whole story, beginning with the scene in the Square on Boxing Day and continuing up to the conclusion of his re-enactment of the hunt with Tom Two. Green listened carefully, breaking off only once to remark that an infusion of debris from a horse's hoof had made a remarkable improvement to the quality of Trooper Scott's normally inadequate tea. He was sad, but philosophical about the likelihood of Robert's guilt.

'I suppose we might all become murderers if somebody pushed us too far. Remember Adam Barker? You couldn't meet a nicer person, but he ended up killing when he became desperate.'

'I suppose you're right there, Lance. Thanks for listening, by the way – it's good to be able to talk to someone about it. We didn't want to say anything to Uncle George, because we think he's already made up his mind that Robert did it. He won't let us go to the kennels today.'

'Well, if I've got one piece of advice, Tom, it's that your uncle knows what he's doing. If that's what he says, you've got to treat it as an order. Keep well out of things.'

'We are – it just seems a bit tough being stuck here, uselessly.'

'I bet it does, but being miserable isn't going to help anyone. Get on with something completely different. Any old routine task will do, and it'll take your mind off things.'

'Thanks, Lance – we'll do that.' Unable to think of anything further, but unwilling to end the conversation, Tom changed the subject. 'Anyway, Lance, what news back at the barracks? Did you ever find out what happened to Lang's sister?'

'Yes, I did, because number three gun team have been boasting about it ever since they came out of their comas. It's not something that you need to know about – I'll just say that if tonsils could conceive, she'd be expecting quads. Lang's very embarrassed and the rest of us are wildly jealous.'

Tom heard Trooper Scott suggest that number three gun team would be happy to oblige their lance bombardier, if asked nicely. This was followed by the sound of a hoofpick bouncing off a skull and a cry of pain. 'Thank you for that helpful suggestion, Monobrow – it wasn't quite what I meant. I'd better go, Tom One – I've got a grudge to work off. Phone me when you get more news, or I'll see you when you get back on Tuesday.'

The Toms stayed in the tree for a while after the telephone conversation. They swapped places and Tom One experimented with the strange view of his house turned topsy-turvy. It looked in a slightly better state of repair when it was the wrong way up.

'The lance bomber's right, you know.' Tom Two prodded a defunct bird's nest thoughtfully. 'We need something to keep us occupied. It's at times like this that we need a harness room of our own – I reckon all life's problems can be sorted out in a harness room. If Hitler and Chamberlain had gone to clean a couple of saddles together, the Second World War would probably never have happened, and we'd still have our Empire.'

Tom One returned his head to the horizontal. 'There's something in what you say, Two. We haven't cleaned our boots yet – we could light the stove in the garage and sort them out there. If we liberate some beer from the pantry, we should be able to put the world to rights quite nicely.'

'Let's do it, One. Do we dismount from the magic telephone tree by backward somersault?'

A few minutes later Margery, watching from her bedroom window, saw the Toms heading towards the garage, a pair of riding boots dangling from each hand. She was pleased that the troopers were considerate enough not to fill the kitchen with the smell of polish. It never occurred to her that each boot contained a bottle of beer.

* * * * *

Ashley spent another half hour in the churchyard, ending up at the grave of Ellen Cleghorn. The small collection of flowers which had accompanied her on her final journey had been removed some days before and the mound of earth looked stark and comfortless. The detective shuddered, only partly from the cold, then looked at his watch. Half past three: the time when Stephen Trevis had suggested that tea might be served in the Rectory. Ashley folded away his notebook and left Ellen Cleghorn to nurse whatever secrets she might have taken with her.

Mrs Trevis came from a Chagford family: she had been pleased to return to the town when her husband was offered the living and she proved to be a great source of information about the decline and fall of the Freston family. The three sat around the kitchen table and Ashley jotted down yet more notes as she reminisced, delving into her extensive knowledge of Chagford history.

'I know the problems started when one of the Frestons was killed in the First World War. At least, he wasn't killed, but he was very badly wounded. He came back, and even got married, but died a few years later as a result of his wounds.'

Ashley consulted his notes: 'That would be William Freston, who died in 1925. I thought it was odd that his was another military grave, when he died so long after the fighting finished. Am I right in thinking that he was Katherine Stone's father?'

'That's right. Katherine was born the year before and there was another child, who was born a month or two after he died. I remember my mother saying what a sad sight it was, seeing the widow, at the funeral, pregnant with a child who would never know its father.' She paused to top up the teapot.

'The other child was called Emily, and she and Katherine turned out very different – this is still all according to my mother, of course. Katherine had all the looks and that hard edge to her that sometimes comes with glamour. She served

157

in the ATS during the Second World War and once she'd seen London, she wasn't going to come back to Chagford. She sold her share of the farm to Emily's husband – we'll come back to that in a minute – and then she also got married.'

Ashley remembered Peter Masters telling him about Katherine's American husband: 'The New York lawyer attached to the US Air Force?'

'That's right. He died three or four years ago and Katherine returned here, which was when I first met her. She came to church a couple of times, until she took against Stephen, and I chatted to her after a service. What she said then, was that she wanted to be near her surviving relatives, and I suppose that's an understandable instinct, when you're old and alone.'

Ashley felt up-to-date on Katherine Stone, nee Freston. 'And Emily?'

'Emily was the nice homely girl – in looks and in attitude. She married into the Brookes family, hence Katherine's relationship to Robert. She died in the nineteen eighties, not long before her son shot himself. You know about that, don't you?'

'I do: your husband told me about it the other day.' Stephen Trevis nodded acknowledgement of Ashley's statement. The detective continued: 'So up to Boxing Day, Katherine Stone and Robert Brookes were the only surviving descendants of the William Freston who died in 1925?'

'That's right. It's strange how families can shrink as well as grow, isn't it?'

'Indeed. What about Evelyn Warren? Where does she fit in?'

'Rather more distantly – you have to go back a generation and then move across. It's not helped by the fact that Evelyn often refers to 'Aunt Katherine,' when she was really some sort of cousin. Hers is rather a sad story, as well.'

Somehow, Ashley had expected this: the Frestons seemed to be a doomed race.

'There was a gap in the generations, when I was searching

around the graves, so I couldn't sketch out a very good family tree of Warrens. I thought at first that a Warren must have been cremated, but then I found a John Warren on the Second World War memorial. Would that be Evelyn's grandfather?'

'Yes, I think so: he was killed during the Italian campaign and he's buried out there, of course. Evelyn's father was only a boy at the time. When he inherited his share of the farm – but that came a few years later – he did his best to keep it going, but he had very bad health. Poor Freddie Warren was almost a medical encyclopaedia in his own right: he was born with a weak heart and a weak spine and then, just when he'd recovered from prostate cancer, he developed diabetes, and there were other complications as well. Evelyn nursed him like a saint. He'd sold the land to pay medical bills, so they both had to live in her little cottage, until he was carried off with pneumonia about four winters ago.

'We all hoped that Evelyn would be able to enjoy some freedom once he'd gone, but the next thing was that Katherine Stone came back from America and started treating her like an unpaid servant, so her life was no better than before….'

Stephen interrupted: 'Worse, because at least her father was a genial old boy, when he wasn't in pain.'

His wife nodded. 'I just hope that Katherine has left her a packet in the will – she deserves it.'

Ashley noted that the contents of Katherine Stone's will had remained secret in at least one part of Chagford. He felt it best to move the conversation on.

'Tell me, if you can, how the original farm was carved up between the various strands of the family.'

* * * * *

CHAPTER SIXTEEN

- OKEHAMPTON POLICE STATION -

By a quarter past five, the old classroom was beginning to look occupied. Various notebooks, photographs, and sheets of paper were dispersed over a large table in the middle of the room; a set of hunting clothes hung from a wire coat hanger, and two whips protruded from the pair of mahogany-topped boots on the floor below. The blackboard was now covered in writing: on the side nearest the windows, Sergeant Craggs' authoritative upper-case script gave the likely timings of Katherine Stone's last hours; at the other end, Ashley was getting himself covered in chalk as he drew up the Freston family tree. Harry had been dispatched to buy beer and sandwiches: these now occupied a third table, towards which the constable was shooting hungry glances, not liking to be the first to start eating.

Inspector Simkin sat on the central desk, among the scattered documents, watching Ashley write. He had removed his jacket, revealing a brilliant purple silk backing to his waistcoat. This was a distinct improvement on Craggs, who had only revealed yet more surplus flesh, the outline of a vest, and a pair of sweaty armpits when his own jacket had been discarded. The others were giving the armpits a wide berth; a fact of which the sergeant seemed unaware.

Ashley finished writing 'Evelyn Warren (1956 –) and stood back to admire his work. The three policemen gathered around and began to trace through the generations of Frestons, Warrens and Brookeses:

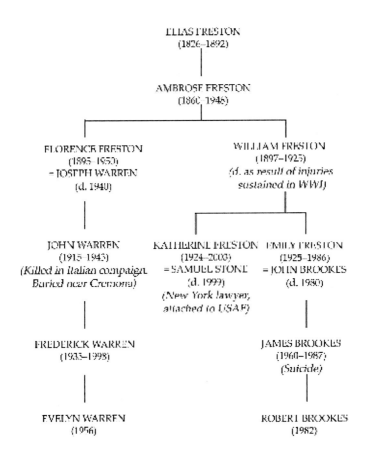

ELIAS FRESTON
(1826–1892)

AMBROSE FRESTON
(1860–1946)

FLORENCE FRESTON
(1895–1950)
= JOSEPH WARREN
(d. 1940)

WILLIAM FRESTON
(1897–1923)
(d. as result of injuries
sustained in WWI)

JOHN WARREN
(1915–1943)
(Killed in Italian campaign.
Buried near Cremona)

KATHERINE FRESTON
(1924–2003)
= SAMUEL STONE
(d. 1999)
(New York lawyer,
attached to USAF)

EMILY FRESTON
(1925–1986)
= JOHN BROOKES
(d. 1980)

FREDERICK WARREN
(1933–1998)

JAMES BROOKES
(1960–1987)
(Suicide)

EVELYN WARREN
(1956)

ROBERT BROOKES
(1982)

'So we pass,' the inspector summarised the contents of the chart, 'From Ambrose Freston, dying as a dinosaur in 1948, still farming extensive land, to Evelyn Warren and Robert Brookes, just over fifty years later, with no land and no money.'

'Though not without hope of some coming in.' Craggs tapped Katherine's name with a ruler. 'It's fairly obvious to see that if she dies intestate, Robert Brookes will cop the whole pile – Evelyn Warren will be nowhere. First cousins, twice removed, aren't very high in the pecking order.'

Simkin pursed his lips and nodded. 'Let's come back to the will later – we've more up-to-date stuff to share around, before going back on old territory. Anything else, Mr Ashley?'

'A small thing, but it caught my interest. When Ambrose Freston died – and, as you say, he must have been an old fossil by that time – he divided the land equally between Frederick Warren, who was still only a boy, and the two sisters, Katherine and Emily. This was a source of much bad feeling on the part of the old girl, Florence Warren, who felt that, as her father had had two children….'

'Herself and William?'

'That's right – that the land should be halved, with the Warrens taking one half and the daughters of William Freston dividing the other half between them. The land, you'll remember, was pretty Spartan, so although there was quite a bit of it, it was difficult to run it at a profit once it was divided. The difference between a third and a half might have represented the divide between poverty and survival. The resentment was especially great, because Katherine had already married her up-and-coming American lawyer and had no need of her over-large, as they saw it, share of the inheritance.'

The inspector studied the diagram for a few moments. 'I'll bet you anything that Ambrose the Ancient made a new will between the death of John Warren out in Italy, and the marriage of Katherine.'

Ashley declined the wager. 'I'm sure you're right: we could even check up with Peter Masters, if we felt it was important enough. Ambrose would probably have divided the farm equally between the Warrens and Emily Brookes if the will had been made after Katherine's marriage. And then, who knows? Both halves might have been farmed successfully down to the present day.'

'So are you suggesting a family vendetta?' Craggs managed to make it sound as though Chagford was a vicious outpost of Corsica. Ashley shook his head.

'Even if there was one half a century ago, I'm not sure that I can see Robert or Evelyn keeping the flame of old animosity alive. Katherine would have done, of course, if she'd felt herself wronged by the division, but she did rather better out of it than she might have expected. No, my guess is that any active trouble died with Florence Warren. Still, it's an interesting circumstance.'

It felt like a good time to attack Harry Sefton's supplies. As Craggs observed, serious detection required a bottle of beer in one hand and a ham sandwich in the other. Appropriately equipped, they turned to the notes of the two policemen.

Simkin waved a dismissive hand at two small collections of paper.

'We didn't get much from the scene of the crime or the house that you don't know about already. There was nothing to be found on the lane itself and any evidence that might have been gained from the grass verge was pretty much obliterated by one of your chaps walking his horse.'

'So I heard him say. I think my nephew would have known enough about criminal investigations not to do that, but his friend is new to this sort of thing. I think he was rather embarrassed when he realised that he could have destroyed important traces.'

The inspector seemed unconcerned. 'To be honest, I don't

think it matters: this isn't going to be a case that turns on a footprint or even a bloodstain. Also, my hunch is that we wouldn't have found anything important there anyway. Just a few signs of her slipping into the ditch, probably.'

'And we've got plenty of those in the ditch itself.' Craggs indicated a selection of freshly-developed photographs, spread out at the far end of the table. Ashley wandered over and inspected them. Half had been taken by daylight and showed little of interest beyond a broken twig here and there or a slide in the mud. The remainder of the collection had been taken by artificial light, and showed Katherine still lying face down, her neck twisted and the wounds in her skull. Ashley saw how easily the Toms could have mistaken the clotted blood for mud, enabling them to cling to the idea that the death had been no more than an accident. He returned to where the policemen were examining the day's notes. 'And the house?'

'Plenty of documents concerning extremely healthy bank balances and investments. She obviously had the knack of moving money about at the right time.'

'Shrewd old cow.'

'Thank you for that, Sergeant. Nonetheless, point taken. I think, Mr Ashley, that your friend the solicitor is going to find that he's underestimated her fortune.'

'Very nice – for someone.' Once again, Craggs hit the nail on the head. Ashley could see why Harry Sefton was intimidated by the sergeant; for himself, he rather admired the blunt hatchet of his detecting technique. He decided that it was time to show the policemen that he, too, had information about the contents of Meldon Dene. 'Did you find the furs?'

Simkin gave an appreciative smile. 'We did – and we were very amused, particularly by the fox stole. I think that's one piece of information that we don't need to keep to ourselves.'

'Too late I fear. The pleasure of disseminating the gossip has been taken from us. I got it from the rector's wife via Betty

Trenchard.'

'And if that fat old bag knows something, the whole village does.'

'Spot on, Sergeant Craggs.'

Simkin turned to the real evidence of the day.

'First thing. One of our chaps drove Evelyn Warren into Exeter to carry out a formal identification of the body. All very straightforward. She was quite plucky about it, so they got her to answer a few questions while she was there.' Simkin picked up a small notebook and passed it to Ashley. It contained Evelyn's description of the argument in the town Square and then her account of the period between the hunt departing and her parting from Katherine Stone on the outskirts of Chagford. This information was new to Ashley; he studied it carefully, while Simkin provided a commentary.

'As you can see, we've summarised Evelyn Warren's timings on the blackboard. According to her statements, she went back to her cottage with Betty Trenchard and Katherine Stone immediately after the hunt departed. That was about eleven thirty, or a little afterwards. Katherine's blood pressure was up again, because she'd realised that they were all going to ride along the bridle path on her land. She was supposed to be staying for luncheon at Evelyn's, but insisted on getting back to Meldon Dene as soon as possible in the hope of finding some damage to the path, so that she could take action against the hunt. Once they'd waited for her pressure to go back down, Betty Trenchard went home....'

'About midday.' Craggs contributed the timing.

'That's right: and Evelyn and the old girl just had a bowl of soup, which had been prepared in advance. Then they set off again: Evelyn couldn't be sure, but she thought that they left at about a quarter past twelve.'

Ashley confirmed all this in the notebook. Evelyn stated that she had deliberately taken a back route to the edge of the town, in order to avoid meeting anyone who might have remonstrated with Katherine. They had avoided the Square by walking down an alley and through the churchyard to get to the road which led towards Meldon Dene. She had parted from her aunt at about half past twelve and returned home by the same route. She had seen nobody either on the way out or on her return and, as far as she knew, nobody had seen her. Here the notebook dried up.

'If we stick to Evelyn for a moment,' Simkin reached for another notebook, 'Craggsy and I called on her at the end of the afternoon.'

'Proper perky, she seemed,' Craggs grinned. 'She obviously enjoyed her ride home in the police car – she must have been driven back by one of our more rugged and handsome colleagues.'

'Well, that certainly narrows down the possibilities.' Simkin got back to the point. 'We just asked her a few questions about Katherine Stone's will – without giving anything away, of course. She knew that a will existed, from passing references, but she didn't know when it had been drafted or what it contained. Obviously, she'd sometimes wondered about what would happen to all the money, but she assumed that the bulk of it would go to an animal charity, and just hoped that she'd be left some small token. She didn't think it likely that Robert would get anything, or any of the American in-laws either. We left it at that, and drove back here.'

He returned the notebook to its place. Ashley observed that Evelyn's guesswork had been fairly accurate, 'But then, it doesn't seem to have required any great deductive powers, especially if Stone dropped the odd remark here and there. What about Robert? You've carefully saved the big business of the day until last – how long will it be before you've got him here in person and not just his outer representation?'

Ashley nodded in the direction of the hunting clothes and

equipment and the others followed his gaze. For a moment, it seemed to Ashley that Robert himself occupied the heavy scarlet jacket and waistcoat, and that his legs filled in the gap between the clothes and the boots beneath them. The sagging metal coat hanger, unsuited to bearing such heavy clothes, gave a passable impression of a noose.

Simkin seemed to share his imaginative powers. There was a grim satisfaction in his voice when he answered Ashley's question.

'About twenty-four hours, I reckon. Not more.'

* * * * *

Betty Trenchard shot steaming water into a large teapot and ambled back to Evelyn Warren's kitchen table, where she placed the pot on a raffia mat and covered it with a woollen cosy.

'We'll just give it five minutes and then you can tell me all about your day while we drink our tea. And look what I've brought with me….'

She bent over a wicker shopping basket and produced a carefully boxed Victoria sponge cake, which she transferred to a plate. 'I know it's well after tea-time, but I thought you might need something to tempt you to eat – you must keep your strength up, or where should we be?'

'Betty, how very kind of you – I'd love a piece. Will you join me?'

'No, Miss Warren, I mustn't. I made it specially for you, and went out to buy proper flour, so's you'd enjoy it. I daren't eat any of it myself. The jam probably wouldn't do me any good either – it was from a jar I had in the pantry from before they diagnosed me.'

Evelyn cut a small slice of the cake. 'Well I think that's so thoughtful of you, Betty – and it tastes delicious. There's no danger of my losing my appetite while this is in the kitchen.'

Betty poured tea and they compared their days. It was characteristic of Betty that, having announced that she had come to hear about Evelyn's experiences at the mortuary, she should begin with an account of her own time in Chagford. Evelyn produced little gasps at every stage of Betty's story: she listened intently as the overweight woman's chins and jowls wobbled their way through the arrival of the solicitor and the detectives, the evidence concerning the will and the signing of the statement. At the end of a long and circumstantial coda, concerning wills past, Betty paused to sip tea. 'And that's about it, Miss Warren – quite the most exciting day I've had for a long time. Well, apart from the day before, I suppose, and the day I collapsed in the hardware store....'

Typically, a potentially interesting tale dwindled into anticlimax. Evelyn interrupted what could have been a tedious ramble through Betty's memories of the mildly stimulating interludes in her otherwise placid and uneventful life.

'So, Betty, they actually made you sign a statement?'

'Just as I said, Miss Warren. Mr Masters – he's a stuffy old stick, I say, but he seems to know his job all right – well, he drew it all up, legal-like, to say that I'd never knowingly witnessed Mrs Stone's will and that none of the conditions of will-signing had been observed. Then I signed it and so did he and Mr Ashley and that nice young policeman. Handsome boy, I thought – of course, the policemen all look young these days....'

Evelyn allowed Betty to continue her gentle monologue, while she examined the implications of the written statement. There was something solid and incontrovertible about a document signed and witnessed by a solicitor, a detective and a policeman. She felt rather frightened by it.

Having covered the subjects of men in uniform, the excellence of National Service, and the spinelessness of modern youth, Betty's soliloquy finally ran out of steam and ambled into the buffers. 'Now, tell me about your day, Miss Warren – I'm that curious to hear how you got on.'

As Sergeant Craggs had observed, Evelyn had enjoyed her day. Of course, identifying the body had been unpleasant, but the mortuary had been beautifully clean and hygienic, with gleaming stainless steel surfaces and a polished floor: she had enjoyed seeing this strange place as much as if she had been visiting a National Trust property or an interesting museum.

The police, too, had been wonderfully kind. She had been driven into Exeter by the reassuring constable who had helped break the news of Katherine's death to her. They had travelled along the picturesque back road, past Castle Drogo and through Drewsteignton and then shot along the A30 at an incredible speed, which she had found exhilarating. Constable Harris explained that he could have driven much faster with his blue light flashing, but that there would be all hell to pay if his superiors found out. He had sat in on the questions as well, after the identification, bringing her tea, and then taking her to luncheon in the police canteen. That had been the best part, sitting at a Formica table, watching the Exeter police coming and going: plain-clothed men and women conducting important conversations in low voices; uniformed officers chatting more freely; and an exciting table of leather-clad motorcyclists, with their helmets on the floor at their feet, laughing loudly at the anecdotes from the morning's haul of erratic drivers. The motorcycle policemen had left the canteen just as Evelyn was finishing her meal, and they had paused at her table to exchange greetings with Constable Harris: she had been close enough to them to inhale the leathery smell of their uniforms and to sense the muscular strength of the legs within the close-fitting trousers.

On the journey back to Chagford, Evelyn had felt brave enough to raise the subject of her driver's colleagues: 'I thought your friends looked awfully smart.'

Constable Harris had laughed. 'Yes, the motorcycle cops get to wear some good kit, don't they? They're an entertaining bunch as well – we're all going out for a drink tonight, when we come off duty. I once thought of going into that side of policing myself, but they don't have as much job variety as I do.'

Evelyn had briefly pictured herself riding pillion behind Constable Harris, her arms folded tightly around his waist and her diminutive body tessellating with his black leather legs and torso as they hurtled down the A30, the powerful motorbike vibrating beneath them, overtaking cars and lorries, weaving through the traffic with breathtaking urgency. Variety, she had concluded, unwinding her window to counteract the hot rush of blood to her cheeks, was a very overrated commodity.

All this Evelyn recalled as Betty Trenchard poured more tea and waited for her reply. She calculated that Constable Harris and his friends would be drinking together now, pints of beer, probably, or lager. Perhaps there was a bar in the police station, and they still wore their uniforms, with their tunics casually unzipped, as they had been at luncheon, and their inverted helmets wobbling on the table, with heavy leather gloves tucked inside. It was a pleasing thought.

'Oh, there's not that much to tell, really, Betty.'

* * * * *

CHAPTER SEVENTEEN

- CHAGFORD LANES -

Harry had been looking forward to the drive back to Chagford. Lacking the courage to interrupt the deductive processes of Inspector Simkin or Sergeant Craggs, he had stored up a number of questions to put to the less intimidating Ashley.

Ashley, however, is taciturn and morose. From the window of the passenger door, he stares out into the darkness, making no attempt at communication beyond the steady tapping of his fingers on a cardboard folder which rests on his knees. The young constable, falling back on his own resources, reviews some of the events of the day, hoping to be able to find his own answers.

Robert had been surly and uncooperative when they had arrived at the kennels. He was vague and monosyllabic in his answers to perfectly reasonable questions, professing to have no memory of the timings of the various stages of the hunt and no interest in the fate of Katherine Stone.

'What's that to do with me?'

'Mr Brookes, a woman has been murdered.'

'I repeat, what's that to do with me?'

'Given that you were her closest relative, Mr Brookes, I

should have thought it had quite a lot to do with you.'

'I don't think of her as a relative.'

'Whether you think of her as such or not makes no difference, Mr Brookes; she was still your relation and her death must necessarily be your concern.'

'Are you saying I killed her? Because I didn't.'

The inspector had remained admirably calm and Sergeant Craggs had limited himself to taking notes, probably realising that any sarcastic comment he might be tempted to pass would only inflame the situation further. Robert denied any knowledge of Katherine Stone's will; either of the existence of such a document or of its contents. He had never thought about the disposition of Katherine Stone's estate after her death, and had no reason to suppose that he would be concerned in any way: he neither expected nor wanted any of her money.

To Harry, at any rate, that last statement had rung true. All through the interview, he had willed Robert to calm down, to use his common sense and not dig himself into trouble; but he had been impressed with the vehemence of Robert's denial of an interest in his great-aunt's money. If he was lying, he was a good enough actor to fool at least one of the three policemen in the room.

Grudgingly, Robert had allowed them to take the hunting clothes he had worn the previous day. The boots, breeches and jacket were obviously his best set; the clothes were still spattered with mud, so it was easy to believe him when he identified them as the relevant articles. The boots had been sponged down, ready for polishing: out of the corner of his eye, Harry had seen Craggs and Simkin exchange glances when they noticed the cleanliness of the footwear relative to the breeches and coat. Robert had been uncertain which hunting shirt he had worn, so Harry had been given the unpleasant task of rummaging through the laundry basket. He had removed the two shirts nearest the top and one about a third of the way down, which was inexplicably damp. Finally, they had taken Robert's two smartest whips, leaving behind an older specimen, which had clearly not been used for some time.

'He's on the run.' Craggs had spoken for the first time as the car drove away from the kennels. 'The huntsman hunted.'

'You know, Craggsy, that sounds almost like a classical epigram. But is our Actaeon running out of fear, out of guilt, or simply because he realises he is the obvious suspect?'

Craggs had made an expansive gesture, knocking the steering wheel and causing Harry to swerve the car. 'Means, motive, opportunity – what more do we want? I reckon we could pull him in now and get it to stick with a jury. Manslaughter at any rate – we might need a bit more for murder.'

So Harry wonders, like the Toms before him, whether the killing was the result of momentary anger. He has seen enough of Robert already to appreciate the force of his temper: could he, provoked for a second time that day, have brought the handle of his whip crashing down onto the eggshell skull of the evil old woman? Unlike the two troopers, he has seen the doctor's report, which has been faxed through to the station. There are three wounds to the skull: like Venn diagrams, they interlock, with two outer strikes causing damage, and a central blow which has actually penetrated the already fractured bone. The doctor had suggested that the wounds were caused by a blunt, cylindrical object, administered with significant (but not necessarily immense) force; he had himself suggested the possibility that the round-ended handle of a hunting whip might have been employed. The third wound would have been sufficient to kill, even if the neck had not already been broken: the doctor had declined to speculate on which of the injuries had been the immediate cause.

Harry runs through the remaining details of the doctor's report and wonders if they have any significance. The old lady's stomach was empty apart from liquid matter and a small amount of bread. That bore out Evelyn Warren's statement, that Katherine had taken only soup for her lunch. No water was found in the lungs: a circumstance which means nothing to Harry. In contrast, the estimated time of death is easy to understand: at the scene of the crime, the doctor had announced that the body had been dead at least three hours and not more than five. That means, some time between noon and two o'clock. Given Evelyn Warren's evidence, that can be narrowed down to some time between half past twelve and two o'clock: which fits in nicely with the various accounts of Robert Brookes' absence from the hunt.

It all seems plain to the policeman: Harry knows enough about criminal activity to be aware that the obvious solution is often correct. Craggs is convinced that it is just a case of deciding whether to proceed with a manslaughter charge or to press on for murder – so why is Mr Ashley so irritable? In the police station, he had not raised any objections to the information provided, nor questioned the conclusions that Simkin and Craggs had reached; rather he had withdrawn into himself, before deciding, rather abruptly, that it was time to get back to Chagford. Now he is sitting, gloomy and brooding, almost like Robert Brookes in one of the sulky silences of his interview.

The car approaches the turn-off to Chagford; Harry slows down and signals right. The change in speed serves to jolt Ashley from his trance. He adjusts his seating position and stops drumming his fingers.

'I'm sorry, Harry, I haven't been much of a travelling companion this evening.'

'That's all right, sir – I could see that you were deep in thought.'

'Deep in mud, more like – though I suppose that's a slight improvement on Robert's position at the moment.'

'You're right there, sir. What do you think they'll go for? Murder or manslaughter?'

'I'm not sure. If we suppose for a minute that Robert did kill Katherine Stone and he admits manslaughter and starts to co-operate with your colleagues, my guess is that they'll leave it there. On the other hand if, having killed her, he refuses to co-operate, it would be quite understandable if they were bloody-minded enough to go the whole way: I'm sure that Sergeant Craggs would argue for that. They're the two straightforward courses.'

Harry thinks for a while as he negotiates the narrow, winding road to Chagford.

'And the course that's not straightforward, sir? You mean, if he *hasn't* killed her, don't you?'

'You're learning, Harry. Suppose, for a moment, that Robert is innocent. In the first place, we're in danger of committing a huge injustice; second, someone else is getting away with murder. I know that all the circumstantial evidence is stacked against him – just one solid piece and they'll arrest him, I'm sure. But I can't help thinking that something's not quite right.'

'What's that, sir?'

'If I knew that, Harry, I could act on it – but I don't. Maybe in here.' Ashley taps the cardboard folder. 'I've got a copy of the medical report; I'll study it tonight and see what I can make of it.'

The car draws into Chagford.

'Well, best of luck, sir. I know he was an awkward sod today, but everyone I've spoken to says he's a good sort, really. It'd be good to see him in the clear. Shall I drop you at Waye Lodge, sir?'

'Thanks, Harry – no, hang on a second. Are you in a hurry?'

'Not really sir – I go off duty after this. Why do you ask?'

'Have you got time to visit the scene of the crime?'

'If you think it will help, sir, I'll happily spare the time.'

They are in the Square. Instead of turning right, in the direction of Gidleigh, the stable and kennels, and Waye Lodge, Harry turns left, and drives past the church and out towards Meldon Dene.

* * * * *

The garage was home to a battered old Daimler, innumerable spiders and a family of field mice who hibernated in a cosy pile of discarded rugs and armchair covers in the far corner. Every so often, a small, bleary-eyed rodent peeped out to see what the Toms were up to, checking whether it was safe to go back to sleep again.

The troopers had assembled a large trestle table, which served as seat, work surface and bar. Squatting cross-legged at either end, they had polished their everyday boots and given a brilliant shine to their best pairs, all the while putting the world to rights and drinking steadily from their collection of beer bottles. Three pairs of empty bottles now stood to attention in front of four pairs of boots, the effect resembling an oversized and eccentric chess set, with two pawns missing. The last pair of bottles was in the process of disposal.

'So, One, you invite me to your home, put me in a freezing cold bedroom; you expect me to climb half-way up a tree to make a telephone call; and you bring me to a rat-infested shed, constructed entirely out of asbestos and string, and you call that hospitality?' Two paused to swig beer, swaying slightly as he tilted his neck back. In the process, he revealed a streak of boot polish across his jugular. Tom One laughed at the effect and then realised he had similar marks all over his clothes.

'That's about right – you wouldn't get treats like this with Louise Trotter. Are you having a good time?'

'Bloody marvellous – apart from the dead body, and even that would be exciting if we didn't think Robert had done it.

Bit of a bummer to make a new friend on Christmas Eve and then find out he's a murderer the day after Boxing Day. Do you think your mother will realise we've been drinking, by the way?'

Tom One shook his head so violently that the bottles and boots rocked from side to side. 'No – as long as we stay within a ten-foot radius of Aunt Lav, mother will just think she's hit the cooking sherry again. Mind you, it might be worth sneaking up the back stairs and sleeping it off for an hour before we reappear. We can hide the bottles under Uncle George's bed at the same time.'

Two finished his bottle and placed it carefully in the King's Rook's Pawn position at his end of the table, pausing to focus carefully on the pleasing artistic juxtaposition of glass and leather. 'You know, we could sell this for a fortune to a modern art gallery. Good idea, by the way – a snooze to sober up. Let's go: by half section prepare to dismount from trestle table – dismount!'

The descent from the trestle table was less smart than Two's commands, and a right turn towards the garage door was similarly wobbly. They gave up attempting to drill and crept an unsteady path through the darkness back to the house, leaving the boots and bottles for later collection. Five minutes later Tom Two lay supine on his bed, snoring loudly; Tom One occupied an armchair in the same room, curled up under Two's service jacket, like one of the hibernating field mice. He dreamed pleasantly of beer bottles marching up and down in review order, while the troopers drank champagne from their riding boots.

* * * * *

The lane is pitch dark, so Harry leaves on the car headlights as he and Ashley walk to the place where Katherine Stone had fallen. A torch from the car boot provides light into the ditch itself.

'I know we won't find anything here, Harry. Your chaps are pretty efficient when it comes to clue-hunting at the scene – but I want to try to picture it all happening and, psychologically, that's most easily done *in situ*.'

'I can understand that, sir. Pretty creepy, isn't it?'

'Yes, though my guess is, a lot of that is due to the artificial light. Now, Harry, I want you to use your imagination. You are Robert, up on your horse, with your whip in your hand – that's right, the torch will do nicely. You've just ridden along the bridle path and now you've come out into the lane and you see Katherine – that's me.'

Harry's white teeth smile through the distorted darkness. 'Okay, sir – that's a lot of imagining, but I'll do my best.'

'Now, let's take the manslaughter scenario. We've met by chance; I see you coming out of my bridle path and I wave my placard, knowing that it will frighten your horse. In all probability it will rear up as it did in the Square. You, hot-tempered and angry, will yell some admonition and perhaps as the horse comes down, bring your whip down on my head. Do it gently, by the way – we don't want another body in the ditch.'

'All right, sir, I'll bring it down softer than a rubber truncheon.'

'That's a great relief – I think. So, here goes.'

Ashley waves his cardboard folder: 'Fox murderer!' Harry staggers off balance: 'You stupid bloody woman!' He regains his position and brings the torch flashing down towards Ashley's head. Now Ashley staggers, almost falling into the ditch. They abandon their adopted characters. The detective looks satisfied.

'Good. Now Harry, I want you to compare what just happened with the details on the medical report. How many times did you hit me?'

'Once.'

'How many times should you have hit me?'

Harry starts to see what Ashley is getting at. 'Three times.'

'And which of the three was the fatal blow?'

'The third one.'

'So, then, forget the rest of the play – just try it. Two taps and a smash.'

Harry raises the torch and brings down two moderate blows in quick succession. He lifts his arm to its full extent to bring down the third strike, but Ashley has moved and the policeman's torch continues its journey through the air until it comes down to his side.

'Well?'

'It doesn't work, sir, does it? It didn't feel right doing a small blow first. That would be the big one, surely, wouldn't it? Especially if the horse had reared up, because that would give extra impetus. And, like you did, she would have moved, whatever order the blows came in. They wouldn't be neatly together like they were on the X-ray.'

'You're doing well, Harry. Next thing: in our confrontational poses, where do the blows fall?'

Harry pauses to think, giving a small swing to his torch. 'On your forehead, sir – you're looking up at me.'

'That's right. But the blows actually fell?'

'On top of the head, sir – if anything, slightly to the back.'

'So we have to imagine Katherine Stone just staring straight ahead, or even bowing slightly to meet her fate. Does that sound likely?'

'No, sir.'

'Conclusion?'

Harry shrugs his shoulders. 'That Robert Brookes is innocent, sir?'

For the first time in hours, Ashley smiles. 'I don't think we can go quite that far yet, Harry – but we can conclude that

179

the killing didn't take place in the obvious manner that we've all been imagining. Thanks for your help – you've given me a lot to think about. Now, you need to get back to Okehampton and get some rest. I'll walk from here – it will help me mull things over.'

'Okay sir, if you're sure. And thanks for letting me in on that – I've learned a lot.' Harry heads back towards the car, then turns round again, hesitating. 'One thing, sir?'

'Yes, Harry?'

'Do I keep this to myself, sir?'

Ashley shakes his head. 'I can't ask you to keep a secret from the inspector and Sergeant Craggs – that wouldn't be right. By all means mention it – preferably at a time when they've just come to the opposite conclusion.'

Harry grins. 'I'll do that, sir – and let you know what their reactions are.'

He climbs into the car and starts the engine. Ashley steps off the road to allow the car past and waves to the retreating vehicle.

Just under an hour later, he arrives at Waye Lodge. The Toms, sober again and smelling unnaturally of peppermint, are building up the fire in the sitting room.

'Hello, lads – any plans for the evening?'

'Not particularly, Uncle George. Any suggestions?'

'Yes – why don't you go and see Robert? I'm sure he could do with some company.'

* * * * *

CHAPTER EIGHTEEN

- THE KENNELS AGAIN -

'Okay, One – first of all your uncle won't let us go to see Robert and we assume that's because he thinks Robert is the murderer. We do a re-enactment of the crime and come to the same conclusion. Now he comes home and sends off to the kennels after all. What are we supposed to think? Are we off to take tea with Jack the Ripper, or is Robert in the clear?'

The Toms walked through the darkness along the Gidleigh Road. Wrapped up against the weather in tweed caps, waxed cotton jackets and green woollen army gloves and scarves, they were shadowy figures, having decided to develop their night vision rather than rely on torches. Tom One's shrug was invisible.

'I'm not sure what to think, Two – though I know he wouldn't let us go if he still thought Robert was guilty. When Uncle George is being cagey, it can mean a number of things. Sometimes, he just wants to keep us all guessing, so that we can see how clever he is when he chooses to reveal his information. Other times, he keeps quiet when he can't prove anything and doesn't want to look stupid if he's wrong.'

'Fair enough, I suppose. You don't think he might be sending us on a mission, do you?'

'How do you mean?'

'Well, I don't really know – I just thought he might want us to find something out, but that if he *told* us to go clue hunting, we'd be really clumsy about it and mess it up; whereas if he says nothing, we might notice whatever it is of our own accord. Then, when we got back, he'd question us so subtly that we weren't even aware of it – and we'd have provided valuable evidence. Do you see?'

'No. Sorry, Two – I lost you about five clauses ago.'

'Oh well, never mind. I've been reading too many spy stories, I expect. Here we are. Presumably we feign ignorance of everything, just like you always did with the map-reading instructor at Pirbright?'

'That wasn't feigning, Two – that was for real. Just knock on the door and let's get out of the cold.'

Robert, to their surprise, was washing up. Clean plates were stacked on the draining board and mugs and cutlery were arranged haphazardly around them. A pile of saucepans soaked in the sink and a gas ring was burning under a frying pan filled with soapy water.

'Are you feeling all right Robert? We rather assumed that you didn't do housework until the clocks went back.'

Robert acknowledged Tom Two's opening sally with a frown rather than a smile. 'Well, to be honest with you, chaps, I'm sort of exorcising the place. I had the police crawling round here this afternoon, poking their noses into everything and making me feel like shit.' He flung his tea-towel aside and flopped into a chair. 'I think I made a bit of an idiot of myself, actually. Getting on with this helped take my mind off it a bit.'

Tom One clucked sympathetically. 'The same with us – we spent most of the afternoon polishing boots and drinking beer. Come on, we'll lend a hand.'

Once they got down to it, cleaning the cottage was quite fun. Even with three people, there was too much work for a single evening, so Tom One and Robert concentrated on the kitchen and Tom Two tidied, dusted and polished in the sitting room. After an hour, there was a mutual decision that their domestic catharsis had gone quite far enough and they lounged around in front of the fire, Robert drinking scrumpy and the Toms sticking to beer. The Toms, having polished four pairs of boots already, decided that one more was neither here nor there and that they could be getting on with Robert's while they chatted.

'I really appreciate that, chaps – but you can't. The police took them. All my hunting clothes as well – at least, the ones I wore on Boxing Day.'

Tom Two whistled between his teeth. 'That sounds bad. Did they say why?'

'No – but it's obvious, isn't it? They want to find bits of old Mother Stone on my kit. Blood, or some of that DNA stuff that they're always talking about on the television. They think I did it and they want evidence.' He paused to take a mouthful of scrumpy. 'Mind you, they can spend as long as they like going over it all and they won't find anything – because I *didn't* kill her, in case you were wondering.' For a moment, Robert glared at the Toms; then he remembered they were his friends.

'Sorry – it's been a difficult day.'

'No problem, Robert.' Two, sitting sideways in the armchair again, bounced his heels together placidly. 'But isn't it a good thing that they've taken your things? Once they've found nothing on them, they'll realise they were wrong to suspect you.'

Robert took some temporary comfort from this, before scowling again. 'I bet they'll just come back poking around again, looking for other things. God knows what.'

Two continued to be unconcerned. 'Well, let them. If they keep drawing a blank, they'll eventually look elsewhere for the killer.'

'Yeah – I suppose you're right.' Robert threw another log onto the fire and began to prod it into position with the poker. 'It just feels as though they've got it in for me at the moment – and I reckon most of Chagford thinks I did it too, after what happened in the Square. I don't reckon I'll be in the clear until they find out who really did it, and at the moment they're looking in the wrong place.'

The Toms exchanged glances as Robert concentrated on the fire; this was the feeding line for some impromptu detective work. Tom One indicated to Two that he should make the first move.

'So where do you think they should be looking, Robert? Who had a reason for killing her?'

Robert finished adjusting the logs and squatted by the side of the fire, his legs hunched up and his arms folded. 'Well, nobody liked her, remember? Once the shock has died down, I shouldn't think anyone will be sorry she's dead.'

'Yes, but that's not enough really, is it? One and I wouldn't have shed many tears if a well-placed landmine had taken out most of our instructors on basic training – but we didn't go out and kill them. Do you know of any specific reason why somebody might have wanted her out of the way? You must know more of Chagford politics than we do.'

Robert nodded. 'Not that I'm saying any of these people did it, mind – I wouldn't wish on them what I've been through today. According to Colonel Hargreaves, the Rector couldn't stand her. She was always writing to the bishop, complaining about this, that or the other. And Primrose Armishaw was livid with her because she got her planning permission for a barn conversion blocked. Primrose wanted to turn it into four holiday cottages, which would have meant that she could afford a full-time hand at the livery yard. That would have made a big difference to her; she's not getting any younger – or smaller, for that matter.' He relaxed his position, stretching his legs out in front of him and leaning back on his arms. It was good to examine the murder from a different point of view. 'That's everyone I can think of.'

Two continued in his detective role. 'What about financial gain, Robert? Do you know who gets all the money?'

'No.' Robert shook his head. 'I'm sure I don't come in for any. I imagine she'd leave some to Evelyn, because she's done a lot for her – but I can't see little Evelyn as our mad murderess. The police were banging on about the will as well today. Best part of two million pounds, they reckoned she was worth, but they didn't let on who's going to inherit it.'

This was a dead end; the conversation flagged, and they drank in silence for a while. Eventually, Tom One asked Robert when the hunt was meeting next. 'If it's before we go back on duty, we'll come and see you set off.'

'It should have been the day after tomorrow, but the Master's cancelled it. He reckons the murder will hit the Sunday news-papers and that if we meet on Monday, we'll have every reporter for miles around on us. Maybe we'll get some in by the end of the week – New Year's Day is always the next big one after Boxing Day.'

'We'll be gone by then – that's a shame.'

Robert had a bright idea. 'I tell you what, though – with no hunt on Monday, Primrose is going to want a lot of horses exercised. Do you fancy coming out for another hack tomorrow? It'd be good to have some company and I'm sure I can get Primrose to trade off the charge against some grooming or tack cleaning, if you didn't mind. What do you think?'

The Toms thought it sounded an excellent idea. 'I think mother is expecting us on Church Parade in the morning, but after that would be great.'

'Yeah – the Colonel wants me to go tomorrow as well. He says it's the right thing to do, and that if I sit with him and Mrs Colonel, folk will realise they're backing me. If we rode out

185

after that, there's a pub out at Throwleigh where we can tie up our horses and get a bite of lunch. How would that be?'

'About a million times better than Aunt Lav's turkey risotto. Let's do it.'

* * * * *

Tap-tap. Smash.

Two inadequate blows and a final, crashing strike, cutting into the other wounds, like the upper row of a set of Olympic rings.

The rhythm runs through Ashley's head as he lies awake, trying to organise the evidence into a credible picture. Musically, two quavers and a crotchet; the short-short-long of Morse Code (which letter?); the triple metre of a cantering horse.

Robert on his horse, cantering towards the old lady, whip outstretched like a cavalry sabre? No – no chance for a second strike at the skull.

Robert halting his horse and striking? Again no – for all the reasons analysed with Harry.

Robert dismounted, horse tied up somewhere along the bridle path? Lying in wait and striking from behind? But waiting where? There are trees lining the bridle path, but none in the lane: nowhere to hide. And still the three wounds refuse to fit a theory.

Unless Katherine was already dead.

Already lying in the ditch, neck freshly broken, snapped in the fall. That would explain the position of the wounds and the apparent willingness of the victim to remain immobile during the pounding of her skull.

But why wound a dead body? A body, fallen into a ditch – an accident, maybe, a slip of the foot. Why make it obvious that a murder has taken place? Just let the body lie there – check that it is motionless and that life has passed from it, then steal away, safe.

186

Stupid to give the game away: or incredibly clever?

Ashley hears the footsteps of his nephew and Tom Two, returned from the kennels. He wonders whether to call them in and hear their news, but it is late: tomorrow will do just as well. He listens to them, moving past One's room and halting outside Two's at the far end of the passage. The turning of the door handle, followed by the closing of the door produces a soft sound of two clicks and a thud.

That rhythm again.

* * * * *

'So, what do you think, One?' Two, having flung a hot water bottle under the sheets of his bed, began the task of changing one set of warm clothing for another, while One, his jacket discarded, but still in cap and gloves, sat in the armchair once more, hugging his own warm rubber bottle.

'About Robert?'

'About anything, really. Yes, start with Robert.' Two flung off his daytime shirt and hurriedly pulled on an old rugby shirt before the cold hit his bare chest.

'Well, if Uncle George thinks he didn't do it, that's good enough for me – and I'm really glad we went to see him tonight.'

'Me too. What about Primrose and the Rector? What did you make of all that?' Two began a similar lightning change on his lower half, kicking off his old shoes and removing trousers and underpants in one movement. He pulled on a pair of track suit bottoms and leapt into bed, gathering the sheets around him, so that only his head was uncovered.

Tom One watched, amused, as his friend writhed around to create more warmth. 'I don't know if the suggestions will come to anything, but we've got a pretty useful day tomorrow. We can observe suspect number one at church in the morning, and then suspect number two at the yard in the afternoon.'

'Before presenting your uncle with a neat little dossier in the evening? Should we say anything to him, by the way?'

'I don't see why we should, unless he asks. He's been keeping things to himself all day, so I vote we do the same - after all, it's not as though we've got anything conclusive to tell him. Let's see what we pick up tomorrow.'

'Fair enough.' Two gave a wide yawn. 'What time is Church Parade tomorrow?'

'Nine-thirty – we'd better get some sleep. Two?'

'Yes?'

'Will you be all right tonight? I'll stay if you want me to.'

Tom Two took a while to think about it.

'No, it's all right, One – I'll be fine. But, well – thanks.'

'No problem. I'll say goodnight then.'

Tom One returned to his own room.

* * * * *

Chagford sleeping: Hounds, horses, farmers and townsfolk, all refreshing themselves against the morning.

Robert, at the kennels, calmer for the visit of the two troopers.

Primrose in her house adjoining the stables, and Stephen Trevis in the Rectory, unaware that they will be under observation tomorrow.

Evelyn Warren, dreaming of Constable Harris.

Betty Trenchard, dreaming of wills.

Ellen Cleghorn, no longer able to dream of anything.

* * * * *

CHAPTER NINETEEN

- NEW SUSPECTS -

There was a general churchward surge the next morning. People who would normally have spent the Sunday after Christmas lazing in bed, felt the need to congregate together and the nave was comfortably full.

During the Rector's sermon, Ashley allowed his attention and his eyes to wander. He looked around the church, picking out familiar faces: Colonel and Mrs Hargreaves, sitting in a front pew with Robert between them; Evelyn Warren, with the alto section of the choir; and Betty Trenchard, tightly squeezed amongst the flower-arranging Mafia, nodding complacently at the idea of God taking on human flesh. Then there were Farmer and Mrs Crane, marginally less hideous in their Sunday best; Mark Overland, hung-over and unshaven, and Mrs Trevis, at the organ, providing an aleatoric backing to the Christmas carols. Notable absentees were Primrose Armishaw, presumably busy at the livery yard, and Peter Masters, gritting his teeth through the modern rite Catholic liturgy in a tin hut on the outskirts of the town.

The Toms, sitting on either side of him, seemed to be giving their full attention to Stephen Trevis. Ashley was mildly surprised at this, thinking it unlikely that either of them had experienced a religious awakening in the last few days. He noted, with amusement, that the soldiers had forgotten to pack any smart shoes, so were once again wearing their best riding boots under their trousers. The metal quarters on their heels had made an alarmingly authoritative clicking on the granite flagstones as they made their way to the pew, suggesting an approach to religion that was totalitarian, rather than devotional.

The sermon included a clever paragraph about the death of Katherine Stone, which made it quite clear that, whilst the parish was shocked and grieved at the passing of a member of the community, yet God's redeeming work continued; that redeeming work which, planned from the beginning of all things, originally saw light on Earth at the first Christmas….

Ashley was aware of the Toms bracing their bodies at the mention of Katherine Stone. There was a definite pricking up of ears (in Tom Two's case, they seemed to expand by at least an inch in all directions), followed by an equal decline as the sermon came back on course. He wondered what they were up to.

Refreshments were served in the Parish Room after the service. Bach's sheep grazed randomly on the organ as the congregation filed out of the church and across the road, where Norah Dyer presided over a pair of huge urns. Ashley found himself in a corner with Mark Overland, who was drinking black coffee from a large mug. A second mug was on standby on a window ledge.

'Party last night, Mark?'

Mark nodded, and immediately regretted it. 'Bellringers' Christmas thrash. Did you notice that there were only four bells ringing before the service this morning? The others didn't quite make it.'

Ashley understood: 'I didn't actually count the number of bells, but I noticed a certain erratic quality to the ringing.'

'Yes – a right old *carillon*, as the joke goes. It's all Katherine Stone's fault.'

'Really?'

'Ernie Yeo had the bright idea of toasting the health of whoever had done her in – then we decided to complete our Christmas peal, only using whisky tumblers for bells. Every time it was your turn to ring, you had to sing, 'Bong!' and drain your glass. I forget how many changes we rang before it all got a bit out of hand.'

'I think I get the idea,' Ashley sympathised. 'What time did you get home?'

'Pass. I know we got chucked out of the Buller and moved on to the Globe, but after that, memory gets a bit hazy. Actually, George, if you'll excuse me, I think….'

Mark made a rapid exit in the direction of the lavatory, leaving Ashley standing by himself. He looked around for the Toms: what on earth were they doing chatting intently to Stephen Trevis? Did they harbour doubts about the Virgin birth? Or perhaps they were trying to lie their way onto the flower-arranging rota? Ashley was curious enough to head over towards them, but his nephew and Tom Two promptly made their excuses and headed off to get changed into riding kit.

'The Spirit seems to have moved our two young soldiers today, Rector.'

'Has it heck as like – I was getting a good old grilling from them.' Fortunately, Stephen Trevis seemed amused rather than indignant. 'Did you put them up to it?'

'Not at all. What information were they after? And were they at all subtle in their extraction of it?'

'About as subtle as my dear wife's organ playing. They began by asking if I'd enjoyed the Boxing Day meet and what my opinions were concerning the incident with Robert's horse and Katherine's placard. Then, before I could pause for thought, it was, "Where did you go after the hunt headed off? – What were your movements between twelve hundred hours and fourteen hundred hours?" And, "Is that stain on your cassock communion wine, or cranial blood which spurted out of Katherine Stone as you struck her with the Processional Cross?"'

The Rector's voice grew higher and more manic with each interrogatory remark. His voice came back down to normal as he added: 'I'm exaggerating, of course, but you get the idea. I haven't had such a thorough Gestapo-style going-over since my wife opened my credit card bill a few years ago.'

Ashley grinned at the thought of the troopers' direct approach. 'Yes, I can see them being better at the jackboot-in-the-groin technique than the "softly softly" approach.'

'That's right. I couldn't help noticing that they even had the correct footwear under their trousers: I assume they've gone off to invade Poland now. Do you fancy a sherry at the Rectory, by the way? The crowds seem to be thinning out – they'll be gone in the next few minutes, and I'd love to know how things are developing. And have you seen the newspapers? We're on the front page.'

Ten minutes later, they wandered back to the Rectory, where Ashley devoured the accounts of the murder in the Sunday newspapers. Over a second sherry, he revealed a minimal amount of information concerning the case, as he gently extracted from the Rector a detailed account of all his movements on Boxing Day. He was on his way back to Waye Lodge before Stephen Trevis realised that the detective had succeeded where his young apprentices had failed.

* * * * *

The ride across the moor was the best yet. Somehow, the miserable circumstances of Robert's life encouraged him to take a devil-may-care approach to the hack: the Toms, infected with the same spirit, and fired up with two pints of beer, followed him fearlessly. At breakneck speed, they shot across the open country for mile after mile, pausing only when it was clear that their horses needed to rest. From Throwleigh, they headed south-west, charging up Kennon Tor and Hound Tor; then, turning through ninety degrees, they galloped in the direction of Fernworthy Forest. Robert chose a track which followed the contour line, so that for much of the time they were running on level ground, even though the surrounding terrain rose and fell dramatically.

Eventually, they had to slow to descend to the North Teign. They gave their horses a long rein and sat well back in the saddle.

'God, that feels better.' Robert removed his hard hat and allowed the wind to blow through his damp hair. 'How's Old Crazy going for you, Two?'

'Living up to her name.' Two was mounted on one of Colonel Hargreaves' hunters, the grey mare being still short of a shoe. 'Very sensitive to the touch as far as the accelerator goes, less responsive to the brake.'

'That sounds about right – she's always up there with the hounds on hunting days. Do you want to try a jump or two on her?'

'Sure – let's have a go.' At any other time, Tom Two would probably have hesitated. Today, however, was not a day for playing safe.

'Good on you – at the bottom of this slope, there's a place where we can jump across the Teign, rather than fording it. Just keep your heels down and give her some rein and she'll look after you. You as well, One?'

'Go for it.'

The ground levelled out. Replacing his hat, and instructing them to follow behind him, Robert spurred on his horse, curved around in order to approach the river at right angles and sailed effortlessly across.

There was no time for the Toms to worry or to recall their

basic jumping lessons: their horses, without waiting for instructions, hurled themselves after Robert's mare and, in succession, they found themselves launched into the air. For a few magical, terrifying seconds, they flew over the running water, before touching down with a landing which must have looked considerably less elegant than Robert's. One nearly continued his flight over the top of the head of the chestnut gelding; he managed to sit back just in time, clinging on to the pommel of his saddle for dear life.

'Wow!'

'Okay?' Robert enjoyed the sight of the troopers getting back breath and adjusting their balance. 'Primrose Armishaw fell off there a couple of years ago – we thought she was going to dam the river and create another reservoir.'

'I'm glad you waited until we'd got across before you told us that, Robert.' Two wriggled his left foot back into the stirrup. 'Ignorance was bliss, wasn't it One?'

'Well, it usually is in my case. How did we look, Robert?'

'You're doing fine, both of you. Come on – we can run all the way to Fernworthy now, and then we'll jump some logs in the forest.'

'Logging', as Robert called it, turned out to be great fun. Some trees had fallen of their own accord across the tracks through the forest; more lay in clearings, felled by the foresters and awaiting transportation to the sawmill. No more than the height of fences they had jumped in the riding school, they presented little technical challenge to the Toms, but somehow they had all the thrill of a cross-country course about them, with their irregular spacing and haphazard angles. Robert devised a short course of about fifteen jumps, which they first ran through in file behind him and then as an individual exercise. As it was impossible to knock fences down, the result was an inevitable tie.

They walked the horses to the reservoir on the eastern edge of the forest, then dismounted and allowed the hunters a rest and a drink.

After a few minutes of idle chatting and skimming stones over the surface of the water, Two looked at his watch: it was already half past three. 'The sun's going down Robert – hadn't we better head back soon?'

'Yeah, I suppose so.' Robert suddenly sounded depressed. 'Frankly, I'd rather stay out here – there's not much to look forward to back home at the moment. Did you see the papers this morning?'

One answered while Robert bounced a few more stones across the reservoir. 'We saw the headlines and the photograph in the *Telegraph*, but we haven't had a chance to read the article yet. Is it bad?'

'The *Telegraph* is all right, according to the Colonel – he had them all delivered this morning, just in case. Some of the others take a really anti-hunting line. One of them – I forget which – has managed to get hold of a picture of that fuss in the Square. It makes it look as though I'm causing all the trouble. The Colonel's had the dailies on the telephone as well, so it'll be in them tomorrow.' Robert threw a flat stone with particular violence. It bounced across four or five times before sinking. 'Come on – we'll have an easy plod back. We'll go through her bridle path as well. I've got to do it sometime, so I may as well get it over with while I've got you two with me.'

The light had gone completely by the time they reached Katherine Stone's path. A few stars and a slender moon were sufficient to guide them along the lanes, but as they passed through the trees, they were in complete darkness. Tom One was powerfully reminded of the experiences of two days ago, as he pressed his body flat along his horse's neck and felt low-lying branches brush accusingly along his spine. It was good to be able to straighten up again and to move into the comparative space of the lane beyond.

'Where did you find her?'

Tom One was rather surprised by Robert's question. He had taken it for granted that the whipper-in would know the exact spot where Katherine had been killed: but then, of course, if he hadn't murdered her, there was no reason why this should be so. 'Ten yards or so out from the bridle path. We were still hunched over our horses, otherwise we might not have spotted her. About here, I think.'

They paused. In daylight, they might still have been able to discern signs of Katherine's last movements: even, perhaps, the odd footprint on the verge from Ashley's experiment with Constable Sefton. In the darkness, however, there was nothing. Tom One tried hard to imagine Stephen Trevis standing there, bludgeoning the old woman and hurling her into the ditch. Then he attempted the same process with Primrose Armishaw: neither scene seemed very convincing, but who knew?

'Let's go – there's nothing to see here.' Robert set off and the Toms followed. All the way down the lane they remained silent, just listening to the clopping of the hoofs against the metal track and thinking private thoughts. They reached Chagford and, for a few minutes, rode beneath clear street lamps; then, in the Square, among the multi-coloured Christmas lights which flashed on their polished boots and bridles. Finally they took the unlit road that led past Waye Lodge and up to the livery yard. The horses knew the road well: the Toms copied Robert who had allowed his reins to hang loose and taken his feet out of the stirrups. They felt beneath them the familiar sensation of a horse lengthening its stride, knowing that home and food are at hand.

The police were at hand, too. Sergeant Craggs stood outside Primrose's office with a dejected Harry Sefton and another uniformed constable. Their car was parked nearby, its headlights shining threateningly into the eyes of the horses and their riders.

They arrested Robert on a charge of murder.

* * * * *

CHAPTER TWENTY

- WHISKY WITH PRIMROSE -

Four depressed people sat in Primrose Armishaw's dilapidated office. The Toms managed to occupy a single armchair, with One actually on the seat, leaning against the left arm, and Two balancing on the right arm and leaning against the back. They also shared a whisky tumbler, taking alternate sips from opposite sides of the glass. Ashley had possession of the second tumbler and the hard office chair next to the desk; while Primrose herself overflowed from the remaining armchair and drank from a pint glass that was normally used to store pens, rulers and other odd desk clutter.

Even after dramatic events such as deaths and arrests, horses have to be groomed and fed. The troopers had found a sort of relief in the routines of the stable, picking out hoofs and brushing down with extra thoroughness in order to put off actually thinking about the scene they had just witnessed.

Fortunately, Robert had kept his temper. There had been a moment when it looked as though he was going to turn his horse around, spur her on and gallop out of the stable but, if such an action had occurred to him, a second thought prevented it. He had dismounted, given the reins of his mare to Tom Two, with instructions to look after her, and surrendered himself quietly.

Tom One saw Harry Sefton make a slight movement behind his back: he was replacing his handcuffs in their case. There had been an obvious sense of relief among the policemen and, even in his distress, Tom One realised that this was as much for Robert's sake as for their own.

At Tom One's suggestion, Primrose had telephoned Ashley while the troopers got on with their work in the stables. By the time they had finished their tasks, he was seated at her desk, jotting down notes in a small book. The Toms had fallen into the remaining chair and Primrose had poured drinks, the whisky bottle clinking erratically against the glasses as she did so.

Ashley closed his book and looked up. 'I'm sorry boys – that was the scene I was hoping to prevent you witnessing yesterday.'

Tom One took a sip of whisky and handed the glass to Tom Two. 'We'd worked that out, Uncle George. It could have been worse, I suppose – if he'd put up a struggle, we'd have found ourselves getting involved.'

'One way or another.' Two was relieved that he had not had to make a choice between loyalty to his friend and the Crown he had sworn to serve. Primrose agreed with him: 'I'd have taken a pitchfork to them if they'd tried anything nasty – I didn't like that sergeant.'

Two brought the conversation back to safer territory: 'What happens now, Mr Ashley?'

The detective shrugged. 'For Robert, a long sequence of unpleasant interviews and a lot of very boring interludes. Peter Masters will look after him as far as the interviews are concerned. As for the police – well, they'll try to get him to admit to the killing; when that fails, they'll charge him anyway. He'll go before a magistrate, who'll remand him in custody, and eventually it'll come to court – and then Robert will go to prison for a very long time.'

There was a long silence. Primrose, quivering all over, passed the whisky bottle around.

'So do you think he did it after all, Uncle George?'

'It's not what I think that matters, Tom – it's what the jury will think. The police will find it easy to show that Robert had reasons for wanting Katherine dead and that the time of her death coincides with his absence from the hunt – we've known all that from the start. Now, it seems, they have the extra piece of hard evidence they were looking for. If they're right, it all adds up to a pretty damning case.'

'What's the new piece of evidence, Mr Ashley? Have they told you?'

Ashley nodded. The inspector had telephoned him that afternoon.

'They found Katherine Stone's blood on his hunting shirt.'

The silence that followed this statement was followed by a strange exploding sound and a primitive howling, as if of some wild beast in pain.

Primrose Armishaw had burst into tears.

Unable to cope with female outbursts, the men made their excuses as best they could and wandered down the lane to Waye Lodge. Somehow, the darkness was rather comforting: it saved them the trouble of trying to put on brave faces. Privately, Tom One felt like a good cry himself: the emotional contrast between the uninhibited joy of their cross-country ride and the awful, helpless sensation he had experienced as Robert climbed into the police car, was bewildering. He left the talking to his uncle and Tom Two, and stumbled vaguely through the darkness, blinking back tears.

'Mr Ashley, you still haven't told us what you think about all this. Is that because you don't want us to know yet, or was it because you didn't want to say anything in front of Miss Armishaw?'

For a few seconds, there was only the sound of their footsteps on the road. Then Ashley replied. 'Partly the latter – I don't seriously suspect Primrose, of course, but one can't be too careful when a crime is involved. And partly because I really don't know what to think. When I came home yesterday, I'd been trying to reconstruct the killing with the help of Constable Sefton, and we'd worked out that the obvious solutions simply didn't fit the facts. All the objections we had then are still valid, as far as I can see – but there's no denying that finding the victim's blood on the shirt of the accused is strong evidence. If I'd been the police inspector in charge of the case, I'd have had to arrest Robert, just as Inspector Simkin has.

'Suppose, for a moment, that the blood had been found on Robert's coat, or breeches, rather than his shirt. Suppose also that Katherine Stone had only one wound in her skull. Then it would be fairly obvious that Robert, still on his horse, had cracked her over the head – perhaps in a moment of anger – and been spattered with her gore as a result. In that case, he'd be well advised to admit to manslaughter and plead mitigating circumstances. Lots of people would give testimony about his good character and, with any luck, he'd get off with a fairly short sentence. Do you understand so far?'

Tom Two nodded invisibly. 'Yes, sir, I think so.'

'But now, consider the facts as they really are. The blood is on Robert's shirt – so we have to assume that he removed his scarlet coat, his stock and his waistcoat before he struck her. That rules out manslaughter at once: a moment of madness doesn't give you time to strip off, let alone dismount, which is implied by the removal of clothing. We also have to assume – as I worked out with Harry last night – that Robert was lying in wait for her in a place where there was no obvious place to hide, whereas a few yards on, in the bridle path, he could have placed himself behind a tree quite easily. Finally – since this is the only way that I can make sense of the three cranial wounds – we have to assume that she was killed by her neck being broken as she fell and that the blows to the skull were administered immediately after death. What does all that mean to you?'

Tom Two mulled over the points in turn. 'I don't know, sir.'

'No – neither do I. At least, I know this much – either Robert Brookes is a completely incompetent murderer, or someone in Chagford....' Ashley paused to open the gate to Waye Lodge: 'is an expert.'

Margery and Aunt Lavinia came up trumps. Remembering Primrose Armishaw's kindness to her, Mrs Noad put on an overcoat, attached a hat to her head with a frighteningly sharp hatpin, and strode up the hill to the stables. Aunt Lavinia, diagnosing Tom One's distress more accurately than Ashley or Tom Two, marched her great nephew upstairs and put him in her own bed, complete with electric blanket and fan heater. A minute later she returned with a hot whisky toddy, then left him to sob in privacy.

Downstairs, Ashley and Tom Two continued their speculations in front of the fire. Two, brighter and more quick-witted than One, proved to be a very useful partner in detection, asking questions which displayed considerable penetration. They re-enacted several possible scenarios for the killing, beginning with the same one that Ashley had performed with Harry Sefton the previous evening. As Ashley had said on the way down the hill, the only version which made sense was the one in which Katherine was already dead when her skull was smashed – and that raised as many questions as it answered.

'Let's try that again, sir, and this time I'll be the old lady. If we change characters, we might get a new angle on it.'

'Good idea. So – you're walking along the lane, with your placard on your shoulder. That's right, the poker will do. The door leading to the kitchen is the direction of Chagford, and the bridle path begins where the curtains are. The real distance is about two or three times that, of course. I'm hiding – where?'

'In the ditch?'

'Too muddy – and slippery as well. I might not be able to get out of it.'

'At the start of the bridle path?'

'It's possible – and then I run out to attack you. But why don't I just wait for you to come into the bridle path?'

Two paused for thought, twirling the knob of the poker in his ear. Then he exclaimed: 'Because I've already seen you, sir! You haven't hidden yourself very well and I've seen your white shirt among the trees – we did a lot on camouflage and concealment on our basic training course, and white things really stick out.'

Ashley was impressed. 'That's good thinking, Tom – it also fits in with our first possibility, that the murder was a pretty clumsy job. Right then, I'm behind the curtains, with my shirt showing.'

He moved into position. Tom began an elderly walk across the room, halting by the fire. 'Who's there? I can see you!'

The curtains parted and Ashley shot out, brandishing Tom One's riding crop. For a second they struggled together – and then Tom Two really did fall over, swearing as he toppled towards the fire.

For a fraction of a second, Ashley simply thought the soldier was acting very well; then, as Tom Two crashed into the fireguard, and sent the irons and dogs clattering onto the stone hearth, he realised the potential danger of the situation. Quickly, he grabbed Two by the shoulders, pulled him away from the flames and then sat him upright on his haunches.

In the process, he covered himself in blood.

* * * * *

'Thanks, Margery – you're a brick.'

Primrose and Margery sat in the kitchen of the small cottage which adjoined the livery yard. This time, Margery had made the tea, employing the few minutes it took to boil the kettle in rummaging around for matching cups and saucers and a milk jug. Her fingers itched for scouring powder and bleach, and she had to remind herself that she was on a humanitarian mission, not a hygiene crusade.

'It must have been pretty awful for you, Primrose. Sugar?'

'Thanks.' Primrose helped herself to four lumps. 'Not as awful for me as for Robert, of course, but still fairly bad. They were hanging around for about an hour before he came back from the moor and the tension was unbearable. They didn't say what they were going to do, but it wasn't hard to guess – and, knowing Robert, I thought there might be a struggle and all sorts of dreadful things. Then, when your brother said that they'd found blood on his shirt, it just all came pouring out of me. Silly, really, but there it is – I'm fond of the boy, and I don't like to see him in trouble.'

'George is upset about it as well. After the inspector rang him this afternoon, he had a long conversation with Peter Masters about what to do. He said that he still thinks Robert might be innocent, but he doesn't know how to prove it. Perhaps the real killer will give himself up.'

Primrose put her teacup directly onto the table. It was obviously some time since she had bothered with saucers.

'To be honest with you, Margery, I thought that Robert had done it all along. I just hoped that he'd get away with it.'

* * * * *

Two was not seriously injured, but he had struck his nose on the fender and blood flowed freely from both nostrils. He held a sodden red handkerchief in one hand and Ashley's cleaner one to his nose. Cupping the cloth in his palm, he pinched the bridge of his nose with the fingers of the same hand. Ashley held a third handkerchief at the ready.

'It serves me right, Mr Ashley – I was still wearing my spurs, of all stupid things. It was all right when I was acting Robert, but when we swapped roles and you jostled me, they got caught up and I lost my balance.'

'Are you sure it's not broken, Tom? I can get the doctor out if necessary, or Margery can drive you over to Okehampton hospital.'

'No, sir, it's all right, really. I think it's slowing up now, anyway.' Two withdrew the handkerchief and examined the crimson patches, before gently exploring a nostril. Satisfied that the flow had ceased, he stood up to admire his wounds in the looking glass, and approved the gratifyingly violent streaks of blood across his face, in his hair and down his sweater. 'I look a proper mess, don't I sir? Like the aftermath of a nice night out with the Paratroop Regiment.'

Ashley was relieved by the return of the soldier's sense of humour. 'I'll remember to turn down an invitation from them, if ever I get one.'

'Very sensible, sir – no-one comes away from the Paras looking any prettier. I'd better go and have a wash, hadn't I?'

'I think that's a good idea. I'll clean up the fireplace while you're doing it.'

Tom looked down: the brasswork around the fire was still shedding red droplets onto the hearth, where a pair of small, dark puddles were doing their best to congeal, in spite of the heat from the flames. 'It certainly adds a touch of realism to our re-enactment of the murder, doesn't it, sir?'

'You never spoke a truer word, Tom. If you give me those handkerchiefs, I'll soak them in the kitchen sink before they dry out. My sister can put them in the machine tomorrow.'

The trooper left the room and Ashley mopped up as best

he could with the third handkerchief. In the kitchen he found a plastic bucket and put the sodden rags in to soak. After a minute, the water had turned a bright red, so he poured it down the sink and ran fresh water into the bucket before returning to the sitting room.

From an armchair, he gazed into the flames of the fire and spotted several traces of blood which he had missed earlier. There was something about the whole episode that worried him: was it just the vision of violence that had brought him so close to the spirit of the murder itself? Or was there more to it than that? Tom's suggestion that Robert – or somebody – might have been spotted and challenged by Katherine Stone was a good one, but it still left unanswered the question of the three wounds in the skull. For the hundredth time, he asked himself why anyone would wish to strike a dead body; and for the hundredth time a solution failed to present itself.

He poured himself a drink and decided to try a new angle: the will. There was something odd about the will: not just the wording, of course, or the contents, but something else. He tried to picture Katherine writing it, putting her signature at the foot of the page and locking the paper away until first Ellen Cleghorn and then Betty Trenchard called. It was a shame that Ellen Cleghorn wasn't alive to back up Betty Trenchard's evidence.

Ellen Cleghorn.

The inspector was going to check with the doctor that Ellen Cleghorn's death was entirely free from suspicion. Had he done so? Or had the events of the day caused him to overlook this detail?

Ashley went into the cold hallway, picked up the telephone receiver and dialled Okehampton police station.

* * * * *

205

CHAPTER TWENTY- ONE

- MONDAY MORNING -

Half past six. The Toms, in breeches, wellingtons and baggy sweaters, are at the livery yard, mucking out and feeding the horses. They came via the kennels in case they could be of use there as well, but John, the elderly huntsman, and Colonel Hargreaves had everything in hand. Primrose, however, is grateful for their offer of help, and they are glad to occupy themselves with familiar tasks. From Primrose's cottage, the tempting smell of smoked bacon brings evidence of their promised reward. It mingles with the scent of the horses around them: the combination is a comforting one.

Ashley, in pyjamas and dressing gown, has slept badly, troubled by dreams of blood gushing from Tom Two's large ears. He has rekindled the fire in the sitting room and is drinking tea, contemplating his morning tasks. His conversation with Harry Sefton the previous night had elicited the fact that Sergeant Craggs had indeed checked up on the facts concerning Ellen Cleghorn's death and that the doctor was convinced that it was entirely natural.

'He and the inspector were talking about it this afternoon, sir, just before we got the results through about the blood on the shirt.'

'Thanks, Harry – I just wanted to check. I hope I haven't interrupted you in anything important.'

'No, sir, you haven't. The inspector and Sergeant Craggs are in the interview room with him and the solicitor now, and I'm surplus to requirements, so I'm just hanging around. Anything else I can do to help, sir?'

'I don't think so Harry, but thanks. Is Robert staying there tonight, or are you taking him to Exeter?'

'He's definitely here tonight, sir – after that, I don't know. I've primed the chap on duty to be decent to him, so he'll be as comfortable as circumstances permit.'

'That's kind of you, Harry. I'll see you tomorrow, I dare say.'

So, Ellen Cleghorn is legitimately dead and, short of digging her up, there is no way of finding out otherwise. Yet still the will troubles. Perhaps another visit to Betty Trenchard will resolve some things?

Robert, in breeches, rugby socks and hunting shirt, squats on the hard bed in the police station. His cell is at least warm, and the policeman makes a powerfully strong mug of coffee. In a way, now that he has been arrested, Robert feels more relaxed: at least the horrible, cold fear of anticipation has passed. Peter Masters has instructed him to say nothing unless he has a legal representative with him and that simple plan of action saves him further thought.

He looks around the cell. The police have taken his braces and spurs. His boots stand bow-legged beside the bed on which he is sitting, the red hoops on his rugby socks giving an unnatural touch of colour to the dingy surroundings. On a small wooden table are his hard hat, his riding gloves and a copy of the New Testament.

Half past six. Has anyone fed the hounds? How will Primrose cope at the yard?

Harry, in nothing at all, has another hour before he has to get up. Rising at half past seven will give him plenty of time to shower and make himself look smart for the day's work. Anyway, he deserves whatever time he can steal to relax and doze after the labours of the weekend.

He rolls over and pulls his duvet more tightly around him. The street light outside his window shines through a gap in the curtains, so the familiar contents of his room are fully visible, in spite of the early hour. His uniform hanging on the wardrobe door; his helmet and peaked cap on the lowest of a set of bookshelves. His notebook, baton and handcuffs on a table.

Harry thinks of yesterday's arrest, grateful that no force had been necessary. A few months ago, he had chased a teenage thief through the streets of Okehampton and had taken great satisfaction in the rugby tackle that had brought the offender crashing to the pavement. He had enjoyed pinning the youth down by kneeling on his shoulders, and closing the steel clasps around his wrists. Even then, the lad had tried to wriggle out of his captivity, so that Harry had been forced to restrain him further by placing his size eleven police boot between the thief's shoulder blades while he stood up to radio for assistance. The crowd had applauded, and Harry had felt very much the hero of the day – had looked forward, indeed, to the next time he could apply the handcuffs and stand, like a big game hunter, with one foot on the day's bag. But there would have been no pleasure in tackling Robert. Between them, he and his colleague would certainly have won any struggle, but to remove all dignity and self-respect from a person he rather liked, and for whom he felt sympathy, would have been a dreadful thing. Mr Ashley had been right when he said that there were grim times ahead.

* * * * *

'Tea and bacon butties in the harness room, boys.'

Primrose staggered through the yard with a thermos flask tucked under one arm, a plateful of doorstep sandwiches, and three mugs hooked onto the chubby fingers of her free hand. The Toms hurriedly finished grooming, cleaned their hands by the simple process of running them through their sweaty hair, and followed the smell.

'You know One, if foxhounds gain as much pleasure from sniffing after a fox as I do following the line of those bacon wedgies, then I want to be reincarnated as a hound when I die.'

Tom One concurred. They followed the trail avidly, stormed the harness room, and attacked the sandwiches greedily.

'Thanks, Miss Armishaw, this is great.'

'Tuck in lads – no, I won't have one, they're all for you. I'm on a diet – and before you even think it, I know it's having no effect, but I still feel guilty when I break it. Stick the cat outside, if you don't want him sniffing around – on the other hand, if you give him a bit of bacon rind, he'll be your friend for life.'

Tom One peeled off a length of rind and played games with the cat, dandling the fatty skin above it until a paw hooked the food and the creature retired to its warm saddle blanket in triumph.

'The colonel rang to send his thanks for calling on the kennels on your way up. He's got a feeding rota going for the next few days, but says if you'd just check that everything looks all right whenever you go past, he'd be very grateful. I've said I'll pop down in the car once a day as well.'

It was impossible to answer with mouths full of bread and bacon, so the Toms grunted and nodded, leaving the talking to Primrose. 'If you fancy any riding later, most of the hunters could do with a bit of exercise. Obviously, I can't let you out on the moor without a guide, but I should think you could find your way into Chagford and up to the top of Meldon and back – if you didn't mind doing that three or four times with different horses, it would be a great help.'

Tom One gulped, sending a large piece of pig down his throat. 'That sounds fine, Miss Armishaw – we're glad of the chance to do any riding. We've only got about half an hour's worth of stable routine still to do. Two, if you finish off that bit of grooming, I'll nip down to the house and pick up our boots and hats, so we can set off as soon as we're ready. What do you say?'

Still unable to say anything, Two gurgled assent, so One took a final swig of tea and pulled on his jacket and cap. Grabbing a third sandwich for the journey, he set off. Primrose watched him walk through the yard and vault over the gate.

'Like me, your friend seems much more cheerful this morning. It's amazing the difference a good night's sleep makes, isn't it? Especially when the next day is as glorious as this one.'

Tom Two finished his sandwich and nodded agreement. The sun was now up and the clear, cold beauty of the day proclaimed it to be perfect for hunting – except, of course, that the hunt had been cancelled. 'Yes, Miss Armishaw – poor old One was quite cut up yesterday. As our lance bombardier says, there may not be much going on under his busby, but he feels things quite deeply.'

'I think your lance bombardier's got it right: when you don't have the right words to express your feelings, you end up keeping them to yourself, and they grow very strong. I must say, Tom's mother was a good egg last night. I could tell she was itching to snap on a pair of rubber gloves and squirt disinfectant everywhere, but she kept her instincts under control and looked after me beautifully. I haven't had a matching cup and saucer since the fiftieth anniversary of VJ day at Throwleigh – and I didn't even know I owned a milk jug.'

It was just after nine that the Toms walked the first pair of horses into Chagford. The first person they saw was Ashley, who was hanging around outside the country clothing shop, idly inspecting an umbrella stand full of walking sticks. Hearing the sound of hoofs, he glanced up and smiled in recognition.

'Morning chaps – you're looking very smart up there.'

'Thanks Uncle George – what about you? Have you developed a gammy leg, or something?'

Ashley seemed puzzled for a moment, then realised he was still holding onto a walking stick. He replaced it in the stand. 'No – I'm just killing time before going to see Betty Trenchard. I have this awful hunch that if I arrive before half-past nine, she'll still be in her nightdress, and I don't want to have to add to my large collection of recurring nightmares. Are you going far? We could meet for luncheon somewhere.'

'That would be good, Uncle George. We're just doing a shuttle service up and down Meldon to exercise the hunters, so we could meet back here, if you like.'

It was arranged, and Ashley watched the two troopers ride past the church and out of sight. For a moment, and not for the first time, he envied them their straightforward, uncomplicated life. He would certainly rather be galloping up Meldon Tor now than preparing to listen to Betty Trenchard's stream-of-consciousness babble about Katherine Stone, wills and medical conditions.

The thought of her diabetes and gluten allergy gave Ashley an idea. He went into Norah Dyer's stores and bought a box of diabetic chocolates, which could form a useful pretext for his visit. They would have been a present for Aunt Lavinia, or something like that, and when the family had spotted they were diabetic chocolates, Margery had suggested giving them to Betty Trenchard. Ashley was fairly sure that if he arrived on a simple errand of that sort, Betty would soon let out any information she might know; whereas if he questioned her more

211

formally, she would be on her guard. Amazingly, Norah Dyer failed to question his purchase, busy as she was in recounting the latest episode in the saga of Mrs Farmer Crane's cystitis. 'On Christmas Day, too – I dare say she'll never pull another cracker in her life….' He crept quietly out of the shop and bumped into a scowling Peter Masters.

'Morning Peter – you look as though a rival has just found a loophole in one of your documents.'

Peter abandoned his frown. 'Nothing that bad, I'm relieved to say – and anyway, the only rival here is an old codger in Moretonhampstead, who wouldn't spot a loophole until he'd hanged himself in it. No, I was fuming about that bloody Trenchard woman. I've asked her to keep up the cleaning at Meldon Dene, but since she hasn't got a key, I arranged to meet her there at nine o'clock this morning.'

'Let me guess: trying to counteract the excesses of Christmas, you walked all the way up there, and she stood you up.'

'Spot on. I would have telephoned her to remind her, because we made the arrangement on Saturday, and a lot has happened since then, but she's ex-directory. Goodness only knows why – I'd have thought she'd be quite glad of a few obscene phone calls. I'm on my way there now, to slap her over-large backside and point her in the direction of an honest morning's work.'

'Then our tasks coincide – I was on my way to pick her brains.'

'Well, I hope you've brought your tweezers with you then. Betty may have a big, big body, but she has a tiny, tiny brain, as I'm sure you've realised. Shall we go together?'

They strolled across the Square, in no particular hurry to reach the place that Peter described as the 'World Headquarters of gluten-free pastry'.

'By the way, George, I had a call first thing this morning from a friend in London – he confirmed that Katherine's handing the will to me makes no difference in law. It's definitely invalid.'

'So Katherine officially died intestate and Robert is now her heir. Will the animal rights charity try to contest anything?'

'They'll be wasting their money if they do. As for Robert being the heir – well, if he's found guilty of murder, of course, he won't get a penny of it…'

Peter Masters broke off. They had turned the corner that brought Lamb Park into view. Also visible were an ambulance, with its light flashing, a police car, and a small crowd. Standing by the police car, Harry Sefton was speaking into his radio. The door of Betty Trenchard's house was open, hanging awkwardly on its hinges.

Ashley casually dropped the diabetic chocolates into a litter bin. 'I think, Peter, we've just found out why Betty didn't make her appointment this morning.'

* * * * *

CHAPTER TWENTY-TWO

- DEATH OF A DIABETIC -

'Four beers and a shandy, gents?' The barman offloaded the pint glasses from a tray. 'Your sandwiches will be along in just a minute.'

In a secluded corner of the Ring O'Bells, Ashley and Peter Masters shared a table with Constable Sefton and Toms One and Two. The two soldiers had returned from exercising horses as the other three walked into the Square and had realised immediately that the presence of Harry Sefton meant that there was a further development. They had ascertained that Betty Trenchard was dead, and then, for an awful moment, it seemed as though Ashley was going to send them away. Peter Masters, however, pointed out that the incident was now a matter of public knowledge, so there was no reason why the troopers should not be in on the discussion. Harry raised no objection either; he just seemed pleased to have some younger people around.

'So are you going to put us in the picture, Mr Ashley, sir?'

Ashley took a mouthful of beer before replying. 'Well I would, Tom Two, if I knew what the picture was showing. Beyond the fact that it's still life, rather than a landscape, I'm fairly confused. Harry – you were on the scene first. Let's have your story.'

'All right, sir.' Harry enjoyed the sight of four faces giving him their full attention. 'The call came through to the station just as I reported for duty – it was an ambulance call, of course, but they always come through to us as well, just in case. When I wrote down the number of the house, I thought it might be Mrs Trenchard's, so I checked up her address in the old classroom and then got the constable on the desk to put a call through to Inspector Simkin over in Exeter. Then I drove straight here.

'Apparently, the postman had tried to deliver a parcel that wouldn't fit through the letterbox. When she didn't answer the door, he looked through the window, and saw her on the floor in the kitchen. He went to the house next door and rang 999, but he couldn't gain entrance to Mrs Trenchard's house, because it was locked up. The ambulance chaps had to break the door down to get in – they arrived at just after nine o'clock, and her doctor arrived at about the same time. I got here about ten minutes later, by which time they were in the house and gathered around the body.'

Sandwiches arrived and Harry broke off his narrative to devour one, leaving the Toms feeling as though a commercial break had just interrupted a very exciting television programme. With nothing better to do, they helped themselves as well.

'Did you catch any of the medical conversation, Harry?' Ashley knew that a more experienced policeman would refuse to pass on details of this kind in front of an audience, but Harry was still new to the game.

'Yes, sir – I even jotted it down when I was outside again. I had to come out after a bit and keep an eye on the crowd. That's when I saw you, of course.' The constable pulled out his notebook and consulted his jottings. 'The doctor reckoned she'd accidentally overdosed on her insulin, sir. The stuff was all there on the table, with the syringe and everything. He said that she'd only recently been diagnosed with diabetes, so perhaps she confused the symptoms of....' He stared at his notes for a moment: 'Hypers and Hypos is what I've written, sir – does that sound right?'

Ashley nodded. 'I'm no medical expert, but diabetes is a fairly straightforward question of keeping a balance between insulin and blood sugar in the system. If you have too much sugar, the treatment is to inject insulin, and when it's the other way around, the easiest thing is to eat a sugar lump. The effects are pretty instant. Presumably, if you mistake the symptom, you make things significantly worse, though I'm surprised it was bad enough to kill her outright. Did the doctor suggest how long she'd been dead?'

'Some time between eighteen and twenty-four hours, he guessed, sir. She'd obviously had her Sunday lunch, though, because the remains of her meal were still out, so eighteen hours seemed most likely. Her *rigor mortis* had pretty much worn off, which was just as well, when it came to getting her out of the door – I had to give the ambulance chaps a hand, she was so heavy.'

Tom One risked the wrath of his uncle by interrupting: 'So it's not another murder, then?'

Harry shook his head. 'The inspector doesn't think so. Sergeant Craggs even tore me off a strip for bringing them out on a false alarm, but the inspector said I was right to be cautious. He had a look around and took some photographs before they put the body in the ambulance, but I think he only did it to make me feel better and to wind up Sergeant Craggs.'

'They'll do tests on the body, of course.' Peter Masters' observation was half question, half statement of fact.

'They're going to sir. In fact, they're probably doing them right now, and on the dirty lunch things as well as on the body

– but the inspector said it was mainly just to reassure ourselves that it was an accidental death, rather than because he's suspicious. I'm sure you can work out why, Mr Ashley.'

Ashley could. Robert Brookes' movements were fully accounted for from the moment he left church – when Betty Trenchard was still very much alive – to the time of his arrest. If the body was found to be overflowing with arsenic or strychnine, the inspector would have to begin reviewing his interpretation of the case, otherwise there was no reason for him to revise his ideas. He explained as much to his nephew and Tom Two.

'So what you're saying, Uncle George, is that we hope she has been poisoned, because then Robert will be in the clear.'

'And his arrest will have turned out to have been a good thing, after all.' Two shared Tom One's enthusiasm. Ashley felt rather sorry to disappoint them.

'I don't think it will be that simple, chaps. Remember those re-enactments we did?' He looked from Tom Two to Harry Sefton: they both nodded. 'Well, we came to the conclusion that if Robert really did do the killing, then he's a fairly useless murderer. The converse also holds – if Robert is innocent, then, somewhere in Chagford, we have a really clever killer at work. And a really clever killer isn't going to shoot a whole load of poison into Victim Number Two, when the main suspect can't possibly have been available to do the job.'

The Toms, deflated, looked at Ashley as if he were a bombardier who had just told them that their kit wasn't up to scratch. Two made a final suggestion: 'What if the real killer didn't know that Robert's movements could be accounted for?'

Ashley shook his head. 'Put yourself in the place of the clever killer, Tom Two. You've done away with Katherine Stone and everyone thinks that Robert is the murderer. You now want to move on to your next victim – let's say you plan to give her cyanide. Wouldn't you do your best to find out what Robert's

217

plans were, so that the suspicion was still on him?'

'I suppose so, sir, though I'm not sure how I'd go about it.'

Peter Masters butted in. 'You've got to remember, Tom, that in a small place like Chagford, most people know what everybody else is doing practically all the time. It wouldn't have been hard to find out what Robert was up to after church. If he had gone to luncheon with the Hargreaves, it would be a fair guess that he'd walk home between about three o'clock and three-thirty. Then again, if, after the service was over, he was seen heading out on the Gidleigh road, you could work out that he was going home for a quiet meal and would be by himself for a while. As it was....'

Tom Two got the point. 'As it was, sir, he left the church hall with us. I suppose it was pretty obvious that we were going riding together. We were talking about it as well, so we could easily have been overheard.'

'There you are then: our intelligent terminator reasons that Robert will have witnesses to his movements for the next few hours, and decides not to pump the cyanide into the next victim just yet. So, one way or another, we don't expect any dramatic news from the *post mortem* results.'

The symposium lapsed into a general silence, only broken when Harry looked at his watch.

'I said I'd relieve Ernie Yeo about now, if you'll excuse me, gentlemen. We've put a guard on the front door of Mrs Trenchard's house until the carpenter can come out and fix it. Mr Ashley, I'm sure the inspector will let you know of any developments.'

'Thank you, Harry. Feel free to pass on any of our speculations to him – though you'd be sensible not to let him know that you told us what the doctor said.'

Harry blushed, realising his mistake. 'Thanks for the tip, sir – and thank you for the lunch, Mr Masters.'

'That's a pleasure, Constable Sefton. Actually, I'll walk with you as far as my office – it's about time I did some work today. Will you excuse me, George?'

The policeman and the solicitor departed. Ashley and the Toms surveyed the table: the pile of sandwiches was much reduced, and the glasses were empty.

'Shall we get some more beer in, Uncle George, or do you want to head off?'

Ashley contemplated the possibilities. 'Do you chaps have any more horses to exercise?'

Tom One shrugged a vague assent. 'Primrose asked us to do as many as we felt up to. We took six out this morning – there are still a handful back at the yard. Why, Uncle George?'

'Because what I really feel like doing is blowing all the cobwebs of muddled detection out of my brain and getting some fresh air and fresh thinking. A run up to Meldon and back would do me the power of good and it might get some ideas flowing. Would you mind?'

'That'd be great, Uncle George. It's good to know that there's something we can do to help. You don't mind, do you, Two? I'm sure Aunt Lav will put a poultice on your saddle sores, if necessary.'

Two clicked his spurs affirmatively. 'You've just made me an offer I can't refuse, One.'

* * * * *

Primrose Armishaw squeezed herself into the driving seat of her Morris Traveller and released the handbrake. It was downhill all the way to the kennels, so there was no need to turn the ignition key – though it was important to check that it was there. She had occasionally forgotten this precaution and found herself at the bottom of the hill with no civilised means of getting back up again. The car moved slowly at first, but gained momentum as it passed through the gate, the combined

219

weight of the car and its occupant proving an efficient aid to kinesis. Halfway down the hill, Primrose was already using the brake.

Since Robert's arrest, the cottage had been locked, but there was a bunch of keys under a granite stone by the doorstep. Primrose let herself in the front door, passed though the hallway and kitchen, and went out into the bitch-hounds' main compound. For a moment, the animals seemed to think that Robert had returned. They set off in joyful chorus, leaping everywhere and anywhere and wagging tails in each other's faces. Crowding around Primrose, whose horsy smell was pleasingly familiar, they demanded attention, so that she nearly fell over backwards under the pressure of paws on her thighs and stomach. She made a fuss of any head that was in reach and retreated.

'Sorry, no food girls – not until later. And someone's going to come and exercise you tomorrow. Get your head out of the way, you stupid hound, or it'll get shut in the gate.'

Back in Robert's kitchen, Primrose looked around and noted with surprise its comparative cleanliness. Perhaps Margery Noad and a squad of crack para-cleaners had made a lightning raid during the whipper-in's enforced absence, ruthlessly scouring pots, pans and work surfaces into submission. More likely, the Master had asked Evelyn, or somebody, to come and put things in order. The sitting room was tidy too, though the anonymous cleaner had obviously been too squeamish to enter the bedroom or bathroom.

On an impulse, Primrose put the kettle on and made tea, carrying her mug through to the sitting room, where she eased herself into an armchair. A deserted cottage was a good place to do a bit of thinking.

Poor Robert. A rotten childhood, what with his father killing himself and his mother having to get by on very little money. Then this, just as everything seemed to be coming right for him:

just when he had his own cottage, a job he loved, his hounds, his horses, friends in the town – his whole life before him, in fact. Not like her, knocking on sixty, past riding for anything more than an hour, past running the yard on her own....

She looked around at his possessions, inert and soulless without their owner to bring meaning to them. The mounted foxes above the fire: she remembered him coming back with one of them after his first day with the hunt, and the Master promising to send it to the taxidermist. His copper hunting horn, which he was learning to blow in readiness for the day when he was promoted from whipper-in to huntsman; his books on kennel management; a photograph, hanging proudly from the picture rail, showing Robert astride his hunter, handsome in his scarlet coat, boots and spurs, all ready for the day's sport. He should be sitting here among these things, not her.

A resolution began to form in her mind.

* * * * *

Looking in one direction, Ashley could see Chagford: in the other, he was able to watch his nephew and Tom Two racing their horses backwards and forwards across the common. They had been down there for half an hour, messing around and wasting time, while he put his thoughts in order. At the moment, it appeared that they were pretending to be skirmishing, using their crops as swords and engaging each other in single combat.

Ashley himself had dismounted and was seated on a granite boulder. He held his hunter's reins loosely in one hand, leaving the horse free to nibble the short, inadequate grass that grew at the top of the tor.

The ride had been a good idea. Forced to concentrate on equestrian matters, he had been able to unclog his mind: now, the solitary peace of Meldon Tor, glorious in the winter sunshine, was enabling him to draw new patterns and create links between ideas which had previously been unrelated. He hadn't solved the crime – or crimes – by any means, but he had shed a lot of useless clutter. What he needed to do now was to bounce a few ideas backwards and forwards with Tom Two.

Standing up, he waved to the riders below. They responded, and the next second were galloping up the path, Tom One in front, leaning forward, his seat out of the saddle, urging his horse onwards and upwards. Ashley gained an insight into the mind of an infantryman in the line, bracing himself to face a cavalry charge. Perhaps, like the Life Guards at Waterloo, the Toms would be unable to stop, and would come to a sticky end on the downward slope to Chagford?

Tom One chose not to display the recklessness which leads to glory or disaster: instead, he began to rein in his horse before he reached the summit, reaching his uncle at a brisk trot, his seat falling and rising with the motion of the horse.

'Who did it then, Uncle George?' He halted, and stood up in the stirrups, looking over Chagford in the hope of spotting a murderer.

'Tom, you twit, if it were that easy, I'd have solved it over the weekend – just like the police think they did. I need to throw some thoughts in the direction of an intelligent person.'

Two joined them, trotting slightly less smoothly than One. He caught the end of Ashley's sentence. 'So One just gets to hold the horses, does he, sir?'

'That's about it. If you'd like to leap off, there's room for both of us on this rock, and I won't get a crick in my neck talking up to you.'

Two jumped down, handed his reins to Tom One, and removed his hard hat. 'All right, sir – fire away.' He bounced himself onto the boulder and indulged in his favourite occupation of clicking his spurs together.

'Point one. We take it as a working hypothesis that Robert

is innocent. We are therefore dealing with a very clever killer, who has not only managed to avoid coming under suspicion, but who has managed to throw suspicion on somebody else.'

'I've got you, sir.'

'Good. Question one follows: was the suspicion deliberately directed towards Robert, or would any member of the hunt have done? Even given that our killer was very clever, the bolting of that hound certainly couldn't have been planned.'

Tom Two tapped out a jazzy rhythm with his spurs. 'Do you think, Mr Ashley, sir, that the killer had a bit of good luck and a bit of bad luck? The good luck was that hound breaking away from the hunt, so that Robert was absent for about the right amount of time – and the bad luck was us. If my horse hadn't cast a shoe, no-one would have come back along that path until after it was really dark and they probably wouldn't have seen the body in the ditch. The hounds would have smelled it, of course, but that's not the way they went back to the kennels.'

Ashley mulled over this suggestion: it was a good one.

'I see what you mean. The body wouldn't have been discovered until the next day, so a whole load of people would have come under suspicion, not just Robert. You could be right – let's move on.

'Point two. We have a very dodgy will, which is certain to be declared invalid. Within the space of a month, the writer of the will and both witnesses are dead. Question two: is that just a coincidence?'

The jazzy rhythm slowed and changed to a soft leathery thud, as Two tapped his toes rather than his heels. 'Pass, sir – I don't really understand anything about wills. It certainly sounds fishy, though, doesn't it?'

'Very, and here's the fishiest bit of all. Final point – for the moment, at any rate. If Robert is innocent, according to our working theory, we have to account for Katherine's blood being found on his shirt. How did it get there? And why not on his coat or breeches? Has our clever murderer planted it on him? If so, did that happen after it became clear that Robert had absented himself from the hunt, or was it just a lucky coincidence? Or is there some other perfectly natural explanation for the bloody shirt, just waiting to be discovered?'

Tom began alternate toes and heels, turning his feet into the percussion section of a marching band. 'I know one thing, sir – Robert never used to bother locking his door. He told us, when we went down there on Christmas Eve.'

'Really? I wasn't aware of that. It would make the planting of a bloody shirt easier, if that's what happened.'

'The other thing you said, sir – about a lucky co-incidence. Wouldn't two pieces of luck be one too many, if you see what I mean? Supposing it had been John, the huntsman, who had had to leave the field for some reason – well then the shirt planted on Robert would have been a nonsense, wouldn't it?'

Ashley took a long time to think. 'If you're correct, Two – and I think you are – our murderer has deliberately intended that suspicion should fall on Robert from the very beginning, not just as a convenient afterthought.' He stood up and wandered over to Tom One, who was waiting patiently, seated on one horse and holding the reins of the other two. Ashley took back control of his own horse and put the reins over its head.

'Last question – I promise. Did the killer want to throw suspicion on Robert because of the incident in the Square, in which case he is simply, as the Americans would say, the 'fall guy'; or is there a particular reason for wanting him out of the way?'

Two also headed towards the horses. 'Do you need a leg up, sir? I reckon it will be safer than using that stone as a mounting block. Have you got a hold? Right – one – two – three!' Having propelled Ashley up, Tom Two vaulted into his own saddle and gathered up his reins. 'I don't think Robert has really got any enemies, sir. I should have thought it more likely that the killer saw the episode in the Square and thought that they could cash in on it. Or is that another example of too much luck, sir?'

'Possibly. Thanks, Two, that's been a great help.' They began to walk their horses back down the tor. 'Do you play chess, by any chance?'

Two seemed amused by this change of subject. 'I used to at school, sir, but the chaps at the barracks aren't really into that sort of thing. Pool and darts are more in their line. Why do you ask, sir?'

'Because I want you to imagine Robert as the white king, in a position where he seems to be caught in a dangerous mating trap, but where the correct response will actually turn the attack onto black. I'm sure there's a way out of this case, but the correct move eludes me – for the moment. We'll play a game tonight, if you like – I don't think there's any more detective work to be done at the moment.'

'All right, sir – I'll look forward to it. I tried to teach One when we were hanging around on basic training, but I didn't get far.'

'I liked the ones with the horse's heads,' contributed Tom One.

'You see what I was up against, Mr Ashley, don't you?'

* * * * *

CHAPTER TWENTY-THREE

- TWO MURDERERS? -

Mrs Trevis saw Ashley and the Toms ride past the church as she went in with her watering can. The Christmas flowers were fading now, but if she looked after them carefully, there would probably be enough to make up a decent arrangement by the altar for next Sunday. She wandered around the displays, topping up the water where necessary and removing any flowers that had already withered. The sight of Ashley put her in mind of dead Frestons, Warrens and Brookeses, and the remembrance of the Freston family, once important in the area, now dwindled to almost nothing – the name, even, extinct – troubled her. At the flowers under the brass War Memorial, she paused to pick out the name of John Warren, killed out in Italy during the Allied advance. William Freston did not appear among the victims of the First World War, having died after the plaque was hung. Mrs Trevis wondered if any parish debate had taken place on the subject, or if, by that stage, everybody wanted to forget the War and William had just received a civilian funeral, the military headstone being added later.

As she progressed towards the High Altar, James Brookes came into her mind. She had known and liked James and she recalled the tears she had cried on hearing the news of his death: now, speculating on the awful spirit of desolation that must have been upon him that night when he shot himself, she felt her eyes stinging once more. At the altar she knelt and prayed fervently that Robert would not attempt a similar escape from his present troubles. She kept her eyes open, frightened, lest in closing them, she should picture Robert in his cell, an improvised rope – perhaps his shirt sleeve or a torn sheet from his bed – around his neck. Surely he would be cleared soon? Would not the police realise that Robert was no murderer? For once, the figure of Christ, hanging from the Cross, failed to provide comfort.

Footsteps sounded on the granite flagstones, and she hurriedly brought her prayers to a close, feeling an Anglican and middle-class embarrassment at being discovered indulging in solitary religious practices.

'Hello Alice – I hope I didn't disturb you?'

'No, Primrose, of course not. Were you looking for Stephen? I'm afraid the dog took him for a walk at about opening time, and I haven't seen him since. I came in to water the flowers and do a little organ practice – I didn't play very well on Sunday. I kept thinking of all the recent trouble and I played even more wrong notes than usual.'

'Bad luck – don't let me stop you. I'll just take a pew and hover for half an hour, in case the Rector comes back.'

Mrs Trevis now felt honour bound to play the organ for a few minutes and she cursed herself for feeling that she had to give excuses for being in her own church – and to Primrose Armishaw, of all people, who hardly ever set foot in it. It would never occur to Primrose, of course, that musicians didn't want an audience when they practised, but then she probably wouldn't recognise a wrong note if the pipe fell out of the case and hit her on the head. With this comforting thought in mind, Alice switched on the instrument, selected a piece of music that had the quadruple advantages of softness, slowness, facility and brevity, and meandered her way through slushy chords, of the kind where the odd extra note in the harmony is neither here nor there.

After a few minutes the movement petered out, with half a dozen repetitions of the tonic chord. Mrs Trevis paused for a few seconds, then switched off the blower and lights and swivelled off the organ stool. Primrose was still there, gradually filling out a pew like a melting jelly in the sun. What did she want with Stephen?

'Can I be of any help, Primrose? I've no idea when Stephen will be back.'

Primrose braced herself: the jelly began to take shape again. There had to be a first time for coming out with it, so she might as well practise on Alice.

'I was going to ask him to drive me into Okehampton. I'm not sure the Morris will make it that far and, besides, I'm going to need some moral support. I'm going to own up. I killed Katherine Stone.'

* * * * *

Tom One agreed to groom his uncle's horse on condition that Ashley made some tea.

'There's a kettle in the office, Uncle George – I'm sure Miss Armishaw won't mind. I wonder where she's got to?'

Ashley put the kettle on and returned to watch the troopers at work. In between hoofs, Tom Two, who had enjoyed his glory as detective's assistant, stood up and looked pensive for a while.

'Mr Ashley?'

'Yes, Two?'

'While you were busy with the police the other day, One and I had a go at some bits of detecting ourselves. We worked out that Primrose Armishaw's movements were unaccounted for after she left the field and, according to Robert, she was angry with Katherine Stone, because the old lady had managed to block a planning application.'

Tom One interrupted his work to join in. 'She wanted to convert a barn into holiday cottages. Apparently, the Rector couldn't stand her either, because she was always writing to the Bishop to complain about him and the bells. We tried to get some information out of the Rector yesterday, but we didn't get very far.'

Ashley laughed. 'I know – but you provided him with some entertainment, so he didn't mind.'

Tom One looked sheepish. 'Oh – so you heard about it, Uncle George?'

'Not only did I hear about it, I succeeded where you failed. Lesson number one in detection, Tom: direct questions very rarely get direct answers. I got him on the subject of dry sherry and within a quarter of an hour, I knew all his movements on Boxing Day afternoon. I'll tell you over tea. Thanks for the bit about Primrose, Two – we'll talk about that as well.'

A short while later the Toms once more occupied a single armchair, drinking their tea from chipped mugs. Ashley had the hard desk seat again, as Primrose's chair was occupied by the cat, who had no intention of making room for anybody else.

'You'll be glad to know that the Rector has no satisfactory alibi: so, presumably, if this case were in the hands of Inspector Tom Marsh and Sergeant Tom Noad, he'd be arrested straight away, strapped over a saddle, and a confession beaten out of him before the sun came up again.'

Tom Two found the idea an appealing one. 'Sounds good to me, sir. Add a desk lamp shining in the face, a bit of sleep deprivation and Tom One digging his spurs in – we'd soon have it down on paper and signed.'

'In his own blood.'

'Yes, well before you get too enthusiastic, let's get back to what he says he did. After the hunt departed, he hung around chatting for a while, then went into the Ring O'Bells for a pint. That turned into two pints....'

'It's strange how often that happens, isn't it, Uncle George?'

'Yes, I've often noticed similar things with gin – but let's get back to the subject. After he left the pub, he accepted an invitation from Mark Overland to split a bottle of claret in the flat above the Vintner's shop. That was all over by about half past twelve....'

'He knocks it back quickly, sir.'

'As I have cause to know – but bear in mind that it was Boxing Day, which was his first day off for a while. Anyway, luncheon was going to be late at the Rectory that day, because Mrs Trevis had forgotten to put the oven timer on before going out to see the hunt off. He then decided to walk off the effects of the drink rather than face the wrath of his wife back at home.'

'So he set off on the Meldon Road?' As far as Tom Two was concerned, the Rector was already convicted.

'Just put that black cap away, Judge Marsh, and pour me some more tea. The Rector says he walked along the Moreton-hampstead Road, because he knew that the hunt had gone out to Meldon and he didn't want his dog to get excited and caught up in things. Thanks, Two – no sugar.'

'That's got a sort of ring of truth about it, hasn't it, Uncle George?'

'It has, but by way of consolation, the Rector didn't meet anyone on his walk, so he has no witnesses to his movements between leaving Mark Overland and returning to the Rectory just after two o'clock.'

'It's sounding suspicious again, sir.' Two, having poured more tea for everyone, bounced enthusiastically back onto the arm of his chair. Tom One was less convinced.

'If he did do it, Uncle George, I don't think he would have tried to stitch up Robert. I can picture him coming across the old lady and getting violent with her – after all, he'd had a bit too much to drink. But wouldn't he have just left it at that?'

'I wonder…. On one level, Tom, you're quite right. Picture the scene: a slightly squiffy Stephen Trevis bumps into Katherine Stone and she starts gloating about getting the bells cut down to half an hour. He loses his temper, or something, and shoves her into the ditch. Perhaps he doesn't realise she's already broken her neck – but he does realise he's in big trouble. He works out that the best way to prevent her pressing charges is to finish off what he has started, so he bashes her over the head….'

'What with, Mr Ashley?'

'Goodness only knows, and that's another weak point in the argument – but let's press on for a bit. Now, according to the Tom One assessment, he simply returns home and lets things take their course. The problem that follows, then, is that we have to imagine somebody else with a grudge against Robert, who takes advantage of the situation to have suspicion cast on him. The alternative scenario is that, either immediately, or some time after he sobers up, he realises what he's done and that he'd better make sure the police suspect somebody else.'

Two gave a short, excited tattoo on his spurs. 'It would have to be straight away, surely, sir – else how would he get her blood onto Robert's shirt? After the body had been found, he wouldn't have any way of obtaining it, would he?'

'Blast you, Two – you're right. I suppose he could dip a handkerchief in the blood and then head off to Robert's house.' Ashley contemplated this possibility. It reminded him forcefully of mopping up Tom Two's blood the previous evening.

'If he was pissed, Uncle George, I reckon he'd have slipped into the ditch, and got himself covered in mud, if he tried to do that.'

Ashley leaned over to the desk and deposited his empty mug. 'These are all good points, but I'm not sure they're getting us anywhere.'

'Shall we move on to Primrose Armishaw, Uncle George? We promise not to try to strap *her* over a saddle and beat the truth out of her.'

'We'd probably never see the saddle again.'

Ashley decided to stop this line of conversation before it got out of hand. 'All right, we'll have a brainstorming session on Primrose – but I don't think we ought to do it here.'

'Do you think the cat's wired up for sound, Uncle George?'

'Idiot: no, it's just a bit much to have uninvited guests in your office, discussing the probability of your being a murderess....'

He paused: there was a motorised clanking in the distance, and the sound of an engine, in the wrong gear, straining up a hill.

'Besides which, here she comes. I suggest we make her some tea and, if any chance to ask about Boxing Day comes up, leave it to me.'

Two dismounted from the arm of the chair and headed for the kettle again. 'It's all right, Mr Ashley, we'll just "act normal", as they say in the thrillers. That gormless expression will do nicely, One.'

Primrose's Morris Traveller gave a *sforzando* squeal as she applied the handbrake before the Morris had come to a halt. It juddered and stalled by the harness room. A moment later, a frustrated and ill-tempered Primrose stood among them.

'Hello chaps – no I won't have tea thanks, I need a whisky, and a bloody large one at that. Yes – that would be kind – pour some for yourselves. And you – hop it before I sit on you.'

The cat stared, transfixed by Primrose's impending buttocks, before shooting out of the chair at the last minute. It jumped onto the desk, and showed its annoyance by lifting a leg in the air and licking itself furiously. Tom Two made an effortless transition from waiter to barman and poured large whiskies for everybody. Primrose drained her glass in one gulp.

'Have you had a stressful afternoon, Miss Armishaw?' Two topped up her glass nonchalantly.

'Stressful? I'll say I have. I had everything sorted out in my mind – what I was going to say and do, and how I'd reply to all the questions. I'd even worked out what to do about all the horses while I was away. And then I messed it all up.'

Primrose realised suddenly that nobody had the faintest idea what she was talking about. Ashley's eyebrows were raised questioningly, Tom One seemed to be focussing on the end of his nose, and Tom Two's ears were practically flapping with curiosity. If she didn't make herself plain soon, he'd take off. She gave a snort, drank some more whisky, and then said:

'I tried to confess to killing Katherine Stone – and everybody just laughed at me.'

"Everybody" now included the Toms. Tom One, who had custody of the glass tumbler, began to choke and Two had to slap him firmly on the back, which almost caused him to fall off the chair. The cat, receiving an earful of alcohol and Tom's saliva, glared filthily at them all and stomped off in search of peace and quiet.

'We're sorry, Miss Armishaw.' Tom One blinked back tears: how could they possibly explain that something which they had just been discussing seriously now seemed totally hilarious? 'We know it's not funny, really.'

Primrose decided that her dignity could fall no lower, so stopped worrying. 'Oh, just shut up, the pair of you – if I weren't so grateful for what you've done today, I'd brain you with this bottle. I suppose it does seem silly, now I look back on it, but at the time I really thought I was doing the right thing.'

Ashley intervened. 'I think, Miss Armishaw, we ought to

send the Horse Artillery to do a round of the stables and then you and I can talk sensibly. Got that, you two?'

'*Jawohl, mein Onkel* – we hear and obey.' Tom One leapt to attention and clicked his spurs. Then he relaxed: 'Sorry again, Miss Armishaw.'

'Yes, sorry.'

'That's all right, I'm off my high horse now. Just check that they're all rugged up for the night and turn the lights out. Then, if your Uncle and I are still talking, there's always plenty to be done in the harness room. Light the stove if it's cold – the matches are in the cupboard where the grooming kits are kept.'

The Toms made a slightly shifty and guilty exit, and Primrose topped up her pint glass and Ashley's tumbler. Ashley transferred himself to the vacant armchair.

'I didn't even get as far as the police station. I went into the church to see if Stephen Trevis would give me a lift and a bit of support. I bumped into Alice Trevis, and she was the one who laughed at me. I suppose I shouldn't say "everyone", since it was only her, but she properly pulled the blanket from under my saddle, if you see what I mean. If that was *her* reaction, what would the police have been like? No point in me driving all the way to Okehampton just so the rozzers could slap their thighs at my expense, was there?'

Ashley did his best to arrange Primrose's snippets of information into a sensible story. He suggested that she went back to the beginning.

'What made you decide to confess to the killing?'

'Oh, all sorts of things. Thinking about poor Robert, stuck there in some horrid cell, when all he's done is bonk a nasty old witch over the head and everybody's glad to see the back of her. Robert's an outdoor person – prison would be a worse punishment for him than for other people. If I'd thought that there was the least chance of his getting away with it, I wouldn't have interfered, but those police chaps were pretty quick to work it out.

'So I thought, well, I've had my fun, and I'm just fat and tired and ready for the knacker's yard now. If I own up to it, Robert could carry on with his life – he could even take on the management here if he wanted – and I dare say the Holloway diet would have done me good.'

Unlike his nephew and Tom Two, Ashley found himself rather moved by Primrose's noble but doomed scheme. He felt cross with them for their callousness, then reminded himself that he would have behaved exactly like them when he was their age.

'It was a lovely idea, Miss Armishaw....'

'Primrose – stupid name, isn't it? Can't imagine what my parents were thinking of.'

Certainly, thought Ashley, Rhododendron or Sunflower would have given a better idea of Primrose's size and her spreading facility. He told himself off for being as puerile as the other two – and without their excuse.

'Well, as I say, er, Primrose, I don't think you were ever likely to get far. It's not uncommon for people to make false confessions – for all manner of reasons – and the police are quite good at spotting it. They'd have asked you lots of questions about how you did the killing, which you couldn't possibly have answered.'

Primrose became defensive. She had worked jolly hard to think up answers to likely questions. 'Such as?'

Ashley shot back an interrogation straight away: 'How many blows did you strike while she was standing and how many in the ditch?'

'All right, I'm not sure about that one, I....'

'What did you do with the murder weapon?'

'Now, I've got an answer for this – but I can't remember what I decided. Oh yes – I used a good wooden stick and then

235

chucked it in the bushes afterwards.'

'Not good enough, I'm afraid, Primrose: they'd have found it. The police are very thorough when searches are involved. Then they'd want to know exactly how you hit her and what sort of wounds you caused – all the things they already know the answer to, but which they suspect you don't. They'd have probably put you in a cell for an hour or so, just to give them time to check that you weren't insane, and then a nice young policeman would have brought you home in his car and made you a cup of tea.'

'Oh well, perhaps it's just as well that Alice saw through me straight away....'

Ashley became serious. 'Now *that* bit, Primrose, is very interesting. Are you old friends?'

'Not particularly – I'm not a regular churchgoer. I see more of Stephen than of Alice, because he'll pop in for a drink when he's walking the dog this way. That's why I thought of getting him to take me to the police station.'

'So Alice was in the position of having someone confess murder to her – someone who was absent from the hunt by the time the crime was committed and who had a reason for resenting Katherine Stone, because Katherine had managed to get her planning application blocked....'

'How did you know that? That was going to be my trump card at the police station.'

'A very low trump, I fear, Primrose. Anyway, to return to Alice: as far as *she* knew, it really could have been you – yet she laughed.'

'Yes, rather hysterically, actually. It took quite a long time for her to calm down – that was what made me chuck the towel in.'

'Thank you, Primrose: you've been enormously helpful.'

* * * * *

236

CHAPTER TWENTY-FOUR

- GAMES OF CHESS -

The good news was that Ernest Yeo, relieved from guard duty in Lamb Park, had called to fix the central heating. He had stuck an old mackintosh over his special constable's uniform, descended into the basement and fiddled around for a good hour and a half, ascending the stairs every so often to take on fresh supplies of hot, sweet tea. Eventually, Margery had heard the roar of a boiler firing up, and the house slowly began to thaw. Special Constable Yeo had then toured the house with a pair of pliers, bleeding all the radiators ('For the first time in years, I reckon, Mrs Noad – it should be done regularly, you know') and frightening Aunt Lavinia in the middle of a raid on the drinks cabinet. He now sat at the kitchen table, the old mackintosh discarded, drinking his second bottle of beer. Margery, bored beyond belief by his tales of central heating systems in the vicinity, was longing for his departure. She was grateful for his time and effort, but couldn't he just take his money and go? And how like Lavinia to disappear in the direction of another sherry, just when she could have done with some support.

Ashley and the Toms arrived through the back door. What

should have been an obvious opportunity for the special constable to leave, was turned into an excuse for yet another bottle: 'Well, I won't say no sir, if you're having one yourself. It's thirsty work, down in that basement.' Abandoning hope, Margery fetched four more bottles of beer, then made a sulky departure for her bedroom. She needed to lie down to recover from her contact with the lower orders of society: at least it would be warm there, now.

'So, Constable Yeo – on duty again. Did you have an interesting session at Betty Trenchard's house? Cheers, by the way.'

'Cheers, Mr Ashley, and to you too, lads. Cold and boring, to answer your question, sir. If anybody seriously thought she'd been done in, there'd have been a crowd, with everybody asking questions, and it would have been quite good fun – but an overdose of insulin isn't going to bring folk out on a December afternoon, is it? A reporter, who was still sniffing around for stuff on Katherine Stone, came along and I got my picture taken by his pal, but they didn't hang around. That was as exciting as it got. Fortunately, Harry turned up on time to relieve me and I went and got out my toolbox and came here to sort out your sister.'

'I'm sure she's very grateful, Mr Yeo.' Tom One adopted a tone of utter sincerity, which lasted about a second, before a suppressed giggle forced its way out, together with some childish smut: 'Her system's been needing a good once-over for a long time.'

'You're telling me – heaven only knows when it last had a proper bleeding. Anyway, I'd best be making a move: it's bell ringing practice tonight and I need to change out of this kit. If you hear a set of changes that sounds suspiciously like "Ding, dong! The witch is dead", Mr Ashley, it might not be entirely by coincidence.'

Ashley saw him out, returning in time to catch the tail end of a ribald exchange concerning the size and potency of the special constable's toolbox. He decided to nip further excesses in the bud by sacrificing the privilege of the first bath to Tom One. 'We'll send up a gin, if you like. Since this will be the first bath of the season when we haven't had to break through the ice to get in, you may as well enjoy a good wallow. Two and I will have that game of chess.'

'Okay, Uncle George – I may be some time. Do you think Aunt Lav will mind if I pinch some of her bubble bath?'

'Top it up from her *Crème de Menthe* bottle and she won't even notice, though she may take to drinking the bathwater.'

Ashley and Tom Two relocated themselves in the sitting room, where Two built up the fire and Ashley poured three drinks, before rummaging around in the games cupboard for the chess set. While he set up the pieces, Two took One's gin upstairs: it was intercepted on the landing by Aunt Lavinia, so he returned to the sitting room for a replacement.

By the time he delivered the drink to its rightful owner, One was already swathed in bubbles, only his head and feet sticking out at opposite ends of the bath. A pyramid of boots, breeches and other clothes stood in the far corner of the room and a pair of spurs hung by their straps from the towel rail.

'Here you are, One - this'll put oil in your toolbox.'

'Thanks, Two - my ratchet was beginning to rust over. You should take your time making your moves against Uncle George. According to his assistant, he can be a devious bastard over the board. I'll see you downstairs.'

Half an hour later, when Tom One descended, in slippers and dressing gown, Two's game had entered its death spasms. A futile series of checks was merely chasing Ashley's king to a position of safety, and Two knew that when he ran out of attacking moves, Ashley would unleash a terrible revenge. Hoping for a mistake, he played on desperately, clicking his spurs together in an agitated rhythm.

His king safely tucked among some friendly pawns, Ashley

paused maliciously. Tom Two had set a final trap: Ashley had a choice of two moves, one of which would give Two the chance to bring a knight into play, forking some crucial pieces. He was clearly willing Ashley to make the wrong move, so the detective, maliciously, took a long time, occasionally hovering with his hand over the piece which Two was hoping he would play, without actually touching it. When Two's spurs had become so fast, it seemed that they would create sparks and incinerate the chessboard, Ashley withdrew his hand and calmly leaned back in his chair: Two, in contrast, was on the very edge of his, seated like a jockey in the forward position: he would probably have started whipping the armchair, if anyone had given him a stick.

After a few more minutes of psychological warfare, Ashley decided to put the trooper out of his misery: he made the correct move, plunging a rook into the midst of the enemy position, and smiled as he watched Two's face change from agitation to disappointment, and then gradually to resignation. Two's spurs slowed, then gave a final "thunk" as he toppled his king.

'You'd seen that all along, sir, hadn't you? You were just letting me think that you were about to make the bad move to wind me up.'

Ashley was clearly very pleased with himself. 'I was, Tom Two – and didn't it work beautifully? You were practically tapping out the *William Tell* overture by the end: it was very entertaining.'

'I warned you he was evil.' Tom One hadn't understood the moves, but he had been on the receiving end of his uncle's cunning in other games.

'By way of apology for my spitefulness I'll let you have the second bath. If you want your revenge after supper, I'll happily play again.'

'All right, Mr Ashley – I'll plan my campaign while I soak.'

The Toms headed upstairs, looking furtive.

By the time Ashley got into his own bath, the pyramid of riding kit could have housed one of the lesser Pharaohs, and the atmosphere in the room was an incongruous mixture of steam and three types of sweat – clean human, dirty human, and horse. There was a distinct municipal feeling to the place, which he found quite pleasing, once he got used to it. Tom Two had made a decent stab at cleaning the bath – thus leaving it, Ashley was sure, in a better state than he had found it – so, having raided his aunt's diminishing supply of bubbles, he sank into the water, sipped his gin, and relaxed.

Mrs Trevis.

Why had she laughed at Primrose? Primrose was certainly strong enough to have killed Katherine Stone: Ashley could even imagine her doing so, in an angry moment – perhaps, indeed, she really had, and was playing a complex game of double bluff? Ashley immediately thought of half a dozen objections to this, so decided to postpone that line of inquiry until later.

Back to Mrs Trevis.

The only reason Ashley could find for her dismissing Primrose's confession with hysterical laughter, was that Mrs Trevis knew – or thought she knew – who the murderer was.

And if you know who a murderer is, you go to the police: especially if somebody has been falsely accused.

Unless you, yourself, are the murderer.

Or you are married to him.

Tom One banged on the door. 'Turkey and gristle curry in ten minutes, Uncle George.'

'Damn! Couldn't you just flush mine down the loo and save time?'

'No – Aunt Lav will be awfully hurt, and she'll probably cut you out of her will. Besides, it's the last night of leave for Two and me, and mother wants us all to have a proper meal together.'

Like Tom Two, Ashley knew when to resign. 'All right – I'll be down in ten minutes. I want a nice small helping and a nice big glass next to it.'

'You've got it, Uncle George.'

The Toms, indeed, were very solicitous towards Ashley, making sure that his wineglass was topped up virtually every time he took a sip from it. As it was their last night, they insisted on toasting the Queen, Prince Albert's Troop, Aunt Lavinia, Margery, Absent Friends, including those Falsely Accused, and – in anticipation – a Happy New Year. After each toast, Tom One refilled his uncle's glass. It was, felt Ashley, a very pleasant evening altogether.

Less pleasant was the game of chess that followed. Fired up with large amounts of alcohol, Ashley flung his pieces into the attack with real aggression. He sacrificed material for advantages in space and time, threatening to penetrate Two's defences the moment he made a slip. Any second now, surely, Two would make a false move and then his position would be smashed apart and his king left vulnerable to the fatal mating combination.

It was about twenty-five moves into the game when Ashley noticed that Tom Two, who seemed vaguely out of focus, was drinking only tea, whereas he himself was guzzling back the wine that he had found waiting by the chessboard. Tom One, ever caring, had made sure that his uncle's glass was replenished between moves. After a further five moves, Ashley realised that his attack was running out of steam. No gap had appeared in Two's carefully-arranged forces, and the bishops that Ashley had sacrificed had martyred themselves in vain. One by one, his remaining pieces were forced to make retreating moves, and gradually Ashley found himself on the defensive, with a significant inferiority of material. Perhaps he could revive his position by pushing that pawn up the board? But no, Two's king's bishop slid along a diagonal and the pawn joined the large collection of captured chessmen that stood in front of Tom Two.

Ashley fell on his sword, avoiding the ignominy of an imminent checkmate. The Toms, grinning so widely that the tops of their heads were in danger of falling off, joined in mutual congratulations.

'You sods! Getting me plastered, so that I played carelessly! I didn't realise what you were up to until it was too late. I wondered why I didn't get a toast over the meal.'

'No point, Uncle George – that was the one toast where you wouldn't have to drink.'

'I did say, Mr Ashley, that I was going to plan my campaign while I was in the bath, didn't I?'

'And it worked really well, Uncle George. I planted that fresh bottle there before the meal, and you thought you were just finishing off the last glass of the one you had at dinner. Incidentally, can we have another drink now? We've had to stay sober all evening – we were on blackcurrant juice during the meal.'

'Well I hope it rots your stomach, you traitor to the Noad-Ashley dynasty. Pour me some of that tea, and I'll try to sober up a bit before I go to bed.'

'Okay, Uncle George. I don't know about the traitor bit, though – Aunt Lav was in on the action. She slugged a whole load of vodka into your curry at the last moment.'

Ashley turned his face to the wall and groaned. '*Et tu, Lavinia!* Mind you, I thought it tasted better than her usual efforts in the kitchen.'

Unsurprisingly, Ashley's night was interrupted and his sleep erratic. He dreamed of Stephen Trevis bludgeoning his congregation to death, while Mrs Trevis laughed hysterically and played jolly music on the organ. Then Ellen Cleghorn, Katherine Stone and Betty Trenchard danced down the aisle, hiding their nudity with veils. They injected each other with insulin and then used their veils to mop up the blood of the

Rector's victims, smearing each other's bodies with the wet, red cloths. The police entered and arrested everybody except Stephen Trevis, and then –

And then Ashley woke, his head pounding and his bladder bulging. He trod a weary and wavering path to the lavatory, where he cursed his nephew and hoped that he was having just as bad a night. Would Margery blame that puddle on her son? Better not risk it.

Tom One, in fact, is awake. He hears his uncle stumbling along the passage and has the grace to feel guilty: as uncles go, Ashley is pretty good. Still, if the Toms clean his riding kit for him, they will be back on good terms before they head back to London.

Tom looks back over the week. He thinks of the murder (or is it two murders?), of Robert, and their friendship, cut short by the processes of the law. He contemplates, with a certain amount of embarrassment, his attempts at detection; and, with a similar amount of satisfaction, the good work he and Tom Two have put in at the stables and the support they had been able to give Robert during his last hours of freedom. The jobs at the stable will fill up their last morning: if only there was something they could do for Robert before they left.

Finally, Tom turns his thoughts to Tom Two. Their rooms were adjoining, and their beds against the same wall, so Two is probably no more than a few inches away; almost as close as when they had slept together three nights ago. That had been a strange experience: entirely innocent in both intent and outcome, it seemed to mark a deepening of their friendship – a moment when a relaxed, easy relationship had taken on a brief intensity.

He rolls over, turning away from the wall which separates them. There is, he decides, no point in thinking too deeply about the significance of it all.

* * * * *

CHAPTER TWENTY-FIVE

- ODDS AND ENDS -

Once in a while, a little miracle occurs. Ashley woke up – admittedly, rather later than usual – with a clear head and no apparent ill-effects from the alcoholic mixture in his system. Perhaps it was those years of solid practice with the gin bottle that had maintained his constitution in readiness for such a crisis; or perhaps it was Aunt Lavinia's suggestion that, before going to bed, he should swallow half-a-dozen of her anti-inflammatory pills. Her doctor had prescribed them for her hip, but she mainly used them to counteract the aftermath of boozy bridge nights at her local Conservative Club. Ashley contemplated filching a bottle from her before he left for London: then again, he must have the names of a few dodgy chemists, lurking in his filing cabinet, who would provide him with regular supplies.

He had forgotten to close the curtains before falling into bed, and a watery blue December sky lit up his room. The trail of discarded clothes, leading from door to bed; the overturned wastepaper bin (what was it doing in the middle of the room, anyway?); and the single sock, still half on his left foot, all constituted valuable evidence for the prosecution in an imaginary trial, *Regina vs.* Ashley, on a debauchery charge, probably. As he tidied up the mess, he pictured himself, unshaven and bleary-eyed, pleading guilty and throwing himself upon the mercy of the court. He might get away with a caution, were it not for his previous convictions on the same charge: 'My client, m'lud, would like a further nine thousand, three hundred and seventy-two similar offences to be taken into consideration....'

There was a gratifying surprise outside his bedroom door. The Toms had cleaned not just his riding boots and spurs, but all his shoes as well. The footwear stood, like a guard of honour on parade, carefully illuminated by a bedside lamp for added brilliance. There was a note sticking out of the top of one riding boot, in his nephew's careless handwriting:

Dear Uncle George,

Sorry about last night – hope you're not too hung over this morning. We've gone to the stables – come on up if you want another hack. The lance bomber says that a good gallop unclogs the system better than a wire brush and dettol.

Tom

PS Two wanted to bull up your suede shoes as well, but I wouldn't let him.

He also wanted to play Reveille outside your door at half past six, but I wouldn't let him do that, either.

Underneath, In Tom Two's rather smarter handwriting was the sentence: *It's all lies, Mr Ashley – hope you're feeling all right this morning. T2*

'Idiots,' Ashley smiled to himself and crumpled the paper into a ball, using one of the riding boots as a temporary receptacle. If there was time, he'd take up their offer of a ride, though he suspected that his morning, late starting as it was, would be fairly full.

In the bathroom he shaved and stuck his head under the shower attachment, then returned to his room and dressed. Margery, who had prepared a glass of liver salts and a speech which began: 'You've only yourself to blame...,' was annoyed to see him enter the kitchen fresh, cheerful and gleaming from the ankles down. She poured the liver salts down the sink and banged the door as she withdrew.

A pint or so of tea later, Ashley wandered into Chagford. He called on Peter Masters to see if there were any developments in the attempt to wring a confession out of Robert, and then set off for a walk along the back road to Moretonhampstead. He ambled along slowly, giving a convincing impression of a nature lover, intent on examining every twig of hedgerow and every puddle of icy water in the ditches. After forty minutes, he stopped at a bend in the road, laughed loudly and retraced his steps. Walking at a normal speed, the return journey was considerably faster.

The church clock was striking the half hour as he came back into the town. Half past ten: he calculated that he could be at the stables shortly after eleven, if he was quick, and get in a decent ride before luncheon, after which, it would be time to take the Toms into Exeter to catch their train.

His plans were knocked off course by Harry Sefton, who emerged from Norah Dyer's stores just as Ashley was passing. The policeman looked fraught.

'Morning Harry – what news of Mrs Crane's cystitis this morning?'

Harry grinned: he had been given the full story. 'Morning, sir – I thought I was never going to hear the end of it. Mrs Dyer seems determined to squeeze every last drop out of that story, though perhaps that's an unfortunate way of putting it, now I come to think about it. Anyway, sir, I'm glad I've seen you – if I hadn't bumped into you in the town, I was going to call on you. The inspector told me to bring you up to date on things while I was over here.'

'That's good of him – shall we do it over some tea? Even by my standards, it's a bit early for anything else: besides, thanks to my nephew, I'd quite like to detoxify for a bit.'

They headed into an otherwise deserted teashop and ordered Indian tea and shortbread. Harry poured, tea first: Ashley guessed that the inspector had been educating him. Certainly not Sergeant Craggs.

'So, Harry, what news? Betty Trenchard turned out to be full to the eyeballs with a rare African poison which is activated by the introduction of insulin into the system?'

'No such luck, sir – it's all very dull. We had the tests rushed through, just in case, but it came up pretty much as the doctor thought. You remember she also had a gluten allergy, sir? Silicon disease, or something like that.'

'Coeliac, Harry, though I'm bound to say that Betty Trenchard did look as though she'd had silicon implanted in all the wrong places.'

'Too right, sir. Well, she'd eaten a helping of some pudding that had the wrong sort of flour in it, and that must have set off her allergy. The doctor thought that the pudding was probably sufficiently spicy that she wouldn't be able to tell from the taste. Then he reckons that she must have mistaken the symptoms for a diabetic 'hyper' and taken her insulin when she shouldn't have done.'

'Are the symptoms similar, then?'

'Not really sir – not according to the doctor – but she was new to the diabetic thing and, as he said, she may have been the biggest button in the box, but she certainly wasn't the brightest. He reckons she made matters worse by taking too much of the stuff as well, but that was difficult to say, because it can disappear from the system very quickly, apparently. So there it is, sir.'

Ashley chewed on a wedge of shortbread: judging from the

taste, Betty Trenchard could have eaten it without danger. 'So as far as the inspector is concerned, Robert Brookes is still the man?'

'That's right, sir. I mentioned our experiment to the inspector and he seemed to take it on board, but then Sergeant Craggs asked how I intended explaining away the shirt with the blood on it – and I didn't have an answer to that.'

'No, nor have I. I gather from Peter Masters that the interrogation process is going rather slowly.'

Harry smiled broadly, displaying shortbread crumbs in his teeth. 'It's driving Sergeant Craggs up the wall, sir. He's desperate to get the case all tied up before the inquest – it's next week, by the way – but Robert won't say a word unless he's got Mr Masters there. Then, when the solicitor arrives, he spends all his time saying things like, "You don't have to answer that question," and, "It would look very bad in court Mr Craggs, if your questioning of my client were seen to consist entirely of leading questions." I tell you sir, the next murder I'm likely to be on is when Craggsy loses his rag and strangles Mr Masters.'

'You sound as though you're looking forward to it, Harry.'

'Well, sir, I'd feel sorry for the solicitor, naturally, but I might be in danger of taking pleasure in the employment of some of his own less-subtle interrogation techniques on Craggs. I suppose he's not a bad sort really, but his sarcasm gets a bit wearing after a while.'

'Have you been on the receiving end much?'

'I have while he's been getting nowhere with Robert, sir. He's been taking out his frustration on me. I was quite glad to get out of the station this morning.'

'I can understand that. What sucked you into the vortex of Mrs Dyer's stores, by the way? Presumably there's no official police interest in Mrs Farmer Crane's cystitis?'

Harry poured out the last of the tea, which emerged from the spout in a very thin trickle, before spluttering to a halt.

'No, sir – there are places where the Long Arm of the Law has no wish to reach. What took me into Mrs Dyer's was the bag of ordinary flour we found in Betty Trenchard's larder. It's got a price label from her shop on it, so the inspector thought I ought to check it out.' He sighed: 'I think I got the history of every grain of wheat in it by the time she'd finished, sir.'

'And was it worth it, Harry?'

'Sort of, sir. She bought it just the other day – Saturday morning to be precise – so she could make a sponge cake to cheer up Evelyn Warren. According to Mrs Dyer, she was going to take it round to her when she got back from identifying Katherine Stone. I suppose she accidentally used the same flour when she was making her own pudding.'

'It sounds all too plausible.'

'That's right, sir. I'm off now to Miss Warren's, just to confirm those details. In fact, sir, if you'd like to come along, I'm sure she wouldn't mind, and I'd be glad of the company. Of course, if you've got better things to do....'

Ashley thought of the moor, rushing beneath the hoofs of a hunter, and of the cold air throwing itself against his face: then he thought of Robert, who ought to be out on the moor himself, but who was stuck in his dingy cell. There was probably nothing to be gained from visiting Evelyn Warren, beyond yet another cup of tea and, presumably, a slice of three-day-old Victoria sponge, but you never knew.

'Of course I'll come along, Harry – I'll be glad to.'

Harry was obviously pleased. He insisted on paying the bill and they walked out into the Square. Here, they heard the sound of horses making an upward transition from walk to trot. Tom One called out 'Uncle George!' and Ashley and Harry turned to see the two soldiers heading in their direction.

'Hello Constable Sefton, we hope you're looking after Robert. Did you get the note, Uncle George?'

'Yes, I did get the note. No, I don't have a hangover, no

thanks to your efforts: and yes, I am pleased with your peace offering, one example of which, as you can see, is even more brilliant by daylight – and that's after a three-mile walk down the Moretonhampstead road.'

'Does that mean we're off the hook, Mr Ashley?'

'Yes it does, Tom Two, but I'm plotting my revenge, so watch out. Good riding?'

'Yes, great, Uncle George. We've worked out that we've got time for a last go just after lunch. Our kit is all packed and ready, so if you'd like to join us, we could put everything in the car, then change at the stable after the ride. It means we'll be a bit smelly on the train back, but Two's used to that.'

'Anyway, Mr Ashley, we think the smell of the horses will send all the girls on the train into a state of ecstasy. At least, it always works on us, so I don't see why it shouldn't for them. Mrs Noad seems to be the only one who's immune.'

'So, Uncle George, do you want to join us for a quick run after lunch? We're back to the yard now, and we'll get a horse ready for you, if you want.'

Ashley agreed. It was, after all, their train that was in jeopardy, not his. He arranged to have a quick sandwich at home, change into his kit and drive them all up to Primrose's yard in Margery's car. 'But first of all, Constable Sefton and I have some business to attend to.'

'Are you going to arrest the Rector, Uncle George? Can we come and watch?'

'No, and *No*. And for goodness' sake keep your voice down. You head off and I'll see you later.'

'All right, Uncle George – we'll see you at lunch.'

The Toms trotted off in single file, with their rising and sitting synchronised. They were clearly preparing themselves for their return to military life.

'Er, Mr Ashley?'

'Yes, Harry?'

'Do you mind my asking what all that was about arresting the Rector? Do you think it was him, then?'

Ashley had an instinctive dislike of sharing half-baked theories: 'And this one, Harry, is not only half-baked, it's unleavened as well. But if you should happen to bump into the Rector, and you're feeling in a mischievous mood, you might like to ask him, how it was that he got himself covered in mud at some time between twelve thirty and two o'clock on Boxing Day.'

The Victoria sponge was still surprisingly fresh, Evelyn Warren having carefully wrapped greaseproof paper around the cut portion, and stored the whole in a tin. She disarmed Ashley by thanking him for his card, pointing out a table full of 'In Memoriam' offerings, several of which were identical. Norah Dyer's stores had only a limited selection.

'It was so kind of you all to think of me, after Aunt Katherine's death. Everyone has been very considerate.'

Ashley wandered over to the table, and located a particularly repellent card, displaying a pair of praying hands, an apparently functionless kitten, and the legend '*At Peace*' in a nauseatingly curly script. Inside, in his sister's handwriting, he found his own name, together with Aunt Lavinia's and Tom One's (who, for this purpose, was simply 'Tom'). There was also a long and lurid poem: Ashley read as far as:

> *Sometimes we must say goodbye*
> *To those we fondly love:*
> *We shed a tear, and wipe our eye,*
> *For they are gone above.*

before replacing the card hurriedly on the table. On the whole, he preferred the poem on Elias Freston's tombstone: at least it was free of sentiment.

Evelyn fussed around Harry Sefton: he wasn't as good-looking as Constable Harris, but he would do nicely to be going on with. She cut him a large slice of the sponge, poured yet more tea, and asked if he had ever thought of transferring to the motorcycle department?

As far as his enquiries went, she was very helpful. Yes, Betty had called on the Saturday, to bring her the sponge, and had made it clear that she had bought the flour specially. Recipes for Victoria sandwiches varied from book to book, but Evelyn was fairly certain that Betty generally used a recipe which specified four ounces of plain flour – it was the one in Mrs Beeton, she thought.

'It was so kind of her. I remember saying before she left, that I hoped I'd soon get a chance to return her generosity. Of course, I never will now. We were going to be cooking together tomorrow: the flower arrangers always have a little get-together on New Year's Eve. It'll seem very strange without her – we've had too many deaths in Chagford recently.'

Harry made an appropriately solemn reply and, shortly afterwards, he and Ashley took their leave.

'Well, that all fits in, sir. It was a pound bag of flour, and it was about half empty, so that seems to be about the last loose end tied up. Unless there's anything you need me for, I'll be getting back to the police station. And thanks for coming with me, sir.'

'That's a pleasure Harry. I think Miss Warren would have liked you all to herself, but she's probably used to disappointment. Any time you need a chaperone, just let me know. Oh – there are a couple of odd things I'd like to ask you.'

'Fire away, sir.'

'We've been talking blithely about the pudding Betty Trenchard ate; what sort of pudding was it?'

Harry laughed. 'Are you after the recipe sir? It was a Christmas pudding and it looked jolly good, too. I'd have happily finished it off if it hadn't been evidence. The other thing, sir?'

'The insoluble problem of the blood on the shirt. You took three shirts from Robert's cottage, Harry; which one turned out to be the bloody one?'

'The damp one, sir. If you remember, I said that there were two at the top of the pile, so we took those, of course. Then there was the damp one, half way down. Nothing else was damp, except the things that had come into contact with it, so I removed that one, just because it struck me as odd. The inspector was very chuffed with me about that. Even Sergeant Craggs forgot to be sarcastic, once he found that that was the one with the blood on it.'

Ashley nodded. 'Quite right too. And what were the inspector's conclusions regarding the shirt?'

'Pretty much what you'd expect, sir, I should think. He reckons that Robert Brookes realised he'd got stains on it, put it in to soak, and then wrung it out and stuck it half way down his basket, intending to take it to the laundrette in Okehampton in the next few days. It does make sense, sir, doesn't it?'

'It does, Harry. It all makes sense.'

* * * * *

CHAPTER TWENTY-SIX

- EXETER ST DAVID'S -

Too late, Ashley realised that the consequence of an early afternoon ride on the moor, followed by a lightening journey to the station, was that he was left looking ridiculous on the platform. Conspicuous in boots and spurs, he gave the impression that he considered the London train to be some sort of tin horse that he intended to mount and ride into the night. The Toms had rapidly pulled on civilian trousers over their own boots, then substituted jackets and ties for their old sweaters, so that they looked exactly as they had for the journey down, and for the services in church.

Inevitably, after the rush, the train was late. They stood on Platform 5, amidst the pile of army luggage, and made the desultory attempts at conversation that always occur at these times.

'Will our friend, Lance Bombardier Green, still be there when you get back, or will he have gone on leave already?'

'He'll be there, Uncle George. Change-over is first thing tomorrow morning, so that the other chaps can get home in time for New Year's parties. Shall we send him your best?'

'Of course. Find out what his New Year's resolutions are and make sure that yours aren't the same.'

'Don't worry, Mr Ashley – none of our resolutions will feature Blondie Lang's sister.'

'I'm relieved to hear it.'

They fell into silence. There was a feeling of dissatisfaction about the whole occasion: they should have solved the murder by now, so that this parting might be a cheerful farewell, a happy ending to the whole mystery. As it was, the business was unfinished and they all felt irritated by this inconclusive end to the holiday. In different ways, but with the same sensation of annoyance, they contemplated the events of the last week. After a few minutes, the germ of an idea occurred to Tom One. At first he dismissed it, but it returned, together with an instinctive feeling that he had to tell his uncle.

'So there's no doubt, then, Uncle George, that Mrs Trenchard's death was just an accident?'

'That's what the police think, Tom: we don't have an easy way out for Robert there, I'm afraid.'

'No, it wasn't that, Uncle George. It's just....'

He was interrupted by an electronic female voice.

'The train approaching Platform 5 is the delayed fourteen fifty-two service for London Paddington, calling at....'

'Quick, One, grab your stuff – if we're lucky, we might get a seat near the buffet.'

Ashley suddenly remembered his avuncular duty, and slipped Tom One thirty pounds for refreshments and a taxi.

'Hey, thanks, Uncle George – we'll drink that toast to you after all.'

'Yes, thanks Mr Ashley, sir. Thanks for everything.'

'It's been a pleasure, chaps.' Ashley hugged his nephew and shook hands with Tom Two before they were carried away with the crowd.

The train drew up alongside the platform. Doors flew open, passengers struggling with luggage disembarked with obvious relief; people who had been waiting an extra half hour on the platform, impatient to begin their journey, surged around, slowing up the whole process. The Toms, identifiable by the green luggage on their shoulders, shuffled among the masses.

Only when Tom One had made it into the carriage did he remember what he had been about to say to his uncle. It suddenly seemed terribly important.

'Hang on there, Two – I'll be really quick.'

He dumped his rucksack in the middle of the gangway, where it blocked the path of other travellers, and fought his way against the tide, until he was back in the space between the carriages. All along the train, doors were slamming: the staff were anxious to make up time.

Ashley was still on the platform, and was obviously surprised to see Tom's head suddenly sticking back out of the window.

'Uncle George – I don't know if this is important or not....'

'What Tom?'

There was a final slam and a whistle.

'I don't quite know how to put this....'

'How about *quickly?*'

The train began to move. Ashley realised that he was going to look like a forces' sweetheart, running with the train, if Tom didn't get a move on. He started walking, cursing his nephew for his inarticulateness. 'Well?'

'It's just that, well, Uncle George, in all the murders we read about, it's the first murder which is carefully planned and seems like an accident....'

'Yes?' Ashley was trotting now: if he tripped over his spurs, he would never be able to show his face in Exeter again.

'And later murders are clumsy and happen in a hurry because the murderer has dug himself a hole.'

'Keep going, Tom.' Ashley was running and panting: he wasn't used to this.

'Well, Uncle George, suppose for a moment Mrs Trenchard *was* murdered....'

The train was travelling too fast now: there was no hope of Ashley keeping up. He slowed down, watching Tom's head grow smaller, his mouth still moving, but his words drowned out by the roar of the engine and the squeal of wheels. Halting, Ashley shrugged his shoulders and extended his arms, to show incomprehension.

Tom made a final effort. He remembered the drill sergeant-major at Pirbright, who had made his commands heard above the strongest of winds and the lowest of aeroplanes.

Opening his throat and cupping his mouth with his hands to amplify the sound, he roared with all his might:

'IT'S THE WRONG WAY ROUND!'

As far as he could tell, his uncle just looked bewildered: he probably hadn't heard. Tom looked out into the darkening sky and the lights of Exwick, suddenly feeling very low. Even if his uncle had heard, it probably wasn't remotely important.

He wished he hadn't bothered. He'd only made a fool of himself.

He kicked the train door with one of his best riding boots, then walked into the carriage, where Two, sitting triumphantly on his kit bag, had found a pair of seats together.

Ashley stood at the end of the platform, confused. The wrong way around? He cursed himself for not bringing his mobile telephone with him; then he could simply have rung Tom's number and had a civilised conversation, rather than that ridiculous sprint down the platform. As it was, he couldn't even ring Tom from the station telephone, because he didn't know his number – it was stored on his own mobile, and he only ever pressed a single key to connect the call. There was nothing to do except try to work out what Tom had been getting at. He could ring him when he got back to Chagford.

Tom, Ashley knew, was a person of instinct rather than of deep intellect. If he told you how much your shopping bill was, or informed you that "he'd worked everything out", it was always worth double-checking the facts. On the other hand, thoughts that occurred to him on the spur of the moment sometimes contained surprising insights. Ashley knew how important it was to follow up his own 'hunches': in the past, they had led him to some surprising conclusions and unexpected successes. It was certainly worth exploring this one of Tom's. Not least, because on the most immediate level of perception, Tom was right.

Ashley paced up and down the London end of the platform as he organised his thoughts. Suppose he accepted that Betty Trenchard was murdered: that would at least have the merit of removing the unlikely coincidence of the death within a month of all three signatories of Katherine Stone's will. Well, if it *was* murder, it was planned with careful simplicity, and had been passed off successfully as an accident: just like the first murder in the sort of books that Tom read, when he was feeling more than usually literary – or, more likely, watched on television. As he said, it was usually the second murder which was the clumsy and brutal one: the one that always gave the game away. The murderer, discovering that there had been a witness to all his careful preparations, is forced to make a fast decision – and a body is discovered with a knife in its back, or a bullet wound in the skull. Something brutal and obvious.

But in this case, it was the other way around: the 'wrong way', as Tom had yelled. The first death could so easily have been passed off as an accident. Even if one blow had been struck before Katherine had fallen in the ditch – which he didn't think was the case – her neck had been so obviously broken that there was no need to hit her twice more. One small wound would have been put down to the glancing of the skull against a stone. How could the same mind prepare Betty Trenchard's death so carefully, and Katherine Stone's so clumsily?

Ashley had become so wrapped up in his thoughts that he had failed to turn around in his pacing. He was now on the main section of the platform, where a sarcastic gang of youths, already celebrating the New Year, suggested that his horse had got on the wrong train. He retreated over the bridge to the buffet, where he ordered a pint of beer and sat in a corner by himself, reviewing his thoughts.

Two murderers? One stupid and careless, the other resourceful and cunning? Of course not.

A single murderer, simply getting better at the craft with increasing practice? Hardly likely.

That left a murderer, planning each death with equal care. Even down to the apparent clumsiness of the first death.

He imagined Katherine's body, lying once more in the ditch, her neck bent at an unnatural angle. He imagined the three blows on the motionless skull: the first two not strong enough, the third, given with extra force, penetrating the thin shell. Then what? A handkerchief in the blood? A visit to Robert's cottage to smear a shirt from the laundry basket? It was possible: but Ashley had a feeling that the murderer had organised things more cleverly than that.

He ordered a second pint, then a third. Halfway through the third pint, he realised that he had been imitating Tom Two by clicking his spurs, and that the girl behind the bar was looking at him as if he were mad. He finished his drink quickly and headed for the car, realising, just as he was about to drive off, that he was well above the legal alcohol limit. At this time of year the police were waiting on every corner, and Ashley had no wish to become part of their Christmas statistics. Unlike Evelyn Warren, the sight of a police motorcyclist did not thrill him.

The taxi rank was empty: all the drivers in Exeter were ferrying people to parties. There was nothing for it but to walk off the alcohol. He went down to the river and, for an hour and a half, wandered up and down, still considering the case. It was a cold, unpleasant interlude.

But it worked.

By the time he returned to the car, Ashley was sure that he knew exactly how both Katherine Stone and Betty Trenchard had died.

He knew why they had been murdered.

And he knew who had killed them both.

But he couldn't prove it.

* * * * *

The rule book of the Officers' Mess is very specific: the duty officer, if forced to spend the evening alone, may order a bottle of champagne, and charge it equally among his absent colleagues. As adjutant, Frank Raynham believed that rules exist to be obeyed, and he had every intention of carrying this one out to the letter. Returning from a round of picket duties, he flung his cape and cap into a vacant armchair and rang for the mess orderly.

'Evening, sir. All by yourself tonight?'

'I am, Robin. What's the most expensive fizz in the cellar?'

'Bollinger, 1990, sir.' Robin replied without hesitation: over the Christmas season, most duty officers were solitary beings. 'There's one in the fridge nicely chilled, sir.'

'Well, let's have it, then. Bring a second glass, Robin – I could do with some company and an idle gossip.'

'All right, sir – thank you.' Robin scurried off, taking the captain's discarded cape and cap with him.

Raynham passed the time by gazing around the familiar room. It wasn't a bad home for an unmarried officer: there were comfortable armchairs; oil paintings of Prince Albert's Troop in action and on ceremonial duties; and bronze statues of officers and troopers, on horseback, playing trumpets or standing at ease with their sword blades resting on their shoulders. There were ash trays made from old brass shell cases; there was a pair of inkwells which had once been the front hoofs of a famous horse, and which were now preserved with silver mountings and engraved inscriptions. The lighting was subtle, the rugs were good, and the club fender around the fire was just the right height for those evenings when a lonely duty officer wished to sink back into an armchair and prop up his feet.

Raynham followed the thought with the action, hooking his spurs over the top of the fender and enjoying the varied illuminating effects of the flickering light on his highly-polished George boots. He was pleasantly aware that, in his duty officer's mess dress, he blended into the room perfectly, so that the scene could have been an exhibit in a regimental museum, or an illustration in a book: 'Life in the Mess in the Nineteenth Century', perhaps.

Robin returned with champagne, an ice bucket and stand, and two glasses.

'So you've had a quiet evening, sir?'

'Quieter than the Moonlight Sonata played on a dummy keyboard, Robin – though I suppose I shouldn't complain. Those who are off on leave tomorrow are either packing or out partying, and those who are returning from leave are *un*packing or out partying. I dare say things will liven up later, but we've got some good chaps on duty in the guard room – I imagine that all I'll have to do is administer Alka-Seltzer and festive fines in the morning. Cheers, Robin.'

'Cheers, sir.' Robin took his drink standing. 'And thank you.'

'It's a pleasure. What's the gossip?'

'Well, sir, number three gun team clubbed together and bought Trooper Lang's sister a fluffy toy woodpecker as a late Christmas present. Fortunately, Lang doesn't get the joke, otherwise there'd be trouble. And Trooper Scott went bum over busby off his horse in the park this morning.'

'Poor show – any ill effects?'

'No, sir. According to Lance Bombardier Green, he fell on his eyebrow, and it cushioned the fall. Excuse me sir, I think I can hear the telephone.'

The call was for Captain Raynham: it was from Ashley, and he sounded very serious.

'Frank, it's George here. I need a favour – a big one.'

* * * * *

Ashley is spending a sleepless night. There is so much to do in the morning, and one mistake will ruin everything. He plans conversations, but their effect is stilted and artificial – he dare not risk that. He is dealing with a very clever person.

Again and again, he runs through the details in his mind. He *must* be right – he *knows* he is right.

Suppose he is wrong?

At four o'clock in the morning, he is just falling into a troubled slumber, when he is brought back to consciousness by the sound of a vehicle pulling into the drive of Waye Lodge.

* * * * *

'One?'

'Yes?'

'Are you awake?'

'No.'

'Sorry – I thought I heard you.'

'Well, with those ears, you can probably hear two dumb men whispering in Australia. Anyway, what is it?' Tom One rolls onto his side and leans on his arm. Across the room he sees a grey, vague Two in a similar position. The barrack lights, partially penetrating the thin curtains, project a cartoon silhouette of Two's ears on the wall behind him.

'The lance bomber and Sorrell – what happened to them? One minute they were in the NAAFI with us, getting Scotty's head in an arm lock and threatening to pluck his eyebrow; the next minute, the lance had been summoned to see the adjutant, and half an hour later, Sorrell had gone as well. Do you think they're in trouble?'

'About their Christmas party, you mean?'

'Perhaps – I don't know. I was really looking forward to telling him all about our week – and then he disappeared. I hope everything's all right.'

* * * * *

CHAPTER TWENTY-SEVEN

- THE BODY UNDER THE STAIRS -

Ashley guessed that Harry Sefton would come on duty at about half past eight. Shortly before nine o'clock, he telephoned the police station and was relieved when the constable himself answered.

'Hello, Harry – are you manning the desk this morning?'

'Is that you, Mr Ashley? Yes – as far as the inspector and Sergeant Craggs are concerned, all the investigating is done, and I'm back on routine duties. I'm bored already, sir, and I've only been here for half an hour. What can I do for you?'

'I want you to pass on a request to the inspector. He'll think I'm being an absolute nuisance and that I'm wasting his time, but you've got to persuade him that it's very important.'

'I'll do my best, sir. I think he respects your judgement, even if he thinks you've got it wrong in this case.'

'Well, that's good to hear. Have you a pen and paper to hand? Good – now listen very carefully….'

By the time the telephone call was over, Chagford would be coming to life. Ashley walked into the town, taking a deliberately slow pace, and carefully controlling his breathing to counteract any sudden rush of adrenaline.

His steady breathing was put to the test when he called at the solicitor's office and met, for the first time, Peter Masters' eccentric and geriatric secretary. She had to withdraw, in order to put her teeth in, before she could respond to his request to see Peter; then, when she emerged from the lavatory, dentured and articulate, she posed a series of intrusive personal questions, apparently under the impression that Ashley had committed a particularly unsavoury crime and required urgent legal aid. He did his best to sidestep these, and eventually found himself in one of Peter's leather armchairs, drinking an indecently early sherry.

'I'm sorry, George: Mrs Allsopp can sometimes be very protective towards me. If it's any consolation, she used to scare the hell out of Katherine Stone. More than once Katherine called to query a bill, and was told that, if she wanted to see me in person, it would cost an extra thirty guineas, so she might as well pay up on the spot. She always did.'

'She obviously had me marked down as a middle-aged delinquent: a serial rapist, perhaps, or a dealer in more than usually bestial pornography.' The sherry was calming Ashley down rather better than the breathing exercises.

'She should be so lucky. Now, what brings you here, George? I think you already know everything I can tell you.'

'I just wanted to double check a few things, Peter. About Katherine Stone's will….'

Standing in the Square afterwards, Ashley hovered uncertainly. Where should he go next? To the church, perhaps? The decision was made for him, when he saw Evelyn Warren stagger out of Norah Dyer's stores, under the weight of piles of shopping. As well as her large wicker basket, she had several plastic carrier bags, which were threatening to burst under the strain of their excessive contents. He ran over to relieve her of the heavier specimens.

'That is so kind, Mr Ashley. It was stupid of me to think that I could manage all these by myself. Normally, Betty would have helped me, but, of course....'

Ashley made sympathetic noises.

'These are all the ingredients for our ladies' group gathering this evening. It's not a party or anything grand, but we have a good high tea together, and then those who have New Year celebrations to attend don't have to worry about preparing a meal beforehand. There's usually plenty of food left over, so if anybody wants to take some back, they can. We've all clubbed in to pay for it, of course.'

'And you're doing all the cooking for it yourself this year?'

'Well, the problem is, that Mrs Trevis offered to help – and really (it sounds a dreadful thing to say) she just *can't cook*. Her recipes are all wrong, she takes short cuts where she shouldn't and her concept of hygiene – well, she just doesn't *have* one, really. Hands straight from the dog, into the mixing bowl. No-one buys her sausage rolls at the fete, and Norah Dyer swears she once found a dog flea in a rock cake. So I thanked her, and said that I really didn't need any help – and after that, I couldn't really ask anyone else, could I?'

They reached Evelyn's cottage. Ashley was the first to reach the front door.

'Just give it a push, Mr Ashley – nobody bothers locking doors here. That's right, then straight through to the kitchen, if you would. Yes – on the table. Thank you so much – you must let me make you some tea.'

Ashley hesitated: 'If you're sure you have time?'

Evelyn put the kettle on and began the task of unpacking ingredients. 'Really, it's no trouble, as long as you don't mind me getting on with a few tasks while we talk. I'd be rather glad of the company, to be honest. Betty and I always used to be so jolly together when we did this.'

There was a pleading tone in her voice. Ashley, to his surprise, experienced a twisting sensation in his stomach. 'You've been through a lot in the last week.'

'Haven't we all, Mr Ashley?' Evelyn poured boiling water over leaf tea. 'Some of the ladies wanted to cancel tonight, but I said we ought to go ahead – and if *I* could face it, I didn't see why they couldn't. There's no point in moping by yourself at home, is there?'

Ashley agreed. 'I'm told the inquest will be early in the New Year?'

'So I understand – in Exeter. They're going to send a police car for me.' Evelyn's hand trembled slightly as she poured. 'I *did* enjoy my ride in one last time, though I probably shouldn't have done, in the circumstances. It seemed to me that the young man who drove me had such an exciting life, compared with mine.'

She handed Ashley his tea, then placed a large chopping board on the table. She retrieved a paper parcel from her wicker basket and unwrapped it to reveal a mound of fresh chicken livers. The inside of the butcher's paper was stained a dull brown; in contrast, the livers themselves were shining and slippery.

Evelyn carefully washed her hands before continuing. 'We always have a large pâté in the centre of the table. It's become a sort of tradition, though I don't know why. I prepare it first, partly because it's the biggest job, but mainly because I dislike handling the livers so much.'

Having washed the livers, she placed half of them on the chopping board, pulled a sharp and gleaming knife from a block and set about her task methodically, building up a neat pile of sliced offal on one side of the board and a smaller, straggling pile of discarded odds and ends on the other. Ashley, who was no cook, was rather fascinated: it was strange to see this fastidious little woman slicing the livers so efficiently.

He brought his thoughts back to the inquest. 'Will you have to give evidence, Miss Warren?'

'The police didn't think I'd have to say much. Only the obvious, really – that I identified the body as being Aunt Katherine. I suppose I'd better not say it like that, though – she wasn't really my aunt at all. It's strange that we never call people 'cousin' in England, isn't it? Aunt Katherine – there I go again – said that people often used to in America. Constable Harris said I might not even be called, but that I ought to be there, just in case. He told me that coroners have lots of powers and like to use them occasionally. To stop them "going cold", was how he put it.'

'I think that's a pretty accurate summary. Every so often, there's talk of phasing out the coroner system, so they like to show that they are important and necessary. And what will you do after the inquest? Will you be able to take a break, maybe even go away for a while?'

Evelyn took a little time to reply. It was clear that she had some secret plan, but wasn't sure whether she should share it. 'Well, yes, I *had* thought of going away for a little while. Nowhere exotic, of course, but it would do me good to escape from Chagford and come back refreshed.'

'Peter Masters must have been to see you?'

Evelyn flushed with embarrassment. 'Oh yes – but I'm not even going to *think* about all that. As far as I'm concerned, poor Robert is innocent until proven guilty and *he's* Aunt Katherine's heir – now that the will has been set aside.' Evelyn swept the pile of sliced livers into a saucepan and placed another portion onto the chopping board.

Ashley persisted. 'But we need to face up to the fact that Robert will almost certainly be found guilty. In that case, of course, he'll be legally debarred from inheriting anything.'

'That's what Mr Masters said. It's awful, isn't it?'

'I agree, but if it does happen, you're going to be very rich,

Evelyn. You won't have to do your cooking in this little kitchen – and that holiday could be to somewhere more glamorous than Bournemouth. It's worth thinking about, just so that you're prepared.'

Evelyn rested her knife. 'That's what Mr Masters said. He talked about investments and that sort of thing, until my head started to whirl. He told me how much interest I'd be likely to lose if I only delayed by a week or so – it was a truly frightening amount. So I have put my mind to it now and then but, of course, I've been thinking of all the *nice* things I could do, and not any of the sensible things. I thought that holiday might be a cruise – the Mediterranean, perhaps. And yes, I *would* like to move to a house with a larger kitchen. Nowhere grand of course – definitely not into Meldon Dene – but somewhere I could entertain a little, and with a good-sized garden. There's only a back yard here, and it would be lovely to throw a garden party in the summer.'

The plans, Ashley thought, sounded tasteful and reasonable. He pictured Evelyn in her large country kitchen, preparing and baking exquisite food for tea parties and informal gatherings. Perhaps she pictured a couple of police cars parked in the drive and some smart young men drinking elderflower cordial and eating cucumber sandwiches, before taking her for a lightning drive up and down the A30? If so, good for her.

Perhaps it was time to go. He could leave Evelyn with her dreams: he might even be invited to one of the parties, and come back to see her, looking less dowdy and enjoying the good things in life.

Then he thought of Robert.

He tried the breathing exercises again, but they didn't work. It was going to be a struggle to control his voice.

'It all sounds lovely, Miss Warren. But then, as we said earlier – a murderer can't inherit.'

Evelyn froze, just as she was about to pass the knife through another liver. Ashley noticed her grip on the knife tighten, and he was relieved that the heavy, oak mass of the table stood between them.

When she spoke, her voice was cold, and lower in pitch than before.

'That's a most offensive thing to say, Mr Ashley. I think, perhaps, that you ought to leave now.'

Ashley did his best to seem nonchalant; to "act normal", as Tom Two had said the other day. He shrugged his shoulders, blandly.

'I could go, naturally – but I'd go straight to the police station and put my case to them. I don't think you'd enjoy your next ride in a police car very much, in those circumstances. Why don't you sit down, and I'll tell you what I think happened? Then, if I'm wrong, you can correct me.'

Slowly, Evelyn lowered herself onto a chair. She also put down her knife, though it was still very close to her, and too far from Ashley for him to be able to win any race for it. He hoped it wouldn't come to that.

'Very well. Let me hear your ridiculous version of events. I'll be more than happy to correct your mistakes.'

'Let's begin with Katherine Stone's will. It was a very unjust document: you had been consistently kind and supportive to her since her return to Chagford and yet she left you virtually nothing. I think you knew the contents of that will and that you resented them.'

Evelyn snorted. 'How could I have known what was in her will? I never saw it?'

'No – but Betty Trenchard did. Katherine Stone may or may not have covered it with a sheet of paper, but it was a very short will. Perhaps a draught displaced the cover, or perhaps Betty accidentally pushed it to one side as she signed. It would only have taken a second to realise that you were largely written out of the inheritance.

'I think that Betty was indignant at the contents of the will and told you of them. Over the next few months, you worked out that it would be much better for Katherine Stone to die intestate. You couldn't destroy the will, because it was at the solicitor's office, but it was badly drawn up, and having it declared invalid would be quite easy, if Betty co-operated.

'And now we come to Ellen Cleghorn.'

An expression of surprise appeared on Evelyn's face; then turned to one of sarcastic amusement.

'So I killed Ellen Cleghorn as well, did I?'

Ashley shook his head. 'Not so far as I know. But Ellen wouldn't have co-operated in overturning the will. She approved of the animal rights charity that Katherine Stone had left her money to – she'd made it the main beneficiary of her own will. Even if the witnessing was irregular, you wouldn't be able to rely on her to support Betty Trenchard's statement: you were stuck.

'But then, shortly before Christmas, Ellen Cleghorn died and your way became clear. At such time as Katherine Stone died, you arranged with Betty that she should inform the solicitor of the irregular proceedings in the signing of the will. She agreed to do so, and my guess is that you gave her some pretty thorough coaching in what she should say. You weren't there to see her performance, but I can assure you it was a very good one.

'Betty didn't realise that, in agreeing to do as you suggested, she was passing a death sentence on Katherine Stone. Your task now was to remove Katherine and to have the murder attributed to Robert Brookes. If Katherine died intestate, Robert would inherit – unless he could be shown to have killed her.'

Evelyn was still frozen and calm. 'And how did I achieve my task? I'm not exactly strong, am I?'

'You didn't need to be. In the first place, you had the brilliant idea of carrying out the murder after the Boxing Day meet

– drawing the antagonism between Katherine and Robert to the attention of a large public. You couldn't have known that there would be a direct confrontation between them: that was a great piece of luck.

'I think there was another piece of luck as well that day. Katherine had very high blood pressure – she had certainly turned a bright red by the end of her session of placard waving. I think that she had a major nose-bleed when she came back here and that you provided her with handkerchiefs and put them into water to soak. That saved you the trouble of obtaining blood from the dead body later. You already had one of Robert's hunting shirts. Like you, he never locks his cottage. Unlike you, he is very disorganised, and wouldn't notice a missing shirt from his laundry basket. If you were clever – and I'm sure you were – you could have put that shirt in with the bloody handkerchiefs before you left to walk Katherine home.'

Ashley paused, to allow Evelyn time to interject, but she was silent.

'You knew that the timing of Katherine's departure ought to be – shall we say – flexible. You therefore took a back route through the churchyard with her, ensuring that there were no witnesses. You continued walking with her after you reached the edge of the town and then, shortly before the turn-off into the bridle path at the bottom of her land, you simply pushed her into the ditch.

'The plan was, that when she was helpless in the ditch, you would kill her with a single blow….'

'From what?' The interruption was snapped and aggressive. Evelyn was beginning to shake.

'At a guess, I'd say the top half of a walking stick. They sell sticks in the country clothing shop, which have handles shaped like the end of a hunting crop. I think you bought one – not in Chagford, of course, you're far too clever for that – and cut it down, here in the kitchen, so that it would fit into your large

273

wicker basket. Once Katherine was in the ditch, you had to lean over and break her skull with it, giving the impression that Robert had struck her from his horse.

'Then you had – not *bad* luck, really – but some unforeseen circumstances. In the first place, the fall actually killed Katherine. If you had simply left her there like that, everybody would have assumed that she had slipped and that her death was a terrible accident. That didn't fit in with your plans at all, so you had to go on with your walking stick plan – and as quickly as possible, so that a doctor wouldn't be able to be certain which injury had come first. Your second problem was that you didn't know how hard to hit her. Too heavily, and you might have got blood all over you, but too softly – well, that's what happened, isn't it? The fact that it took three attempts to strike what would look like a fatal blow was an awkward clumsiness. No matter how many times I re-enacted the scene with the constable or another assistant, it just wouldn't make sense.'

'Afterwards, you came back here, put the walking stick on the fire, then wrung out the shirt and walked up to Robert's house, where you planted the damp garment half way down the laundry basket. That was a nice professional touch: Harry Sefton was very pleased with himself for finding it.

'Finally, you came back here, scoured out the sink, or whatever you had used to soak off the blood – and then, I should imagine, you made yourself a well-deserved cup of tea.'

Ashley came to a halt. He had reached, it seemed, the end of Act One.

'Is that it? I think you'll have to do better than that for the police to re-think the case against Robert.'

'There's more. Two little postscripts to Katherine's death. You couldn't know where the hunt would go, so you hoped that Katherine wouldn't be found until the next day. That

274

would give lots of space for characters to be in the wrong place at the wrong time. With darkness falling by four o'clock, it was a fair bet that, even if riders did return that way, they might not see the body. The two boys who found her, very nearly rode straight past – so it was bad luck that she was discovered earlier than you wanted, or expected. On the other hand, there was ample compensation in the fact that Robert actually absented himself from the field for half an hour – and from your point of view, that was perfect.'

Evelyn was a shade calmer now. It was clear that she thought Ashley had produced all his evidence, and that she considered it inadequate. He let her think this for a moment or two, using the time to calm his own breathing rate again. He saw the beginnings of a victorious smile spread across Evelyn's face, and then continued.

'And now I'll tell you how you murdered Betty Trenchard.'

The smile disappeared instantly.

'Betty's death was an accident – everybody says so. If the police had thought it was murder, they'd have released Robert.'

'They would – and what a brilliant idea it was, therefore, to kill Betty while Robert was in custody. They were happy to carry out the quickest of investigations, confident that they already had the killer of Katherine Stone under lock and key.

'When Betty agreed to testify to the irregularity of the will, she not only cleared the way for Katherine's death – she also drew up her own death warrant. When she put her name to that statement, which Peter Masters drew up, the warrant was effectively signed. After that, you needed her out of the way as speedily as possible – because she knew too much, and she gossiped too much. Who knows? One day, she might even have worked out that you had killed Katherine Stone – and then there would have been trouble. She had to go.

'I think you were with her that Sunday lunchtime. You had bought a gluten-free Christmas pudding – again, not in Chagford – and experimented to reproduce the flavour. As the doctor said, Christmas pudding is rich and spiced, so the disguise probably wasn't too tricky to an expert cook like yourself. When the allergic reaction set in, I think you persuaded Betty that she was having a diabetic attack. You nursed your father for many years, and he had developed diabetes by the end – Betty trusted your opinion. She injected herself with insulin and fell into a coma. And then you injected a second dose. Enough to kill her.'

Evelyn was very agitated now. Ashley was unable to see her hands, which were below the level of the table, but he could imagine them clenching and releasing. Was she going to admit everything? Or did he need to bring out his last piece of information? If, indeed, it *was* information. His last card was a joker rather than a trump.

Evelyn steeled herself.

'You still haven't offered anything that might be real evidence. It's all theory and no proof.'

Time to play that card.

'The police are examining Betty Trenchard's body for the second injecting point. I suggested they start with her feet: that's the last place you'd expect it to be. You might have injected her somewhere else, of course, and then they'll take a little longer – but they'll find it.'

Evelyn should have held out. A few minutes' thought would have told her that Ashley was still on uncertain territory. Instead, she crumpled: there was almost relief in her voice, as she said softly:

'She was so stupid. She never questioned my advice, just injected herself straight away. It was so easy killing her.'

And then, suddenly, the fire came back into her voice. What proof, after all, was a second syringe hole? Betty could have injected herself the previous day, for all anybody knew. Angrily, she voiced these objections: 'There could be dozens of syringe marks on her body – who knows how often she had to take insulin? I don't – and you certainly don't. You still have no proof.'

Ashley smiled: 'Oh yes I do.' He raised his voice. 'Did you get that, Lance Bombardier?'

There was the sound of clumsy movement; of brooms and buckets being disturbed. From the cupboard under the stairs, there emerged a dusty and unnaturally civilian Lance Bombardier Green. He carried an expensive and powerful portable recording machine.

'I got it, sir – and I'm jolly glad to be out of that cupboard. I've been in there since she went out shopping, first thing this morning.

Ashley turned to Evelyn: 'You of all people, should realise the danger of leaving your house unlocked.'

It is difficult to know what is going through Evelyn's mind as she reaches for the knife. Ashley assumes that she is on the attack and, at first, he stands and backs off. Green is less timid. Slowly, step by step, he moves towards Evelyn, speaking calmly, telling her to put the knife down. Ashley, recovering, begins a similar movement around the table.

Evelyn glances rapidly between the detective and the soldier. Will she attack? Which of them? She is not strong, but she has the power of the cornered beast – the hunted fox who, when he can run no more, turns to face his enemies and dies proudly, fighting and resisting to the end. The knife is ruthlessly sharp: its dark, bloody edge contrasts with the rest of the glistening blade.

Evelyn places her left hand to her heart. For a moment, Ashley assumes that she is having an attack, and thinks that all may end peacefully. Too late, he realises that the expert cook is finding a gap between her ribs.

As she turns the knife upon herself, both men rush forwards – but she is already dead.

Perhaps for five seconds, she stands, her face frozen in a look of well-bred surprise. Then her body gives a spasm: blood shoots from her mouth, landing on the table and mingling with the offal on the chopping board.

And then she falls to the floor.

* * * * *

CHAPTER TWENTY-EIGHT

- EPILOGUE -

As Tom Two had said, everything gets sorted out in a harness room.

Ashley, leaning against a work surface, is surrounded by saddles, bridles and soldiers. On the metal frame, which runs the length of the room, Lance Bombardier Green is perched on a saddle, his boots in the stirrups: this is his throne. Squatting next to Ashley on top of the work surface, their knees hunched up, are the Toms, dressed in green coveralls and lace up boots. Two's toes tap a noiseless rhythm against each other, his combat soles absorbing the sound. Functionless, but nosy, a topless Trooper Sorrell pretends to clean a bridle and Trooper Scott, in riding boots and green army sweater, is in charge of making tea. Finally, Frank Raynham sits on an upturned bucket. He has tactfully removed his cap and service tunic, lest his rank should inhibit the flow of conversation. As far as Lance Bombardier Green is concerned, he need not have bothered: the harness room is *his* kingdom, and the Captain's status is that of an ambassador from a distant and unimportant country, with which Green has a vague and flexible alliance. At the moment,

His Majesty is issuing an edict.

'And for goodness' sake, don't stir it with a hoof pick this time, Scotty: it's a generally accepted fact that officers and gentlemen prefer their tea without large gobs of horse shit floating on the top. Use that old riding stick, like a civilised person.'

'Okay Lance. Here you are, Mr Ashley, Captain Raynham – sorry we haven't got any fancy doilies to rest them on.'

Mugs are handed round; their contents contemplated and endured. At Raynham's request, Ashley retells the story of the murders and their aftermath. There are anarchic interruptions from the Toms and occasional questions from the others.

'So, Tom, your remark about things being the wrong way round was the turning point – it forced me to see things from a different angle. If we go back to that chess analogy, I realised that the threat wasn't from the big pieces arrayed against Robert, but from a small pawn which was steadily working its way up to the eighth rank. Evelyn Warren was so diminutive and insignificant that no-one considered her – but the moment one began to think about it, it all fell into place.'

Sorrell looks up from his bridle to ask: 'Why didn't you just go to the police, sir?' He is swiftly put down by Green: 'Hey, Sorrell – who said you could speak, just because you came along for the ride? So, sir, why didn't you just go to the police?'

'Because Evelyn was right – I hadn't any evidence. No weapon, no proof that the second death *was* murder – nothing at all. I didn't know that the second injection definitely existed….'

'And did it, Uncle George?'

'Yes Tom – and it *was* in the sole of the foot, where she hoped no-one would look for it. But that was just guesswork. That's why I needed someone I could trust to conceal themselves in the cottage with a tape recorder.'

Lance Bombardier Green beams importantly: 'Though I still don't see why you didn't get that copper chappy to do it for you, sir. He seemed like a good sort – I'm sure he would have been up for it.'

'You're right, Lance Bombardier, but he would have got himself into a lot of trouble. What we did was all very irregular – the more so since Evelyn killed herself. If Harry had been mixed up in that, he would probably have received a severe reprimand at the very least: as it is, the inspector has passed some very favourable comments about him up the line.'

The next question is from Tom Two: 'And how was the inspector about it all, sir?'

'Surprisingly generous: like me, he'd never considered poor little Evelyn as a suspect. I think he was rather relieved that a miscarriage of justice had been avoided and, above all, that he wasn't around when Evelyn killed herself. Sergeant Craggs was a shade less grateful than he might have been and I think he went and worked off a few grudges on Constable Sefton afterwards.'

The Lance Bombardier nods approvingly: 'Sounds reasonable to me, sir. Here, Scotty – any chance of some more tea?'

Frank Raynham adjusts himself uncomfortably on his bucket, 'And so Robert Brookes is now released, presumably?'

'That's right – he was out first thing on New Year's Day and was changed and mounted in time for the eleven o'clock meet – at which, Captain Raynham, your Lance Bombardier and Trooper Sorrell distinguished themselves by their panache and devil-may-care bravery in pursuit of the fox. Which reminds me – Tom Two, could you pass my bag over?'

In the bag are two fox masks, stuffed and mounted.

'I don't know which was the one killed on Boxing Day, and which one succumbed to the hunting prowess of Lance Bombardier Green and Trooper Sorrell, so you'll have to fight over possession. Robert sent them to the taxidermist and had them mounted for you as a thank-you present.'

Both foxes present aspects that are fierce and cross. Green selects the one which looks marginally more unpleasant.

'If the Toms don't mind sir, I'll take this one – that's just how the lady looked before she stabbed herself. I'll call it Evelyn, after her.'

'That's a lovely gesture, Lance – you're all heart. Two and I will be happy with the other one, won't we, Two?'

'Sure – it'll be good to have something in the room with larger ears than me. So, Mr Ashley?'

'Yes, Two?'

'Just a couple of questions. First of all, what about Primrose and the Rector – where do they fit into it all? And second – what about the will and all the money?'

Ashley is blissfully happy: he has been hoping for those questions.

'You're going to like this. Mrs Trevis laughed at Primrose's attempt at confession, because she thought her husband was the murderer. When he had his drunken wander down the back road to Moretonhampstead, he slipped and fell in a ditch. I found the place where he fell – even five days later you could see the marks and the broken twigs in the hedge. He came back covered in mud and tried to avoid his wife's wrath by getting changed in the vestry and sneaking upstairs for a quick bath. She saw him from the kitchen window and later put two and two together and guessed he was the killer. Stephen is now delighted that she thinks him capable of murder and keeps threatening her with a walk along the road to Meldon Dene.

'As for the will and the money…. I had to be really careful when going through the case with Evelyn, because the whole conversation was being recorded by Lance Bombardier Green. Now, I don't know this, but my guess is that the will was properly witnessed and, although it was badly drawn up, it was a perfectly legal document. However, valid or not, Betty's signed statement undid all that – and I didn't want anything to appear on that tape which might give that ridiculous charity grounds for an appeal. Mercifully, Evelyn took that secret with her, so all the money will eventually go to Robert – after the taxman and Peter Masters have had their share, of course.

'Peter has arranged a bridging loan for Robert, who has made an appropriately large donation to the Gidleigh Hunt, in loving memory of his dear aunt, Katherine Stone. He's also, at my suggestion, sent some money to the home for Elderly and Impotent Troopers, or whatever the charity for retired Patties is. Finally, at the suggestion of Colonel Hargreaves, he's made an indecently large donation to the George Ashley Detective Agency. He's still left with ludicrous amounts of money for himself, I ought to add. Perfect, isn't it?'

There are nods and murmurs of approval all round. Green suggests a second, celebratory mug of tea; but Captain Raynham has other ideas:

'I think Mr Ashley and I were planning to go to the Mess and drink something altogether more civilised, weren't we, George?'

Ashley raises his eyebrows and looks around the soldiers. They wear reproachful expressions – apart from Scott, who just looks shifty. The Lance Bombardier speaks for the Other Ranks:

'It seems a shame to break up the party, sir, especially when the Toms here have played such a large part towards getting that donation for the Old Comrades' Association. Not to mention me in the cupboard under the stairs, and Sorrell coming along as co-driver. And Scotty making the tea....'

And now Captain Raynham allows his eyes to travel around the harness room, resting his glance on four expectant troopers and a grinning Lance Bombardier. He knows when he is beaten.

'Oh – all right then. Who's got a mobile 'phone?'

'Sir – you know we're not allowed to carry mobiles when we're in uniform.'

'That's right, sir – it's against regulations.'

283

'It's on Standing Orders, sir.'

Raynham allows this to go on a little longer before holding up his hand for silence.

'All right, I hear what you're saying. And now, I repeat – who's got a mobile 'phone?'

Five telephones are immediately offered to him. He rings the mess.

'Hello – Robin? That's right, Captain Raynham here. Did you put that Bollinger 1990 for me and Mr Ashley in the fridge? Good – well we need it over in the harness room – that's right, the *harness room* – with seven glasses. Bring one for yourself as well….'

The soldiers all study the ceiling, innocently, while Robin answers. Sorrell busies himself with his bridle.

'Okay, Robin, point taken – if there's another bottle already chilled, bring it over as well…. What do you mean, there are *six* bottles, all ready…?'

Raynham flashes an inquisitory glance at Green, who is taking a sudden interest in a saddle on the other side of the room. The troopers are similarly preoccupied.

'Oh, to hell with it – bring the lot over. If I'm going to be stitched up, it might as well be good and proper.' He closes the 'phone and hands it back to Sorrell. 'Bastards, all of you – especially you, Green.'

'Thank you, sir – it's always good to know we have an adjutant with a real concern for the welfare of his men. When the fizz arrives, sir, I propose we toast first Her Majesty – God bless her – then Robert Brookes for his donation to the Old Fart Fund. Then we'll drink to Mr Ashley for solving the murder; and finally, to your good self, for supplying the Troops with six bottles of the right stuff – which just happened, by unexplained coincidence, to be ready chilling in the fridge. And look, sir – here comes Robin now. He must have had the glasses all ready as well.'

Lance Bombardier Green stands up in his stirrups to give the toasts, and the champagne flows and flows.

* * * * *